About the author

Following a 20 year career teaching Physics it was time for a major and long overdue life altering change;… and time also to write a novel.

Put under a microscope what would you see?
A question where a kiss should be.

Names, characters, businesses, places, events and incidents are either the product of the author's imagination or used in a fictitious manner. Any resemblance to actual persons, living or dead or actual events is purely coincidental.

ISBN-13: 978-1518664571

© *SG Molly 2016*

DTMWWXX

DECREASING NUMBERS

SG Molly

DECREASING NUMBERS

Chapter One

What is yet unknown is yet to be, inner warmth holds tenure; the dead are still living. Monica Hanley would soon be entering the family home: Monica Hanley would soon know. Warmth extinguished. For now, chilling grief and heartache are merely delayed.

A slow lazy old clock ticked away rhythmically in the deathly quiet room trapped in the nineteen fifties. In the corner was a standard lamp barely bright enough to illuminate the shade but grudgingly sufficient to cast shadows and reveal walls adorned with fading paper; floral, bold, vulgar but just right. The magnolia ceiling which in a former life was probably white enhanced the comforting gloom. Engraved in the faded red and black carpet, suggesting colour where not worn down to brown canvas, was a history of paths well trodden. Pictures hung from every wall. Some were mass produced prints. The ubiquitous fruit bowl with a rogue apple caught for eternity escaping its glass prison, another depicting a vase of flowers of no particular note; every image framed with purpose, unspectacular but playing its part. And photographs, just everywhere photographs of smiling children in their school uniforms or on holiday; and graduation pictures from a multitude of decades.

Against a wall sat a glass cabinet displaying hoards of gifts and trinkets, valueless pieces of treasure competing for prominence. Each replayed the ghost of a precious moment when grandchildren, nieces and nephews would hand over their lovingly chosen Christmas presents or mementos from summer holidays, their expectant faces primed for the gushing praise and gratitude that would most assuredly flow from the best grandparents in the world.

Thick velvet curtains draped to the floor shielding the room from uninvited sights and sounds of an era not welcome. A television sat in the corner on top of which was a patched up aerial that had seen better days; and that could not be more true of this particular day. A mirror set in carved wood showing specks of gold paint suggesting grandeur long since departed hung above a simple tiled fire place. A brass companion set sat in the hearth, clearly lovingly polished but long since used, and a stark gas fire of little beauty neither modern nor in keeping with the mood of the room imposed itself where once a coal fire may have blazed before the chimney was sealed off. Yellow flames flickered producing faint dancing shadows on the walls.

On either side of the fire sat two matching chairs, one perched upon a rocking mechanism, and sitting on that chair was an elderly woman rosy cheeked and still. Lying upon her lap was knitting and in each hand a needle, but they lay silent. Across from the woman sat an elderly man, a newspaper on his lap and a pen limply held in his hand. Nestled by his foot was a ball of wool which had cascaded from the old woman's lap, perhaps the last caress that this loving and devoted couple ever shared. For unsuspecting loving kin, this house, which in their minds was still a sanctuary of warmth and comfort, was soon to become a cold empty void of soured memories and haunting despairing torment. The first to experience this would be their granddaughter Monica.

"OK Monica, whose turn is it to go to the bar Monica? I think it might be you Monica. Monica, what do you think Monica?" Hannah shouted turning an empty glass upside down on her head." She was soon joined by others relaying the same message though one girl perhaps should have checked more thoroughly that her glass was empty. She laughed as liquid poured from her hair leaving behind a slice of lemon and a small umbrella; and everyone else laughed also. It was just one of those nights. Nothing could suppress the mood.

"Right, I can take a hint," answered Monica, "but would somebody please come up with me? I can never remember the order and always get it wrong. Please," she pleaded one more time.

"OK I'll come up with you," Poppy volunteered. "We better be quick though, it's last orders soon. I hope there's still enough money in the kitty."

A bewildering array of requests were made from lager to cocktails all with tacky names of blatantly sexual double entendre. Poppy rhymed the whole order off to Monica's admiration and bewilderment. She just never understood how so many people could do that. They each took a tray back to their lengthy double table and the drinks of varying and multiple primary colours found their way to their expectant owners.

"It's absolutely Baltic out there Poppy," moaned Monica. "It is supposed to be summer. I'm going to freeze to death out there!" pointing to her skirt which served no purpose other than to be a fashion accessory.

"I think one of us should be phoning a taxi to get you, me and Hannah back to Abercorrie. Do you have a number?"

Monica took out her phone then after a short discussion turned to Poppy. "Twenty minutes. Twenty minutes till the taxi," she shouted louder up the table to Hannah. So far they had managed to get through the evening without being approached by boys with romance on their mind, or at least their definition of it. Neither had any of them been requested to display assorted ID of dubious validity. Only last week Poppy had her ID checked. All she could find that night was her brother's driving licence. The police looked at it, handed it back to her and moved on. She was not best pleased and thought she would rather have spent a night in the cells than be mistaken for her brother. Already though anyone who was familiar with Poppy knew it was not a subject from which to get some mileage if they wanted to avoid a drink being poured on their head: two nights earlier Jamie Kelly got a drink poured on his head. The girls were actually not however going to be spared the advance by the boys which last orders often prompted. They knew this was their last chance and had invested considerably in liquid courage. In their heads they had rehearsed their lines and also anticipated the fawning replies from the envisaged smiling faces of the receptive girls flattered to have been naturally selected by the forces of evolution.

"Is that your drink that you're drinking?" A couple of the girls looked up blankly, and the boy crumbled inside."Oh my God, what was I even trying to say there? Shit!" the already beaten vehicle of XY chromosomes thought to himself in despair. He bravely continued undaunted, "It's a beautiful colour just like you," immediately thinking, "Oh fuck. Worse!"

There were howls of high pitched laughter which in the right circumstances would be music to the ears of a hormone flooded young male but right now? Crushing! Meanwhile his male colleagues are standing back enjoying the show. There was however one girl whose laughter seemed to be through gritted teeth, and to whom the girls were glancing to her increasing annoyance. Her spray tan had not been a great success and she was most certainly not a beautiful colour unless olive green holds specialist appeal. An awkwardly structured collection of publicly humiliated arms and legs slunk back to his sneering friends at the bar. "Well played wee man. You really need to teach us your technique some time."

The Abercorrie girls said their good byes with kissing and hugging as was now very much the way of things and waited outside for the taxi. They huddled together for warmth, all three tugging down the hems of their skirt in futile resistance to the bitter east coast wind. A car roared up fitted with a gleaming twin silencer which evidently had not been designed and manufactured with silence in mind though most certainly constructed to appeal to a particular clientèle, and to serve much the same purpose as the bell attached to the neck of a troublesome cat. The window slid down and a young face very much in love with itself was joined by another clearly also much appreciated by its leering narcissistic owner, and fortunately for whom not gifted to see himself as others might, his skin being a veritable hormonal battle ground.

"You look cold girls. I could warm you up if you know what I mean." The other looked to the driver in admiration then turned back to the girls with an, "I'm with him," look while basking in the glow of his super slick babe magnet friend.

"Now there's something you don't see everyday," said Poppy. "A booster seat for the driver."

The car roared off in a huff and turned up its base boost in defiant retribution. A taxi arrived and the heat inside was just so welcoming.

"That was a good night," shivered Hannah.

"Yes," added Monica. "It's strange why that is. The same place, the same people but sometimes it's just great yet other times it simply falls flat." They all nodded in agreement.

"We'll just give money to you Monica since you're last off. If it's too much it can go straight into the kitty for the next time."

This they did while Monica took off her high heels. They were used to this ritual as Monica had explained before that she doesn't like to disturb her grandparents late at night, clip clopping up the garden path. With more hugs and kisses the two girls climbed out the taxi leaving Monica alone. Moments later she was waving to the taxi driver and made her way up the path holding her stilettos in one hand and a bag in the other. She reached through the letterbox like she had done a hundred times before and found the string holding the key. She silently turned it and was soon gone from sight; but not for long. Within moments she came running aimlessly and blindly from the house screaming in anguish and terror, howls of despair penetrating deeply and piercing the still silence of the night, then collapsed in the middle of the road as bedroom curtains were parted in curiosity and alarm.

The gentle flickering illumination of the room was now replaced by the severe red and blue beams sweeping across the walls from the police cars and ambulances outside. Within moments of Monica staggering screaming from the house the emergency services were on the scene cordoning off the area with blue and white tape rarely seen in this mostly incident free village. In the living room was Detective Watt, still with the scent of college about him, and Detective Sergeant Jones who reeked of experience. On the coffee table sat a large tin of sweets and lying to the side was the lid with a raffle ticket attached to it.

"Somebody got lucky," said DC Watt clearly about to help himself to some sweets from the tin.

"Don't touch that. This is a crime scene. Did you not actually study crime when you were at Police College?" an exasperated DS Jones snapped sharply who didn't have the highest regard for fast tracked whiz kids. The young detective in truth had no designs on being a fast track anything and like most in his generation just wanted a job; any job. These were difficult times. All his young life he had actually wanted to be a North Sea fisherman; until he met some North Sea fishermen. Thereafter he decided to content himself with admiring these quite extraordinary, courageous and resilient individuals on documentaries from the comfort and safety of his mum's living room. At that moment out from the kitchen came Detective Inspector Buchanan, his mouth still bulging with sweets, the wrappers in his hand being compelling evidence of his guilt.

"I didn't expect you to be here," said DS Jones feeling not quite comfortable with the preceding few moments.

DI Richard Buchanan had raced through the ranks in his early years before Her Majesty's Constabulary had time to realize he was never going to be one of the establishment. His core belief was that criminals should be caught and essentially good honest people should not be endlessly pestered. Indeed the mantra which he shared with every new member of his team was, "Let's catch the bad guys, not make enemies of the good guys." When it came to paperwork he was meticulous with that which he believed helped to secure convictions. The ever increasing cascade of bureaucracy however that fluttered down from above did not receive the attention which the hierarchy felt it deserved. For his quite outstanding achievements in the field therefore he was rewarded with career stagnation, which didn't break his heart. He had a face that had never been comfortable with nor suited to being young and before its time eased gently into that of a warm and trusted favourite uncle.

"I was actually just passing when the ambulance arrived. So what do you know about them? What do you think happened here then?"

"He is or was a teacher at Abercorrie Academy. Joseph Hanley," DS Jones responded.

"Really!" exclaimed DC Watt. "He was my Registration teacher. He looks so different when he's...."

"What? Dead? Scarlet?" Detective Sergeant Jones, after his snipe continued, "He worked beyond normal retirement age. His wife was a retired bank clerk. DC Watt was here before me and I have just arrived. Fortunately! I was just about to give him some in-service training regarding crime scene contamination."

"But what crime? When I arrived the draught excluder was tight against the partially opened living room door on the inside and saw that both the victims had cheeks as red as tomatoes and the fire was still burning with a yellowish flame and blackened with soot. It was as quick as we could get them out for fresh air and administer resus' but we knew it was a complete waste of time. Clearly a lack of oxygen in the room resulted in the combustion producing toxic and fatal Carbon Monoxide."

"I'm very very impressed," congratulated DS Jones in a voice that did not sound very impressed in the slightest.

"That I recognised the symptoms and signs of Carbon Monoxide poisoning? Well actually I did both Chemistry and Biology as part of my degree."

"No not that. I'm impressed that you've actually heard of a tomato! Aren't you originally from Glasgow? I thought the only vegetables you would know would be chips, fries and wedgies."

"Well Sir a tomato is actually a fruit. That's quite a common mistake. You see because it is formed from the ovary at the base of the flower......"

"Oh dear God," interrupted DS Jones, "do you think we could have the Carbon Monoxide back?" This quip and the chip salad reference actually quite impressed the young detective but more than that, surprised him as normally DS Jones was the font of all clichés. When first they met DC Watt thought the sergeant was doing parody but soon came to realise it was not the case after the unrelenting flow of, "I don't button up the back sonny," the truly jaw dropping, "Allo allo allo, what do we have here then?" and the absolutely delicious mixed double,"Don't try to pull the wool over my eyes sunshine, I've got eyes on the back of my head."

Normal service was quickly re-established. "There's just something fishy going here but I can't quite put my finger on it."

"OK detectives," said Inspector Buchanan, "Break. Get to your corners!" after which he began shadow boxing, pointed to the corner of the room and flapping an imaginary towel up and down in front of an imaginary boxer. "Too far huh?" The blank silent responses answered his question. He continued, "In truth I really don't think we will be proceeding with crime in mind either. The windows have been left taped shut from the winter possibly because of the nasty unseasonably cold weather of late, and unfortunately an oxygen starved fire has done to those poor people in the ambulance outside what it has done many times before. And on top of that the doors were locked from the inside."

"But there is a Carbon Monoxide detector on the wall, and also the front door key is hanging from a string under the letterbox. I didn't know people still actually did that any more," DS Jones pointed out, believing that there was sufficient grounds not to dismiss foul play just too rapidly. Inspector Buchanan moved towards the CO detector but hesitated noting DS Jones' disapproving look and put on gloves to keep him happy.

"Well there's a battery in it so it hasn't been whipped out for the TV remote control," like it was in his own house but thought to keep that to himself. "Maybe it's flat. That could be easily tested; or perhaps this could be the problem. Look, the battery is the wrong way round."

In truth even DS Jones didn't think a crime had been committed either and they left to allow procedures and tests to be completed as required. In reality in this quiet and sparsely populated part of the country they rarely got crimes of any real substance or drama far less a murder in the small village of Abercorrie or any of the other scattered communities served by the local school. They made their way back to the police station leaving the scene undisturbed apart from the tin of sweets made yet lighter on their departure. There was however something about the whole scenario that was just starting to stimulate an itch of doubt in DI Buchanan's holistic mind. Perhaps there was indeed, "something fishy" going on.

Outside, still shaking and tearful in the back of an ambulance sat Monica wrapped in blankets clutching the obligatory cup of tea, a cup to which she was completely oblivious. For a second time in her very short life, uncaring fate had been so horribly cruel to her.

Chapter Two

It was the first day of a new session at Highland View Secondary School, now a brand new building, all crisp and shiny, and controlled by an elaborate electronics system, the maintenance of which, as many had said, could not possibly be financed in the years ahead. A committee had previously convened composed of local dignitaries to come up with a name for the school though there was a pretence of weightier objective and broader remit. Regularly they met in a 4 star hotel in a plush conference room with a breath-taking view of the Highlands. After 6 weeks of personal sacrifice, compensated by nothing more than the finest cuisine an internationally renowned chef could offer, and fine wine, and single malt whisky, travelling expenses; more expenses, someone had that spark of genius.

"The answer has been staring at us through the window all the time!"

"What, Window Cleaner Academy?"

Needless to say this spawned an avalanche of witty suggestions, the mirth fuelled by Scotland's finest 12 year old poison.

"Car park Academy, Flasher McNab Secondary....." Eventually they had to concede that their work was done and go their separate ways until summonsed again to come to the aid of their grateful community. The grateful community had mostly thought that calling it Abercorrie Academy like the old school would be the obvious and least costly option. Fortunately this esteemed group of worthies, of whom clearly no woman was deemed worthy, prevented such folly.

The sanctuary of the 7 week summer break was now slain and defeated. There can be few teachers who would deny, at least to themselves anyway, that 13 weeks holiday per year was not an influence on their career choice, but anyone who dared even allude to that during an interview would be as well listing child sacrifice as a hobby on their CV. No, the game had to be played out even though at one side of the table sat three promoted staff who just loved the long holidays facing another who longed for the long holidays. Parody normally took the broad form, "So Mr Liar, what has been the driving force which has had the greatest influence on guiding you towards a career in teaching?" A quick game of mental spin the bottle would come to rest at any one of many acceptable clichés.

The lecture theatre was beginning to fill up with staff in their casual gear. This day and the next would be in-service days; no pupils, so it gave the staff the opportunity to cast aside their suits and ties, and dress as they wished, and for some that was a shirt and tie, and a pair of jeans; and not the sort of jeans that those who wear jeans would ever wear. The Head Teacher, Fiona Dalton was already sitting at the front as were all the senior management team, and the ubiquitous data projector sat whirring, ready to unleash an unwieldy flood of statistics. At the back of the room sat Zander Gordon, a Physics teacher who recognised that after 20 years of teaching, his attitude and approach labelled him a dinosaur and a cynic. He had come into teaching for all the right reasons (plus of course the wrong one) and genuinely thought he could inspire and make a difference. He valued originality and endeavoured to go his own way. He was soon to discover that it was now only acceptable by the teaching establishment to be original and different if it was the same as everyone else was doing. The teachers who had inspired him as a child would now, he believed, be sent to correction centres and fed through the clone machine for having the audacity to try and be interesting and unique. He also held the belief that pupils should know more when they left a classroom than when they came in and those who were disruptive should be thrown out. Unfortunately the local authority did not share this belief. They wanted the number of exclusions to be substantially decreased and the way to do this was to decrease the number of exclusions substantially. Zander could still recall one of their body preaching during a previous in-service lecture. "How can there be effective Learning and Teaching when the child is not in the classroom?"

was the sanctimonious mantra which drove him to the edge of an enforced retirement. Fortunately he only thought to himself and did not voice, "And how the fuck can there be effective Learning and Teaching when these fuck'n howling morons are launching books about the room you sanctimonious prick?" Those around him did wonder however why his pencil was being bent and twisted to shreds.

Zander Gordon had arrived with a new Physics teacher, Matthew McKenzie in whom he saw a kindred spirit. A compulsory transfer due to a slight and transient falling roll had seen him redeployed to Highland View Secondary. "How could there possibly be effective Learning and Teaching in a school with a surplus of 0.2 of a teacher?" thought Zander bitterly thinking about Matthew's situation which had also seen some of his closest and most talented colleagues summarily catapulted from Abercorrie Academy on the whim of a computer algorithm. His contempt for the local authority was never far beneath the surface. In the brief time he had got to know Matthew, he discerned that they shared the same sarcastic sense of humour and they both liked football. What else really mattered? They were also both atheists, a surprisingly rare breed for a Science department. Indeed the number had just gone up 100%. Zander felt he just had to share some of his observations with Matthew to get him up to speed. The first target was actually the Science Head of

Faculty, Colette Murphy who always snuggled in just behind the management team. Matthew had obviously met her but had yet to form opinions for himself on her and all the other Thespians in the unfolding drama.

"Just to give you the heads up lest your ears are irreparably damaged, if anyone in the management team says anything remotely humorous you will hear squeals that would have banshees taking refresher courses in total shame at their inadequacy."

"OK, you've got my interest. I'm guessing you have identified someone as, how can I put this delicately? An arse lick perhaps? Please share."

"Look no further than your own boss. Listen out for a tortured hyena on helium."

Colette Murphy was a figure of considerable substance. Not only was she of a large build, she also looked solid with it, with long wiry salt and pepper hair always scraped and gathered into an explosively tight bun. For her, the purpose of paperwork was the paperwork. It had been speculated that had bureaucracy been in the Olympics her place on the podium would be assured but with the cruel addendum that it would have to be a podium of secure structure. She was a Biology teacher by qualification and daughter of a peripatetic army officer hence perhaps the reason for her accent of no fixed abode. She lived alone in an oppressively warm and humid house which spilled with plants of substantial size and variety. Sharing her jungle she had more cats than could be counted, exotic snakes; and mice, a combination which sat disturbingly with most.

The lecture theatre was rapidly filling up and would deny Zander the opportunity to share any more of his opinions but he still managed to squeeze in one last observation. "There are always people who turn up after Fiona has started to speak. Just watch what they do. Everyone of them will duck down, make a funny face and tiptoe, cartoon style to the back of the room."

The noise in the lecture theatre was starting to become uncomfortably loud, but not loud enough, thought Zander to prevent effective Learning and Teaching. He just wouldn't let go. The Head Teacher, Mrs Fiona Dalton stood at the front of the hall and began to speak. A silence which would have allowed hearing a feather drop on a fluffy carpet; a silence reminiscent of a deserted church in a still dark night, did not ensue. Indeed no-one seemed to notice her at all. No-one apart from Colette Murphy who immediately sat up and clasped her hands on the bench in front of her. What happened next had Matthew slightly bemused. Fiona held up her hand and a few moments later a few other hands were raised, one of them being Colette's, well of course. Soon more and more hands were being raised as the noise level subsided using a technique to calm inattentive classes, or so the theory went.

Matthew turned to Zander and said, "For fuck sake, they're not going to start talking in tongues are they?" A spontaneous laugh erupted from Zander which he only just managed to convert to a fairly unconvincing cough. The eventual silence made it a very bad time for two grown men to try and control a fit of the giggles which didn't go unnoticed by their colleague Christine Graham from Chemistry.

"What are you two smiling at?" she asked.

"I'm not smiling. It's wind," explained Zander making things worse.

Fortunately for them the first bit of news Fiona had to share after the obligatory welcome back was the tragic death of a member of staff. Obviously though it was not news to anyone.

"Welcome back everyone to our exciting new school Highland View Secondary." There was a light hearted groan and much shaking of heads. "Now first of all I was not involved in choosing this name. Highland View sounds more like a retirement home. I thought perhaps that Abercorrie Academy would have made a good name and also saved a couple of hundred thousand pounds." There was a unanimous wave of nods of agreement with Colette Murphy risking whiplash. "Now there are some issues with the new school that I will get back to you about. In the mean time may I suggest that that you do not linger in the automatic doors." Light laughter rapidly waned to slight concern as it was clear she was not entirely joking. "Anyway as you will be aware, during the holidays we lost a valued and treasured member of staff. Mr Hanley, Joseph... Joe was found dead in his home. You will be aware also that the press reported it was Carbon Monoxide poisoning, and though there has been much speculation and gossip we will leave that to others and I will pass on our thoughts and collective sympathy to his family. It is particularly sad that Joe had delayed retirement but I can tell you now that he had planned to leave in three month's time on his birthday. His granddaughter Monica whom many of you will know felt she could not come back to this school to complete her education and has elected to attend a college instead."

The truth was that Monica was familiar with the rumours and one in particular, that he had been driven to suicide by the indiscipline in the school and the personal attacks which had even invaded his online world. Her grandfather was a private man who detested intrusion into his personal life. If it was suicide then why would he sacrifice his beloved wife Claire? What Monica knew was that they were a devoted couple; inseparable and often said to each other how cold and empty life would be without the other. In Monica's mind it made sense. It was just another sad chapter in her tragic life. Ten years earlier she had been dropped off for a sleep-over at her grandparent's house by her mother and father, but a fatal car crash that night ensured she would never return to the family home.

"To another matter", Fiona continued, "and it is one of great delicacy but I know you all personally as a staff and I am confident you will be very supportive and understanding. Other than those of you who are new to the school, and I will come back to you soon I promise and give you all a worthy introduction ..."

"You're not going to make them sing the school song like you did last year?" interrupted Hamish Jones the charismatic and extravagantly gifted head of the Art Department. At this point a stranger standing at the front of the lecture theatre would have been able to spot the newbies. Yes, they laughed with everyone else but embedded in their faces was fear.

"Yes of course after you have taught them and everyone else the song." The uncomfortable truth was that the school did actually have an archaic Latin laced song. "Now back to the matter in hand and please allow me to continue without interruption as I'm sure you will soon appreciate why. You may or may not have noticed that Mr Martin is not with us in the theatre at the moment. He is actually just standing outside." All eyes were drawn to the door. "For some time now, and I feel both flattered and privileged to have had such personal and intimate information shared and entrusted with me,

Mr Martin has not been at ease with who and what he was..... He... I'm making this more complicated than necessary. From now on he wants to be known as Miss Toni Martin. Difficult times lie ahead but I'm sure you will be fully supportive and understanding. I don't need to tell you that children can be cruel. Toni, if you would like to enter in your own time."

If ever there was such a thing as definitive silence, this was it. No one breathed or blinked but just stared at the empty doorway that promised a moment that would surely be engraved in the history of Highland View Secondary School. That moment seemed to last for ever then hesitantly in walked Miss Martin and stood nervously before her captivated audience.

"I know this will be difficult at first but I hope; I know that soon you will get used to me as I really am and as I always have been."

Toni made her way to the back of the room to a backdrop of the silence in a perfect vacuum. Everyone wanted to say something. In fact everyone wanted to say exactly the same thing, which was, she did not look any different at all! Was the zip on her jeans to a different side? Under the circumstances it would have been very wrong indeed to stare. She did however have naturally soft androgynous features and was not cursed with height nor broad shoulders being little more than about five foot six. Just 24 years old he had been very popular with some of the girls for completely non educational reasons. Just how would they react to their "babe" Mr Martin becoming Miss Martin? As time would soon tell, she would need not concern herself and they would take both warmly and sensitively to their new teacher. She sat herself down beside a small group of female teachers from the Maths department. One of them took her hand and smiled warmly while another one said, "I love your hair." Humanity at its best.

With the silence now broken Matthew took the opportunity to ask Zander, "What was her name before?"

"Tony."

"Fuck think of a joke quick before I bite clean through my lip." In due course however Matthew did recover his composure and turned to give Toni a glance of acceptance; an exchanged glance which lasted just a moment longer than anticipated.

It was now time for proper business to be conducted, the culmination of the event being the exam results. Fiona Dalton always allowed her deputies to say their bit first, perhaps to weaken the resolve of the staff before she proceeded to tell everyone how inept they were, but in a positive manner; she had done many courses to this effect. As she was about to surrender the floor to one of her deputies a latecomer arrived on the scene, who promptly ducked down, made a funny face and tiptoed to the back of the room.

"Just a fluke," thought Matthew as Zander smiled at him with a self satisfied grin. As Fiona, having paused, then made to continue, another late comer appeared and the performance was repeated.

"Six lottery numbers now!" Matthew demanded of Zander.

With a look of controlled exasperation Fiona invited Richard Campbell to enthral his audience with the new registration procedure. The next warm up act was Gill Paterson who was tasked with pointing out some of the new first year who would present individual challenges to Learning and Teaching. There can be no more thinly veiled euphemism. There were always special cases though that harnessed attention. There was little Maggie the vampire. A white vampire she insisted what ever that was. So long as sunlight did not fall directly on her face, theatre would be avoided. Then there was Joe who was terrified of stuffed kangaroos. All in attendance were grateful for the heads up on that one. That information had surely averted many a catastrophe. Lastly was big Norman who could see through walls, the advice being just go with it. Last to the floor was Grant Cameron who had to go through safety procedures given that it was a new school. They all said they would be brief and they all lied.

Finally came the headline act, Mrs Fiona Dalton herself. She began, "So if you are familiar with this year's exam results you will appreciate that I'm not exactly inclined to hand out bars of chocolate." At this point Matthew actually jumped in his seat banging his knees on the bench. Right on cue Colette had erupted in a twisted modulated high pitched throttled squeal that could have brought down a bird in flight.

"Jesus Christ Zander I know you warned me but fuck!"

Fiona's controlled exasperation was starting to show signs of weakness and Colette sensed she had judged the moment horribly wrong. Thankfully this drove her to silence for the rest of the lecture. Fiona continued to substantiate her disquiet with bar graphs, line graphs, scatter diagrams and pie charts. The case was compelling; the staff were useless. The truth was that the results were only marginally down on previous years but statistics have the means to exaggerate trends where the will exists.

"So, in two years the results have taken a turn for the worse and I'm open to suggestions as to why and what we can do about it. Anyone?" There was a silence and many looked down at their own feet uncomfortably.

"Find out who has started teaching here in the past two years and sack them," said Hamish who immediately wished he had just looked down at his own feet uncomfortably.

Fiona Dalton continued with more graphs. In the middle of the theatre being inundated by the onslaught was Simon McDonald. He was an English teacher of some experience and had sat through basically the same presentation for decades, if perhaps initially on overhead projectors. He noticed that the bar charts reminded him so much of the Manhattan sky line. He had visited New York during the holidays and his memories of those happy days took control of his thoughts, and fortunately for him time passed more quickly than it did for everyone else as they did not have this salving diversion. His attention was quickly brought back across the pond as he noticed the Head Teacher looking directly at him.

"Well Simon, you looked like you wanted to say something."

"Eh I think that it's perhaps important that we don't over extrapolate the data and produce statistical aberrations." An outpouring of laughter made him wish he really was in New York. It was perhaps the most elaborate answer ever to, "Does everyone think we should take an early break for tea and scones?"

As Zander and Matthew made their way back to the science department, Zander asked, "What room have you been allocated?"

"Lab 6."

"Ah, that was going to be Mr Fuck off's room!"

"Sorry what?"

Chapter Three

Several months earlier Mr Munro had been sitting quietly immersed in his own thoughts, totally unaware that very soon and for ever more, despite having spent over 20 years teaching Physics in that same room, in that same school; very soon his name would be erased, replaced, and his legend would live long after his departure.
In front of him sat a class of teenagers pretending to be Physics students in much the same way as plastic props in a show house pretend to be fruit, loaves....... vegetables. In truth, to be honest to himself, there were a few "good guys" as he labelled them, sentenced by the education system to rot and be forgotten in a swill of low lives. Their crime? They were not sufficiently gifted academically or yet proficient at tests at a random moment in their short lives to get into classes that were not, day upon day, little vignettes of war torn third world countries. Most of the swillfest had not, as they would be quick to remind him, chosen to do Physics if he dared suggest that they perhaps read a few words, or heaven forbid, write something. They had wanted to do either Biology because it was "easy," or Chemistry as you got to "blow things up" but those classes were full so they were "forced" to do Physics and they hated it and it was "well rubbish" and the

teachers were "crap." Selecting subjects which were most suited to fulfilling their desired academic profile was clearly of great importance to them.

Today, Mr Munro thought to himself that they weren't being particularly repugnant nor nomadic. They weren't working, good God no, but neither were they pushing books onto the floor, scribbling words of wisdom on adjacent jotters or just breaking up rubbers into little bits and throwing them about the room. There was nobody demanding to go to the toilet or they would go straight to their "guidy teacher." No-one was suddenly getting the wander lust nor screaming and raging because somebody was looking at them! It helped also that no one had come into the room during the period. That tended to be a trigger for the making of loud random noises. Neither had anyone looked in the window from the corridor which often evoked scenes reminiscent of celluloid moments when a man in a Turkish prison is fleetingly given a glimpse of a woman. The boys hadn't been making farmyard smells, a talent for which they were particularly proud, and the girls hadn't been describing their sex lives in sordid, repugnant detail that would have had squaddies throwing up their breakfast.

So what were they doing? As always the "good guys" were just talking quietly to each other wishing they were somewhere else, or perhaps plotting to dig an escape tunnel. The "talking quietly" concept was actually something which the 16 headed monster with whom they had to share a room just could not begin to comprehend. For them it was always important to shout everything, including, "I'm not shouting," and laugh outrageously loudly at each other's innate comic genius. The most articulately droll were always of course the aspiring footballers and was one of the reasons they didn't need to study. A glittering career lay ahead of them. It was a well know fact that talent scouts from Barcelona, Real Madrid et al, scoured Europe for young podgy indisciplined alcoholic smokers to add to their pool of superstars. What unearthed gems they all were just waiting to be discovered. In 20 years one boy from the school had actually made it into the professional ranks so the prospects clearly were good. Those who weren't footballers all knew an uncle who would get them a job. Yes of course they did.

  So what of the girls? Kylie-Valencia Pratt (celebrities have much to answer for, Stephen Munro often thought to himself) was one of several blond oranges, endeavouring to add just one more layer of foundation to her face. Surely a mud slide was imminent? She was not alone. Many of her fellow 15 year old teenage girls were desperately trying to fight off the cruel uncaring wrath of ageing. Others were mindlessly brushing the hair of the mindless. And why not? Most of them were going to be beauticians and hairdressers anyway. "Just when will the world's most pressing shortages finally be met, food, clean water: beauticians?" was a thought never far from Stephen Munro's mind when sharing a room with classes such as the one in front of him right now. In truth they did not all want to be beauticians. No, there was always at least one that was going to be a vet. "Treated by a vet maybe," being another opinion he often wanted to share with the aspirationally deluded.

His thoughts then turned to his own daughter, who until recently had been a pupil at this school. So what had she achieved? For her six years in the place she had achieved being six years older with a sprinkling of unexceptional qualifications. She made it to the prize giving in her final year but just to collect the tickets at the door. She had been gifted with good looks and in her school uniform gave the first impression that the Head Teacher would like to sell to parents and guests. She had also made it into the Seniors' Year Book. There were various categories all voted on by their peers. The one most likely to become a millionaire, the one most likely to become famous etc. His daughter? The one most likely to sleep with a celebrity. She did also win amongst other things a car air freshener in a school raffle. What fragrance was it? Slutty Girl? Whatever it was it hung from his car mirror and had long since surrendered its powers of camouflage.

Mr Munro was stirred from his personal festival of sarcasm. Something had happened to disturb the calm. This came as no surprise to him. Only a very inexperienced teacher would be lulled into thinking that 40 minutes of broadly civilised peace and tranquillity could be extrapolated to 50 minutes. Loud animalistic grunts were being exchanged between two of the boys as they grappled with each other. The make-overs had stopped and the crowd settled for the drama unfolding before them. At this stage Mr Munro would normally be out of his seat shouting, "enough of that," or some similar such impotent demand, or more accurately, request. Today though he did nothing other than casually look up. Very soon his doing nothing became the focus rather than the feisty young bucks locking horns. Eventually one of them said, "Are you not going to do something about that?"

"About what?"

"He just called my mum a whore!"

Still Mr Munro just sat quietly detached and uninterested, which motivated the boy to come storming up to the front desk, his family name deeply wronged.

"I want you to do something about that!" he spat and spluttered.

Mr Munro casually looked up in his own good time and said, "and I want you to fuck off!"

Stunned silence does not begin to describe the moment. Shock waves rippled across layers of amber coated faces. Hash leaf drawing on desktops came to a complete halt and the good guys just gorged on the beautiful moment. Out strode another from the troop scenting a kill.

"What did you just say to him?"

"I told him to fuck off and you can fuck off too."

"What?"

"You heard. Fuck off."

Out came another.

"And you can fuck off as well."

This was growing beyond their wildest expectations but there were the seeds of resentment starting to grow also amongst the others who had not themselves ever been so instructed. They recalled that only days earlier they had committed classroom crimes which they judged to be much more deserving of such profane reward. Life was unjust.

"Tell me to fuck off," was the ever growing demand, each request granted freely, not grudged in the slightest. Now they were baying to be included in the exclusive gang, a gang which was soon not to be exclusive at all. Mr Munro picked up his jacket and made his way into the corridor followed like a Parental Advisory version of a charismatic evangelist. The timing could not have been better as the morning interval bell had just rung to feed this spontaneous flash parade with all the energy required to grow into a monster. "Tell me to fuck off," soon just became the much more succinct, "fuck off," chanted in unison by an ever growing congregation of followers, and congregate they would as they followed him through the school. This was gaining a life of its own led by the creator as he seized the moment and strutted his stuff down the corridors and into the school grounds, marching like the leader of a band, twirling and throwing his imaginary baton into the air and catching it with extravagant style. A circle of the newly converted formed around him chanting their mantra. Soon he was conducting his choir, raising the volume of one section while dampening another. "Fuck off, fuck off." He then gestured as Moses may have done to open his sea of devotees, and he strode between them to be followed to his car by his battalion of aficionados.

He eased into his vehicle, closed the door of his car: closed the door on his present life, and carefully drove off, the chanting slowly but surely fading into the distance, with his newly found flock of fans shrinking in his mirror. Mr Munro was dead and the legend that would be Mr Fuck off was born. "Fuck off, fuck off....," and fuck off he did, just he himself, his wife, his daughter; and the eleven million pounds he had days earlier won on the lottery.

Chapter Four

It was the first day back for the pupils and they were forming into social groups and cohorts oblivious to the spying eyes above. The staff room in this brand new hi tech school overlooked both the school grounds and the "atrium" inside as the architects elected to called it and with which the Head Teacher chose to run.

"They are starting to take up positions," Zander informed the staff in a strangely theatrical voice as he looked out on the gathering army of pupils. "They are clearly planning something."

"They seem very quiet .... Too quiet," added Matthew immediately recognising the direction things were going.

"Fear not," continued Modern Languages teacher Jacky Forster taking up the baton. "Behind these solid walls and sturdy gates we shall remain safe."

"And with our more than ample supplies," joined in Hamish pointing to the Matterhorn of cakes and biscuits on the table, "we are handsomely placed for a war of attrition."

An alarmingly harsh bleeping noise filled the room then pupils started pouring through the main door.

"Our defences have been breached!" shouted Zander in mock despair, though perhaps not entirely so.

"A traitor in our midst must have opened the portcullis," added Jacky clutching both hands to her despairing heart.

"The doors open automatically," said Colette Murphy. The moment was dead. If bureaucracy was her signature dish she also had a natural capacity for exorcizing levity and joy from a room.

"To your posts and stand strong," added Simon McDonald in vain, endeavouring to keep alive the impromptu skit but the devouring sorcery of Colette had taken another life.

The first day the pupils' return is most certainly not devoted to Learning and Teaching. Pupils, all sparkly and clean, wander like tourists in New York only in their hand they clutch new time tables rather than maps, asking teachers who is Mr X and where is room Y? This term however most of the staff were apprehensive about even leaving their own rooms lest they couldn't find their way back. The tragic death of one teacher plus another leaving before the holidays as a man and returning as a woman added an edge to the gossip and confusion. Also marching through the festival of pandemonium were newly crowned 6th year Prefects leading armies of first year newbies to their various destinations like guides in a theme park. So tiny and innocent looked all the newcomers but only the pathologically naïve would be deluded by the façade as lurking within the groups hid the "special challenges" identified during the in-service days. For some though, remaining low profile even on day one was a trial too far.

"You taught my brother," was often the first tear in the camouflage, usually followed by an indifferent attempt at discretion, "My brother says he's shit."

This bedlam was to be repeated a further five times as the rasping harsh beep signalled the end of a period. To increase the chill factor the beep was accompanied by voiced instructions from hidden speakers all around the school, distorted and bordering on subliminal, embedded in eerie white noise like the words spoken by tormented souls in a horror movie trapped between Hell and Earth. They could have been saying anything and soon the pupils had invented a host of interpretations most often describing the sexual activities of random mothers.

David Stewart, a teacher of Modern Studies, was off time table for the final session of the day, and grateful he was after a really torrid period with some vile 5th year pupils who really did not want to be in a school at all but whose late birthdays denied them parole. He was about to articulate his love for them but one unforgettable experience had taught him the dangers of sounding off when wrongly assuming privacy and solitude. In the previous year he had done just that while thinking he was alone in his room, a memory which he now re-called with discomfort.

"Right now I just want to kill some of these wee bastards," he growled as he packed documents into his briefcase before looking up and discovering he was not alone at all. Standing in front of him was Amelia Rosenberg, a 5th year pupil. If he could consider himself lucky in such a circumstance then he could not have chosen a less hostile pupil with whom to share his affection for the class recently departed. Amelia was a girl of considerable ability, especially in Literature, Art and Music. She was unobtrusively attractive and had a dark but warm individuality and elegant style. With her naturally flowing hair with subtle hints of purple hi-lights, a soft black skirt which draped below her knee, and accessories which alluded to the dark side, she should have been a target for bullying like most of the pupils who refused to conform to the adornments of the dominant sub culture, and yet she was rarely targeted as if protected by some ethereal force which disarmed malevolence.

"You suicidal freaks are all the same, trying to be different," was roughly the encapsulating theme of assault on the free thinkers, the irony always being totally lost on the perpetrators.

"My deepest apologies Amelia. You really should not have been subjected to such an unforgivable outburst."

"It's OK. Though traumatized I have the inner strength to pull through," said Amelia, her gently mocking response carefully chosen to defuse the situation and put Mr Stewart much more at ease.

"I obviously didn't know you were there," added Mr Stewart immediately recognising that wasn't the smartest thing to say either. "I mean even if I had known, I shouldn't have or I mean if I hadn't known I, I can't finish this sentence," he surrendered.

"It really is OK." She didn't have to say anything along the lines of, I won't tell anyone or something similar because they both knew it to be the truth.

"There must be some of your fellow pupils that you would like to see sent to the guillotine or some other such grizzly end, no?"

"Well perhaps, but with your considerable experience I would let you choose."

Pointing to a newspaper attached to the wall Mr Stewart proclaimed jokingly, "It's the parents' fault anyway," the headline preached, asserting its characteristic brand of balanced journalism. At that moment Mr Stewart then Amelia noticed that they too were now no longer alone as he cursed himself for making the same mistake twice within a few minutes. In the doorway stood Shelley, another 5th year pupil.

"Eh Sorry Shelley," said Mr Stewart, "I hope I haven't kept you waiting long. I never noticed you."

"One minute fifteen seconds," she stated looking at Mr Stewart but not quite. He looked back at her in awkward silence feeling just a bit uneasy. It was an effect Shelley had on most people. Eventually he discerned that she was looking just over his shoulder so he turned around to see the wall clock with its second hand.

"One minute twenty seconds.... Right, I'm with you now. So what can I do for you?"

"One minute fifteen seconds," she repeated mechanically but with no hint of annoyance. "Mrs Dalton said I had to give you this envelope," and she held it out.

"That's great, thank you. Just put it on my desk."

"Mrs Dalton said I had to give you this envelope," her outstretched arm rigid and motionless. He took the envelope and began, "Thank you Shell," but she was gone.

Amelia and Mr Stewart exchanged a glance both smiling through guilt at smiling.

"I never did ask was there something you actually wanted to see me about?"

"I have never done Modern Studies before and will not be doing it this year either but I want to know if I would be allowed to go straight into the Advanced course class in 6th year?" The whole discussion was essentially a courteous formality. Of course she would.

David Stewart's mind snapped back to the present from that moment which could have taken quite a different direction had it been any one of several hundred different pupils other than Amelia Rosenberg. It was not long however before his thoughts returned to a further past event somewhat more sinister as he reflected on the sad and lonely life of Shelley, and one day in particular he will never forget.

As her birth certificate would affirm Sarah Jane Primrose was her actual name, twin to Charlotte Abigail. Following a difficult and ultimately traumatic and tragic birth her sibling was left with severe mental and physical disabilities and now stayed in a hospital requiring 24 hour care and attention including assistance with basic bodily functions. There was early fear that Sarah Jane too had perhaps suffered damage yet to manifest itself but as the early years passed she was clearly showing no signs of developmental reversals or difficulties, and was now a pupil for whom academic assessments proved to be no challenge. Such cold data however revealed so little. Why Shelley? It was a name really only fully understood by a small but influential group of her peers, the root of the name lost on all but enthusiasts of nineteenth century Gothic novels. They deemed it an appropriate name and it stuck. She did three sciences, Physics, Chemistry and Biology, and mechanically passed the exams with minimum words and maximum content. Mathematics was despatched with comparable minimum fuss. Her English assignments were technically flawless and demanded high grades but totally void of all flavours of humanity.

Music was the same. How could a piano piece be played so right and sound so wrong? Similarly no amount of colour in her art work could combat the grey monochromatic chill which seeped from her paintings. Her academic produce mirrored her demeanour. She was of dour appearance, always tending to face slightly down but with her narrowed eyes staring slightly up to compensate. Just exactly when she became known commonly and universally, even by staff, as Shelley is unclear but this was the name to which she now acceptingly responded herself.

David Stewart was her Guidance Teacher however and knew so much more. It had always been the case that she turned up to school like she had slept in her uniform with hair that was matted and tangled. It was always frequently commented upon by the pupils that she had a distinct odour. The fact was that she smelt no worse than anyone else but a nasty and unjustified reputation had been invented by vindictive young minds while still in primary school. This is one aspect about which children can generally be cruel and once so stamped no remedy will erase the rank. Although there were constant and frequent clues that all was not well in her home life there were never really sufficient grounds to take action. Even when interviewed with warmth and subtlety Shelley gave no verbal indications at all as to what was happening at home. That however changed one dramatic morning.

David Stewart was in his office very early one day as was the usual case. Only Deputy Head Teacher Gill Paterson and Head Janitor Grant Fleming were also in the building and outside it was a bitterly cold, wet and dark winter's morning. David's peace was disturbed by Grant appearing at his door with his arm around a drenched and shivering Shelley. The Head Janitor was not inclined to allow pupils into the main building at such an early stage of the day but his considerable experience of working with various youth groups and his years spent on a Children's panel made him alert to something out of the ordinary. He left Shelley with him but signalled that he would be informing Gill next door that something was not right.

Shelley curled herself up in a seat but before David could really say anything Gill appeared.

"Shelley, let's get that horribly wet jacket off." Her jacket was just a school blazer and her skirt so short as to offer no protection from the ferocious horizontal rain leaving her exposed legs red raw. Removing her jacket revealed her white school shirt splattered and stained with blood.

"I'll go and get a warm blanket from the First Aid room to wrap around you," Gill Paterson calmly said but realizing that this was no longer a school matter.

With David and Gill in attendance Shelley was interviewed by a policewoman who arrived within minutes and the story which Shelley told, not only left David and Gill shocked but also distraught with guilt that as a school they had done nothing over the years despite their misgivings. Shelley told of how as far back as she can remember several nights a week she lay awake listening to the screams of terror from her mum as her dad shouted abuse at her, evidently subjecting her to physical violence also as Shelley relived the desperate pleas from her mum not to be beaten by who knows what. Frequently also Shelley would be warned by her father what dreadful fate awaited should she ever breath one word to anybody about what was going on in the family home.

On this particular night however, Shelley described how her mum had very quietly crept into her room drenched in blood and told her to slip on some clothes without making a sound. She then gave Shelley a long tearful hug, told her how much she loved her but she was going to have to go away for a very long time and she must go straight to school, tell someone what was going on and never ever return to her home. She then put Shelley in her school blazer and both quietly disappeared from the house. Once out of sight of their home her mother had given her one last long final hug then vanished into the darkness.

Shelley's father of course protested his innocence but to no avail, was consequently jailed and would be subjected to a very strict exclusion order on his release. Shelley was fostered out and at first was passed from family to family but eventually settled with an older couple to get some affection and stability back in her life but was it any wonder that she interacted as she did?

David often contemplated what possessed him to take on the roll of a Guidance Teacher. Yes it had its rewards and being able to play a part in the lives' of pupils beyond teaching Modern Studies had so much to offer, but the terrible down side was all the secrets with which he was burdened. Shelley was perhaps an extreme case but for so many pupils he passed in the corridor of whom he was privy to their difficulties and tragedies, he just marvelled at and endlessly admired how they managed to conform to and get through school life at all, often with such humour and good grace.

So what of Amelia? He recalled her story as he busied himself with routine tasks. She too had tragedy to bare. While only 8 years old she lost her treasured and beloved 4 year old sister Holly to meningitis. It was still so clear in her mind, as she had shared the images of seeing her in a hospital bed covered in tubes and wires. She still remembers also overhearing the talk of removing her arms and legs in a desperate fight to save her life but how they despairingly judged that it would be better to let her "slip away" with some dignity.

"Slip away." Those words haunted Amelia for a long long time as she cried herself to sleep night after night, month after month. "Slip away to where?" When she asked trusted relatives and grown ups around her what exactly this meant their answers not only served to confuse but also to anger. "She has gone to heaven; God has taken her back." Why did God need to take her back? Had she herself done something wrong and that's why God took her away; to keep her safe? She was tormented with guilt and hatred for a long time but reflection and logic, married with intelligence beyond her years moved her on to start seeing the universe and all matters through her own eyes, a universe that did not have nor need a God. In her Guidance notes which accompanied her from primary school, her teacher felt compelled to include a couple of verses Amelia wrote while only 11 years old as she reclaimed her own life free from the shackles of religion and superstition.

Look inward through your tearful eyes
There's nothing there you should despise
Let no more acid tears be spilt
As punishment for absent guilt

No sentient esoteric spark
Guides time through cold and soulless dark
There is no one to loathe nor hate.
No choreographed unfolding fate

What the dreadful event in her life had done was to give birth to a beautiful human being of unrelenting compassion, warmth and empathy.

The now familiar hell-bleep dragged David Stewart back to the present and having had a full period to prepare he had chosen for once just to leave with the pupils rather than work for an extra hour or so. He waited for a couple of minutes to allow the exit storm to subside then made his way through the main door. On departing, a couple of Highland View's finest were still lurking about the doorway as one of them whispered at the top of his voice, his target quite clear, "It's just great to get out of this place and away from these boring old bastards."

At this moment the quite vocal pupil hadn't the slightest idea that many of the said, "old bastards" had secrets which most assuredly detached them from what most would deem boring. There was of course Miss Martin who only 8 weeks earlier had been Mr Martin. In addition however there was the Geography teacher who could captivate a classes' attention but got a rather special thrill from being captivated himself. Could the perceptive young pupil perhaps have been referring to the PE teacher who was having an affair with a senior year boy, or two; or could it be the teacher from the Maths department whose wife had tragically left him and nobody had any idea where she was;

although not quite nobody? He knew. She was exactly where he had left her. Many teachers had secrets and vulnerabilities, and guidance teachers were not immune. Boring teachers indeed, and so many from which to choose.

Chapter Five

John Mortimore was preparing for the freedom that is Friday evening, and like most people often wondered why they were so overwhelmingly out numbered by Monday mornings. As things go his working life was reasonably free of stress. For some staff, that was far from the truth. Somewhere down the line, and for reasons perhaps too subtle to discern; with too many variables to control, they had lost the classroom and were subjected day upon day to unrelenting indiscipline, abuse and disruption from a network of pupils with a scent of blood and cornered prey. Young primary school children, before they had even arrived at secondary level had often already been primed who to target. By this stage the battle is lost, the victim shackled to their own personal hell by the vice like grip of mortgage and debt. Why do some find themselves in this cycle of hopeless despair? Too friendly with the pupils? Too severe? Both traits describe teachers who command the highest respect and those who enjoy none. To those in this tortured imprisonment there is no way out. How they got to where they are is irrelevant. They were either being torn apart while at work or living in dread and fear while not. It may have been apocryphal, though probably not, that one Drama teacher was said to stay up and awake all Sunday night to make it seem longer until Monday morning.

For John though, this was not the case and his easy manner and youthful good looks made everyone comfortable in his presence. For most staff including Mr Mortimore, the weekend was for relaxing, but how he achieved that made him not in any way like most staff at all. His idea of recreation was not something he would want to share with his colleagues; and most certainly not with the pupils.

He packed his brief case with some documents and homework, which never ever saw the light of day, and made his way out the school building. Staff and pupils alike smiled and waved him on his way as he strode to the car-park. Once in his car he drove a few miles to a road junction where turning left would take him home to his bachelor flat. On Fridays however he turned right then drove for a further mile or so where he parked his car and entered a ground floor flat to which he had a key.

The room, for the moment unoccupied, was clean but fairly stark. There was a double bed, a couple of armchairs and a large old sturdy table made from solid wood. Within this room also were basic kitchen essentials all well beyond their guarantee period. The flat was completed by a small toilet and a generous walk-in cupboard. In the corner most strikingly was a strangely large baby's cot. John sat his briefcase down and made himself comfortable in one of the chairs in anticipation of a drill he knew so well. Within about 10 minutes footsteps could be heard outside and in walked a tall good looking woman, young, possibly teenage but skilfully made up to look older. Her command of English was good but she had an Eastern European accent, the origin of which she was always so careful not overtly to share just like her name.

"Hello and how are you today?" she asked not really expecting an answer. Indeed it was extremely unusual for him to formulate any words at all in their regular encounters, limiting himself only to strangely age inappropriate sounds.

"I will get myself ready first, then we will attend to you OK?" and she disappeared into the cupboard to re-appear, after the sound of much erotic swishing and shuffling of clothes, erotic to John's ears at least, dressed as a traditional Victorian Nanny with a long black dress and an impractically frilly white apron tied to the rear with an enormous trailing bow as usual, and he lying naked on the table; as usual.

After much twanging and pinging and sweet smelling powder aplenty filling the room like a scented white cloud, the side of the cot was let down and he was led and guided into it whereupon the side was securely pulled up. Still without a word being said by him his left hand was gently but firmly handcuffed to the bars of the cot followed by the right and then both his feet. He was hopelessly imprisoned, and loving every moment of it.

"I hope you like the lovely new pink dress I've put you in," she said in a teasingly sweet accent. "It just so matches your bonnet, and the white tights are brand new as well as the old ones were getting a bit grubby."

Somehow the explicit descriptions served to intensify his growing state of excitement. "There now, whose a pretty princess?" not a description chosen at random but the word written on his dress in large white print.

"Now princess, there is something I want to discuss with you. You pay me handsomely I know for looking after your needs let's say, but I think the time has come maybe to bring it in line with inflation and that is why I propose the rate should be.... let me think now? What would be fair to both of us?...... Trebled!"

Mr Mortimore, an incongruently dignified social label as things stood at that moment, was annoyed but not alarmed. He knew this day would come and he was prepared for it. As he had long since predicted in his own mind the camera was out and blackmail had played its gambit. He however held his ace card, a card he was soon to discover was made from rice paper and about to crumble in his tethered hand.

"Oh dear, the moment just had to come didn't it. Just so predictable, so in preparation I have done a little bit of research."

"Oh, continue," invited his now somewhat tarnished nanny, disturbingly unperturbed.

"You have always been quite evasive about your background and real name so I did some homework; Trudi, or should I say Corina Petri."

"Homework?" she sniggered openly, the irony not lost on her. "What had you to do? Use crayons to draw a picture of mummy?"

He was firstly getting annoyed. Being dressed like this while discussing finance and immigration policy was not at all for what he had paid good money, but for the first time also there was a real feeling of humiliation, different from the passive but elective degradation for which he parted with cash. Secondly however, it was not lost on him that she was completely unphased by what may follow and fear was starting to tighten his heart. Regaining his composure; dignity was certainly a step too far by anyone's standards, he continued, "You are an illegal immigrant and if you try to blackmail me to meet your reprehensibly extortionate demands you will find yourself repatriated in a blink!"

"Reprehensibly, extortionate ... repatriated! These are awfully big words for such a little baby," and while searching about for something in her pocket she glided towards him, put her hand under his chin and said, "I think we have heard just about enough from our clever little princess. It's time we super glued her gorgeous rosy lips together."

On hearing this he forced his jaws wide open to foil her attempts parting his them to the full, and she immediately inserted a very large dummy in his mouth and secured it behind his head with elastic.

"Oh my God, that was just too easy!" she sneered. "I thought teachers were supposed to be clever. Did you buy your degree on the internet?"

Instead of being dressed as a baby girl, he was now dressed as a baby girl unable to speak. Fear was now replaced totally with crushing panic and he struggled furiously with his shackles but as they were made from flexible but strong rubber he scarcely made a sound save the rustle of the layers of fabric under his dress which now imprisoned him; a sound which normally had such a fervid association but now only served to amplify his abasement.

"You are absolutely right. How could I possibly blackmail you when you could so cruelly have me banished from this wonderful land, with its proud history, brilliant scientists, inventors, whisky; giant babies?"

Casually she started to undress from her costume and pack the clothes away in a suitcase into which followed all her other possessions in the flat that comfortably fitted into the case. She slipped into a pair of jeans, a T shirt and a pair of trainers then took a lighter from her bag.

At this John started to struggle furiously. She was momentarily confused by the sudden activity then she smirked as she interpreted his misguided fear. "Don't panic, I'm not going to torch you but perhaps quite soon you may want to torch yourself. Did you say something? Mmrrmph? What on earth does that mean?" Corina, having lit up a cigarette, really did seem to be particularly enjoying her rather specialist profession today.

"Clearly the time has come for me to disappear into the mist. It's probably a good thing though. Don't want to be stuck in the one place for too long eh?"

She opened his briefcase and casually browsed its content while using the case itself as an ash tray. "What are these now? Discipline reports? I know these two girls or rather where they stay. Wait a minute. These are the 6th year SLUTS that you have mentioned before. Remember? You boasted how you humiliated them in front of a whole class with your razor sharp sarcasm? I'm guessing they don't like you very much."

John Mortimore was in a state of total breakdown as he knew what direction this was going, the hot scarlet colour of his face separated only from his red and filling eyes by bold black mascara.

"I think one of them might just receive a little note through the letterbox quite soon. I suspect they won't have to worry about Saturday jobs for a while."

With that she made her way to the door, the frantic rustling of his desperate but impotent struggle just a joy to her ears.

"Don't panic precious. There should be a couple of familiar faces here soon. Well perhaps not that soon but not to worry. That's a nice clean nappy you have on."

One final sweet smile, followed by the sound of a key turning in a lock, and she was gone, leaving him tethered in an upright position, legs straight but held apart, alone to visualize in horrific mortifying detail the catastrophic outcome that surely lay ahead. By now he was exhausted with struggle and knew further attempts of escape would be totally futile, his soft and gentle bounds being such that he couldn't even endeavour to dignify his situation with bruising or blood. Scenario after scenario sliced through his soul as the hours passed, and then...

"This is definitely the right place. It's the correct number and a blank sticky label on the door like the note said," a voice whispered, but to a backdrop of total silence, was as sharp as a dagger and hideously identifiable. The second would surely inflict the same horror.

"Just what do you think we're going to find?" said the second voice.

"I don't know but the note said, "Welcome to a goldmine, enjoy," so let's just do this."

"But what if it's a trap? What if someone is in there?"

"I'll look through the keyhole. I don't hear anything though."

"Well?"

"Nothing, let's do this but keep the door clear and be ready to run. You've got the keys. I think it will be the big one."

At first there were lots of giggles and shooshing but that was soon replaced by a stark silence and then the turning of a key. John was resigned to the inevitable. Two girls with whom he had had an antagonistic relationship and who he had also belittled for years were about to reap a harvest of sweet revenge. They were both truly obnoxious to him, one in particular and were only subjected to his verbal snipes once he had become totally exasperated by the failure of every technique in the teaching repertoire to get them to be at least civil. Right now though, that was totally irrelevant as the door silently swung open and together holding hands they stepped cautiously into the room then they froze at what they saw. At first they could not actually visually decipher what was in front of them but Corina, having deliberately adjusted the room lights to full brightness for this very moment made sure that in a very short time they most certainly would.

"What the hell is it in that enormous cot thing?" said Chardonnay still whispering with caution. "Is it a shop window dummy?"

"I don't know!" whispered Madonna. "I think ...."

In a frantic maelstrom of a moment the girls were gone and an echoing scream had taken their place: the shop window dummy had blinked.

"A gold mine! A fuck'n gold mine?" said Chardonnay bitterly, both girls putting distance between themselves and the door.

It soon became apparent however that they were not being followed by whatever it was so they stopped and then together without a word cautiously made their way back to the door then once more into the room.

"That's a real person ... dressed as a baby. What the f.."

"Look, her feet; his feet. I don't know but they're handcuffed to the cot," observed Madonna, both starting to talk with increased volume and confidence.

"So are the hands," added Chardonnay. "Whoever it is can't get out. They're tied up!"

Confidence was now really building rapidly and they both strode up to the victim for a closer examination. There was a pause then as one they both yelled out, "THAT'S MR MORTIMORE!" Manic uncontrollable laughter filled the room as they staggered about drunk with bewilderment.

"Quick shut the door. We'll need to quieten down," realised Chardonnay as the situation began to take on a reality. Now somewhat quieter but still giggling Chardonnay opened the enquiry.

"Mr Mortimore, or should we call you Princess?" She could go no further as a duet of merriment exploded from both of them. "Princess," Chardonnay continued, not yet quite in control, "why are you handcuffed to a cot dressed as a baby girl?"

The truth was, both girls were worldly wise and were not strangers to the world of bondage and such things, but seeing their Geography teacher in this predicament had shocked even these streetwise teenagers. Already though it was obvious to a helpless John Mortimore that the game was moving on to phase 2.

"A very pretty baby girl," added Madonna. "Where did you get that lovely dress, and the bonnet? It is simple beautiful. The tights look a bit itchy though and Oh my God, you're wearing a nappy!"

Ecstasy resumed as the girls danced about the room but always looking at their victim; and now they knew that's exactly what he was.

"Mr, eh sorry, Princess," said Chardonnay, clearly ready to step up a gear, "Maybe I'm wrong but I'm guessing that it was perhaps not your choice to be found by Madonna and me, dressed up as a baby girl, tied to a cot with a dummy in your mouth.... Or maybe it has always been your secret fantasy!"

Chardonnay may always have been a nasty bitch but she was quite a clever nasty bitch. Chardonnay was in fact a student of considerable talent who could only fail assessments in any subject if she endeavoured to do so, and on occasions she did just that, so apprehensive was she that she would be "outed" as intellectually gifted. She was also strikingly attractive at 5' 8" with the physique of a finely tuned athlete, and naturally blond hair cascaded around her truly beautiful and fine featured face finished with a flawless complexion.

It was now time for the ubiquitous phone to come out though Madonna was struggling to keep it still long enough to take pictures. This was even worse than Mr Mortimore had imagined despite having had hours to envisage in detail his most impending personal hell. The pictures of course were inevitable but he hadn't anticipated the adept skills of his chief tormentor.

"I can't wait to post these images," screeched Madonna. She also presented as a nasty bitch. She wasn't particularly nasty at all, just gullible and so easily led, and fate had chosen Chardonnay to be her leader whom she absolutely idolised and desperately tried to be a reflection of everything she did, but unfortunately the mirror was not often the best. Unfortunately for her also, far from being clever she was in fact spectacularly stupid. If Chardonnay were to be described as top of the range, then Madonna would be the entry model in more senses that one. "Love has to be shared," romantics might generously have describe her attitude to tactile relationships. The reality though was of a somewhat less generous nature exclusively alluding to slut. She seemed destined to make an appearance on day time TV with some of humanities finest specimens of young men sitting back stage for safety reasons in separate rooms; many many rooms, as the host played Name That DNA in front of a baying audience. Her hair was certainly not naturally blond and her skin a truly unnatural orange. Beneath the layers of cosmetic camouflage lay a face which was actually quite attractive but had long since been denied exposure to the light of day through anything less than a thick barrier of smeared gloop. She was shorter than Chardonnay and carried a bit more weight but nature had kindly ensured that it was distributed in all the right places, enhancing the differences which Frenchmen implore will live long. Indeed her breasts did not demand but absolutely insisted on a second glance. They probably explained why she witnessed a disproportionately large number of low impact car crashes. She possibly had no idea the embarrassment and discomfort she caused her adolescent male peers when it came to them standing up from the concealment of their desks at the end of a school period. When it came to failing exams she was much more naturally gifted than Chardonnay. The reason she was doing a 6th year was simply because she had previously completed five already. There was no prospect of an academic dividend.

Madonna was clearly poised to send the damaging images on their electronic journey.

"No don't!" shouted Chardonnay. "Don't you remember what the note said?"

There was a silence. "No." It was true. It was now over an hour since she had read the note and the content had long since dispersed and faded in her mind.

"Goldmine?"

"What? Oh my God yes, we really should look for that."

"The goldmine is staring at you!" Chardonnay was struggling to contain her exasperation. Madonna's mouth fell open but no words followed. "Mr Mortimore is our goldmine!"

Open mouth was replaced by blank expression and open mouth. Chardonnay knew she trying to teach a snake how to knit. This was a regular experience but right now she had work to do so decided to let Madonna puzzle over this for a few minutes until she had forgotten what had puzzled her in the first place.

"Princess. I'm just guessing here again but I think you probably don't want us to tell anyone about this or show anyone some of these simply beautiful pictures."

"But we're going to so tough shit Mr Baby!" interrupted Madonna, quite pleased with her own wit.

"No we're not!" and just to make sure Chardonnay took the camera from Madonna who had fallen back into her confused state.

"As I was saying, Princess, I think you would like to keep this little episode a secret yes?"

"Yes," he nodded in an exaggerated manner which caused the bell in his dummy to ring out loudly.

"I think teachers probably get a pretty good pay and to be honest neither of us really like doing a paper round or distributing cosmetic magazines and that's where you come in."

Madonna's face lit up. At last it seemed the golden penny had dropped.

"Yes, from now on Mr Baby," she couldn't let that one go, "you will be doing the paper round and handing out brochures but we get the money!" Madonna's triumphant face dissolved as she recognised "the look" from Chardonnay

"You're a clever man Mr Mortimore, though looking at you right now? Anyway, on Monday I will come to pay you a visit at lunchtime and you will reward me with your wit and charm; and two hundred pounds. Do you understand?"

For a second time the bell rang.

"What a clever little princess." At this point Chardonnay realized what the second key was for. "Now I'm going to release one of the cuffs around your wrist then put the key in your ch mitten and then Madonna and I will be leaving. And don't try anything or these images will go viral faster than you can say need a pee pee. Oh and don't worry you can continue with your little pastime. Actually we will insist. It should be fun coming round here from time to time. I'm sure you can afford to run two flats. It will be such a good night's entertainment for a few of us. Drinks, snacks, music..... a teacher in a cot dressed as a baby girl!"

Madonna had become strangely transfixed but her head was jerking and her lips moving. She was trying to see how quickly she could say, need a pee pee.

Chardonnay did eventually release one wrist but not before she gorged herself on more of this delicious feast of retribution for another hour or so. She checked his wallet also but clearly whoever had written the note got there first. After an eternity, well for him at least they departed leaving the key in the inside of the door.

"So who is going to do our paper round then?"

"Shut up."

Chapter Six

It was now the second week of term and the school had settled into some sort of a routine despite the numerous fire drills which had taken place already. It wasn't quite a full class zipping about his laboratory Mr Gordon had discovered when he carried out registration. One of the girls, Pamela Swanson, was absent because her mother had been killed in a domestic accident. Zander could not help pondering that death was becoming a recurring theme in this school, as were fire alarms. As it was a new building it was clearly very important that emergency procedures were in place but none-the-less four drills had seemed rather excessive to Zander Gordon as he watched his 2nd year class bounce about the room reminiscent of a disturbed bee hive. To an observer unfamiliar with 21st century education it would seem like an anarchist led riot. They were in fact clearing away the equipment with which they had been, by experiment and observation, discovering for themselves the basic laws of electromagnetism. That was how modern educationalists wanted it. Teachers were not to impart knowledge to pupils; teachers teach and pupils learn? Certainly not. What a disaster that had proved to be in the previous few hundred years. In truth Zander Gordon was mostly in agreement with the idea of self discovery but the idea that 13 year old pupils may stumble upon the tenets of electromagnetism which the finest minds from André-Marie Ampère to James Clerk Maxwell had taken centuries to theorize seemed just a bit ambitious in his mind. He was actually a naturally gifted teacher who liked to get the pupils thinking for themselves, discussing ideas with each other and carrying out investigations. He also liked to make the pupils really think when asking them questions, getting as many pupils involved as possible and making the discussion open and accessible to all levels of ability. By doing this he was able to get an idea of how well each and every pupil was coping with the course work. His problem though was he was not au fait with the in vogue jargon. He wasn't aware that he was already "embedding day-to-day assessment strategies into learning and teaching" and practising the philosophy that "Assessment is for Learning." Once enlightened though he assumed that everyone would be happy that serendipity had washed him up on the shore of conformity, but no, because he was not formally stating such things in his lesson plans, whatever they were. His plan was to teach and the pupils left the room knowing more than when they came in. His inadequacies did not stop there. Was he listing performance indicators with which he could assess the efficacy of his strategies, then reflect upon them? Was he consequently modifying and updating his

Personal Review and Development records and researching In-Service training courses to meet the needs of his identified weaknesses? Not at all. When he dared ask in the wrong company whether it would be a more efficient use of time just to do these things rather than waste valuable time writing about them, he was met with stares of hostility similar to what atheists may have witnessed at the hands of the Spanish Inquisition.

However, it was now time to ask the class questions about what they had done and in truth they had actually done a great deal. Just ten minutes earlier each group had been using wires and batteries and Bunsen burners and compasses and magnets. They had turned things that weren't magnetic into magnets and they had turned magnets into things that were no longer magnetic. It was with some trepidation however that he moved on to asking questions. As classes go they weren't a bad bunch but a few of them, he knew from experience, would always just take off at a tangent. He would not be wrong.

"OK, first of all I need someone to be the scribe and write on the white board the findings of you young scientists."

From the choice of arms straining to touch the ceiling he chose the one attached to Lorna Little. She could write and spell: some 13 year old pupils are not very tolerant of dyslexia and display their scorn both openly and cruelly.

"Without shouting out, tell me some of the things you discovered today from your experiments. Each group choose someone to be your spokesperson."

This stage went very well and soon the board had various statements about what they had unearthed. Zander Gordon was not fooled though. He had been here many times before. It's the open questions which always derail the train.

"Right, here is what you have told me," and he readied himself with a pen to circle some pertinent discoveries. "You told me that if you heat a magnet with the Bunsen it will no longer be magnetic," and he circled that statement on the board. "So far so good," he thought to himself.

"You also told me that the centre of the Earth is magnetic." Another statement was imprisoned by a circle. "Now put your hands down till I have actually asked you a question. Here is the question". Up shot a couple of hands. "I have still not asked a question ...... That means put your hands down." One hand stayed up. "OK, what is it?"

"Can I go to the toilet?"

"No it's nearly break time just use the sink...... DON'T USE THE SINK!"

A confused boy sat down learning again never to trust adults, especially teachers. The class laughed as Zander thought to himself again, "Will I never learn?"

"Now what else do you know about the centre of the Earth?"

"It's where lions and tigers live!" shouted out a girl in the corner.

"Please don't shout out but no." Her face took on a confused look clearly wondering where the hell they did live then?

After much torture identifying merit in answers where none existed someone pointed out that the centre of the Earth was extremely hot and molten. This fact was written up and circled. Zander was starting to feel that things were going much to plan and proceeded to probe.

"OK, just look at those three statements encircled on the board. Look at them closely and think about them. Something is not quite right."

Mandy McEwan's hand shot up right away. Zander was familiar with Mandy and her alternative thought processes. This could be the train starting to wobble.

"Let's just see who else can come up with something first Mandy. Not everyone is a fast as you, '*nor so off their fuck'n head,*'" he mused then wished he hadn't. Pupils can find it just a bit disconcerting when teachers start smirking to themselves. No one was about to offer an alternative, and one boy was just sitting scribbling on a piece of paper.

"OK Mandy, let's hear your thoughts."

"Sir if you could be any animal what would it be?"

"Oh God she's off," he thought, but felt like his lips perhaps moved; and just maybe also made a sound?

"Mandy. Please stick to the question in hand."

The class were now just that bit more attentive and prepared themselves for the show. They were no strangers to wonderful world of Mandy McEwan either. Scribbling boy however continued to scribble.

"I would want to be a whale." Mr Gordon pulled up the white flag and surrendered all weapons. The room was hers.

"Just think about it. Too big for anything to kill you and you can swim then walk on the land at night when no-one is looking." Zander felt he really had to say something at this point. Even for Mandy that was surreal. He made to interrupt but the moment was gone.

"And they can really jump high out the water. This means they can actually swim and walk and fly."

Zander Gordon's professional conscience got the better of him and he endeavoured to get things back on track but before he could formulate a word it was too late.

"And whales are so intelligent as well. They come up close to ships so they can read the names. They learn the ones that feed them the most then follow them." Within the class were many pupils of considerable ability but fortunately also instilled with a sense of decency. They were however turning blue trying to contain their laughter.

"The thing is though, if they are that clever then why do they keep getting stuck in shallow water and need taken back out to sea?"

By now, Zander was as engrossed as the pupils, apart from scribbling boy who was still apparently in his own private world. "That's a thought. I wonder if the whales are depressed and they're trying to kill themselves but we keep dragging them out to sea again?" She paused but it was just a ruse.

"Remember that man last year who drove into the country and gassed himself with the hose pipe from the exhaust because he wanted to die? Think how he would have felt if a whale had come and dragged him out the car!"

This was just too much. The laughter dams crumbled and were swept away. Mandy wasn't laughing though and really didn't understand why anyone else was. At that point a 6th year pupil came in with a letter which she handed to Mr Gordon, from her expression clearly thinking that Science seemed much more fun than Accountancy. Order was restored, eventually and Zander Gordon finished with, "OK then, I think we might have to go back to some of that tomorrow. There are maybe a few points still to clear up, and Scott," Mr Gordon said looking at scribbling boy, "if Mandy can't get your attention then clearly I am wasting my time. What were you scribbling anyway? Bring it out."

He came out then reached into his pocket and separated a crumpled bit of paper from many crumpled bits of paper and sweets and just things unidentifiable. Zander flattened the bit of paper out to reveal beautifully drawn sketches with notes and arrows about how convection currents in the hot molten core of planet Earth could contribute to setting up an electromagnet field similar to the one they had built today with a battery wires and iron nails.

"What is it sir?" someone enquired.

"Humiliating," answered Zander, the bleeper quickly clearing his lab and leaving him alone to marvel at the genius that periodically passes his way. As the last pupil departed Matthew McKenzie came into the room and was distracted by something outside.

"What the hell was that? Something just flew past the window!"

"Probably just a whale."

"Eh?"

"I'll explain when you have an hour to waste," he said opening his letter.

"If it's the same letter that I got it's just to say that because of all the technical difficulties the new building is having the Head Teacher has decided not to do a school show this year."

Zander laughed at this. "Trust me, the school show being cancelled this year is absolutely nothing to do with the school's teething problems."

Chapter Seven

Fiona Dalton had been at a meeting with the rest of the management team, Gill Paterson, Grant Cameron and Richard Campbell. Also in attendance were two representatives from the local authority. This was an emergency meeting with one subject and one subject only on the agenda, the new school. It was a stunningly attractive building and clearly the architects had wanted to ensure that it would make an immediate visual impact without being quirky. It fitted in with the traditional buildings of the old village and this was by design not accident as it was built from identical stone, or the façade at least, quarried from the same rock as the church, village hall and many other houses constructed over 100 years earlier. Aesthetics aside it had also been thought through carefully in layout at least with function in mind. It was evidently an extremely high tech' building with a central processor system which monitored and controlled everything. The doors, alarms and fire extinguishers were integral parts of the system as would be expected. Monitored also however were the lights, and gas supplies, which again, would come as no surprise to most. In addition to these however was just an endless list of items watched and controlled by this all seeing electronic leviathan. It spied on the traffic and ensured that all vehicles which entered also departed. It did the same with the pupil toilets; count them in, count them out. It monitored computers, printer use, controlled the security cameras much to the annoyance of the janitors who would suddenly be switched to another area or sweep away from events that had caught their attention. It was for the computer to discern what merited observation. Even school stocks and supplies were stored and checked for a need to replenish.

The Head Teacher was aware of this long before the school was completed though and did voice concerns at the time regarding maintenance and servicing costs. She did her introductions then turned to Malcolm Ward, from the council planning department and someone she had come to know over the past year during construction. "OK Malcolm, we are having problems and you are here with solutions. Cheer us up."

"Cheer you up? Well I'll tell you what I know. This is a beautiful building with an equally beautiful finish using some of the finest and highest quality materials." All were in agreement and nodded in unison. "Like all projects however, they had to work to a budget and when it came to the latter stages the finances were becoming a bit stretched let's say and so,"

"they cut corners," interrupted Richard Campbell from the Technical Department and before that an Electronics Engineer.

"Indeed they did, one of the corners being the electronic control system and much of what it operates and monitors. They also cut back on personnel. Not so much numbers but rather on costs."

"So the technicians and engineers they employed. What were they really?" enquired Gill Paterson, a member of the Maths Department.

"I have the feeling that you are all getting ahead of me here. I don't know what they were to trade. They perhaps made very fine cakes or could plaster with skill and elegance. Who knows but they were not qualified electricians or electronic engineers. They must have had some relevant experience and were guided by appropriately qualified staff but that is it really."

"I can't help thinking you have more to tell," joined in Grant Cameron from Computing. Fiona Dalton was happy at this stage to let her deputies engage in proceedings as her background was Biology and Chemistry.

"There is more and I'll let my colleague Brenda Mackie take it from here as she is better qualified to answer your inevitable questions."

"Hi folks. I'll do my best but this is a complicated mess. Basically the electronics hardware they used was also done on the cheap. The control system they used was salvaged from another project and is basically obsolete and out of date. Devices all over the school, alarms doors etc. feed back to the processor and should all have had their own dedicated line of contact straight to the processor. However, as the ancient processor did not have enough dedicated inputs they kind of doubled up and trebled up inputs........OK in some cases it looks like six or seven devices were connected to the same line."

"I think I know where you are going with this and if I'm right it could explain why we are having so many fire alarms going off and lots of other bizarre little incidents. So who designed this patch up job? Was it a dentist, circus clown?"

"Actually," continued Brenda, "whoever did it must have been quite a talented individual. Each device was given an unique signature and a priority system was built in. It just looks like there was some vital logic circuitry missing to prevent what are known as race hazards."

"Oh dear God don't tell me," interjected Fiona, "if we flush the toilet we could summons the Ku Klux Klan!"

Brenda continued but not without difficulty. She quite liked that one. "Such circuitry just ensures that signals arrive in the correct order. Belt and braces so to speak."

"But the belt is slack and the braces are missing," said Richard bringing the technical jargon to a completion. Brenda nodded at what was a fairly accurate précis of the chaos.

"OK, so it looks like the fire alarm perhaps went off because someone used the photocopier at the same time as a van arrived with milk or whatever, but what's the problem? The construction work guarantee lasts for 12 months. They are building a new school in Edinburgh right now. Just get them back in here yes?" but Linda could tell that the faces looking back at her were not saying yes at all.

"The company have done a runner," Malcolm Ward announced.

"Oh my God so they have built half a school in Edinburgh and then disappeared!" said Fiona.

"No not exactly. They have built quarter of a hospital and disappeared."

"Sorry what the f." Richard managed to stop himself.

"Yip. Unbelievable as it sounds, nobody noticed it was the wrong plans."

"To the point though," sighed the Head Teacher, "what do we do in the meantime? Can it not just be switched off?"

"Sorry but that is just not an option. Remember it controls everything in this school including the heating, lighting.... everything. And just turning off some parts won't work either. That just sends a logic signal back to the processor to produce more mayhem."

"So can you give us any advice at all?"

"Yes. Don't use the lifts!" Assuring Fiona Dalton and the management team that they were working on the problem, Malcolm and Brenda made their departure.

"Have they started knocking the old school down yet?" Gill asked as the three deputies made their way back to their own offices leaving Fiona alone to use the situation for a quite lateral purpose. She set about composing a letter to be distributed about the school staff explaining that due to some technical difficulties the new building was having it would not be advisable to have a school show in the coming year. She knew all too well though that absolutely everyone who was at the final night last year would know exactly why she did not want to risk a repeat performance, and she often reflects on how eternally grateful she is that they took seriously and to heart the formal warning that copyright legislation would be, "Pursued to the full extent of the law," if the school attempted in any way to record the show.

Chapter Eight

The final night of the final school show, in the now condemned building, was less than an hour away. For those who had a long association with the crumbling relic it would be no contest as excitement battled nostalgia for pole position. With demolition due to begin within weeks it is quickly forgotten how achingly cold the rooms were in the winter and how suffocatingly hot in the summer. If it was windy outside you could be assured that it would be windy inside also. The flat roofs served to enhance the interior with many water features, and mould decorated the room with shifting patterns. But these issues were of no matter as only prize giving ceremonies, school dances; and school shows seduced the memories of many assembling here this evening.

Even Stephen Munro from the Physics Department, for whom teaching had become something from which he could walk away in a minute (and soon famously would) felt an underlying sadness as he thought back to all the events in which he had been involved. Often he had been the camera man but tonight recording had been strictly banned just in case the school got caught in the copyright web which had been growing uncontrollably in recent years. The show this year had basically been written entirely by staff and pupils but because it contained recognised songs, albeit with significantly altered and customized lyrics, it was considered best to play it safe. Even when popular and recognized shows were performed and recorded by schools, Stephen always thought how ridiculous the whole copyright thing was. "Is Broadway going to be brought to its knees and the West End Theatres turned into penny bargain shops just because of some ropey old videos of truly amateurish production gathering dust on the shelves of proud grandparents?" he found himself once again asking.

Stephen had arrived early as he had to drop off his daughter Michelle to perform her aesthetic duties and squeeze some more money out of their captive audience as they arrived. For some families, finding about £20 or more was a significant slice off the meagre family budget and he really thought that £6 per ticket was quite excessive for a school show. Emotional blackmail however is a powerful beast, and it lay await at the doorway to consume some more unwilling flesh, his own daughter being one of the monster's snapping gorging heads. Like all the others who had been selected to meet and greet, they were pleasing on the eye. As he looked at them however a recurring thought came to him. If society is so vocal in protecting its young then why do we insist in dressing the girls in what is just about the most erotic outfits ever designed by man, and he wasn't being politically incorrect by using the term.

Surely only a man could come up with such a "costume". The girls assembled like a young tribute act to prostitution and made ready to charm some pockets dry.

Stephen was soon joined by Jacky Forster from Modern Languages with whom he got on very well and shared a sense of humour. They selected their seats from the 220 that had been laid out. Strict fire regulations had decreed that 220 was the maximum safe number. With the hall really starting to fill up they both noticed that near the front many people were holding up tickets, gesticulating and pointing quite aggressively at others, most of whom were seated. They were not the type of women with whom you would contest an item at a jumble sale, and indeed could be forgiven for misreading their gender.

"The crowd is turning a bit ugly," said Jacky. This set them both off with uncontrollable giggles feeling just a bit guilty that they could be so shallow. It later transpired that people had been copying and printing off their own tickets hence the considerable over booking. Fiona Dalton appeared on the scene then had a word with the janitors. They returned with an extra 60 seats. Strict fire regulations had been down graded to simply being advisory. As they settled to watch the final moments before the show began, they both shared their admiration for those who can put together such productions. The stage was pre-lit for those arriving to show a street setting convincingly constructed and beautifully colourful. Lighting and sound were getting their final check before the show began, with sixth year boys scurrying about feeling quite cool and important saying, "one two one two," and giving the thumbs up to observing eyes. Most incredibly was the way that year upon year they were able to persuade some of the senior boys with the most street cred' to step well outside their comfort zone to perform on stage. It was never difficult to get girls to volunteer their talents. Was there ever a girl born who was not a naturally gifted singer and dancer? Well evidence would suggest most of them but such things were of no consequence on these occasions.

Ten minutes late, which traditionally means on time, the hall lights dimmed and the stage lighting was turned up. The mini orchestra of five led by the music teacher Miss Muldoon hiding in the hastily constructed pit stepped it up a gear from the underplayed overture which had been greeting the audience in the background, and suddenly the stage was filled with tiny little black figures wearing very bright multicoloured gloves. At first they moved slowly pointing and twirling about the stage but slowly the tempo of the music increased and so too did their pointing and twirling. As the music reached a crescendo it seemed quite miraculous that there were not multiple collisions as they simply flew and twisted about the stage, pointing and ducking and weaving. Suddenly the music stopped and they all froze in a random array of positions. Still they stood, though for some the music had ceased at the most inopportune moment as they balanced painfully on one toe. Eventually though as one they began slowly to lower themselves all wavy and twisty, and melt into the floor. Still they lay and silent parents sat uncomfortably, not really knowing what they were supposed to do. To their relief the stage lights faded to black which was the cue for tension breaking applause, each and every parent knowing that their son or daughter had melted better than any other. Under cover of darkness the little people rumbled off the stage.

The band struck up again and on came a troop of dancing girls wearing knee length dresses in an array of glamorous bright primary colours, the full A line skirts lagging their exotic movements. They smiled confidently as they glided their way about the stage in a broadly synchronised routine. This was always how it was. On the final dress rehearsal everyone trooped home in trepidation following a mostly discordant shambles, the lights going on strike, the sound system coming out in sympathy and young performers basically forgetting lines, forgetting lyrics and continuity silences which lasted for an eternity. Humiliation surely awaited the next day, but strangely, that was never how it unfolded.

Flawless? No but most certainly passable and appreciated by the half filled hall. First nights were always half full. By the second night the young performers are becoming fairly slick and accomplished but by the third night they are world superstars. They perhaps can't sing like world superstars; but neither can world superstars whose voices are "air brushed" by computers. Tonight though the senior pupils just seemed a bit more confident than their counterparts from previous generations. The first half came to an end in the traditional manner which is to get as many on stage as possible singing a long loud final note while slowly raising their arms from by their side to high above their heads. It worked every time.

It was now time for the raffle in which staff did the traditional swirly thing with their finger should their number be drawn, indicating that their ticket be removed and the draw taken again. After all, it is the staff who buy the prizes, buy the raffle tickets, twice: no amount of protestations at the door will fall anywhere other than on deaf ears, so it would be really bad form to collect a prize also. David Stewart, as always, was invited to draw the numbers from the hat and Shelley then despatched the prizes to the lucky winners. This year instead of the multitude of small prizes they had last year which resulted in the show running 30 minutes late, they bundled them in into larger prizes. The first winner held out his hand to receive his prize but Shelley was having none of it. She insisted on seeing the winning ticket. All subsequent winners ensured they had their tickets to hand. Stephen Munro just gave his raffle tickets to his daughter as he left the hall. He had left the building to use his artificial cigarette. There was no need to do so but he said the ritual of going to his old haunts was somehow helping him to quit.

Back in the hall as people returned to their seats for the second half with their fruit juice; fizzy sugary drinks were banned for all including adults but crisps and sweets were OK, the noise from backstage seemed rather excessive given that the show was about to recommence. There was giggling followed by giggly shooshing, and clinking noises. The hall fell silent as the band struck up and Amelia Rosenberg, probably the outstanding talent in the school but not comfortable with sharing, quietly took a seat to the side having earlier completed make-up tasks for the performers. Lights flickered on to reveal a park scene with a bench to the front of the stage. Once again a minor miracle had been performed by the Technical and Art Departments.

The lead girl and boy were sitting as far apart as possible on the bench as scripted. The lead boy however, Craig Ross was once again by his smile and demeanour, displaying more of this mysterious ultra confidence that pervaded the senior performers and indeed confident he was; as confident as a newt.

The opening scene should have shown a coy young boy, sliding slowly and discreetly along the bench towards the beautiful innocent young girl who had captured his heart. Lips poised, theatrically he should then have motioned towards her hoping to plant love's first kiss on her soft awaiting cheek. Craig quite evidently however had made the unilateral decision that sleazy old pervert would give the performance an extra edge, and leering at her made a grope for her left breast. As always at this stage of the performance the leading girl, Wendy Croft, stood up and strode towards the front of the stage announcing, with a despairing hand to her brow, "This is all happening too fast," and she wasn't wrong as she plunged into the orchestra pit landing in the drums.

"Oh no my girl has fallen for someone else!" proclaimed Craig. From where did he dig that out? It served however to make most of the audience believe that just perhaps it was part of the script. Wendy clamoured back onto the stage to the sound of much applause then performed a full but far from steady curtsey. By this point Fiona Dalton was perhaps seeing her pension being used to stoke a fire and tried to make her way unnoticed from the back of the hall to the stage. Suddenly those extra 60 seats seemed like a very bad idea as she tried to squeeze her way through a heaving crowd having the time of their lives.

Our smirking young performers moved towards each other as on came the senior dancing girls again. They flooded the stage clearly filled with the same joy as the leading pair and proceeded to dance enthusiastically but mostly certainly not in crisp synchronisation. One girl fell to the floor but stood right back up like a new born foal and flowed seamlessly back into her routine. A second one fell taking another with her but as before they were unperturbed and returned by instalments to an upright position. In no time at all however it looked like a sniper in the audience was trying to take out the living dead. Down they went then up again but carrying on smiling with their dance routine. Back and forward they stepped, jazz hands in full flow. By the time the Head Teacher reached the stage there were as many on the deck as standing as she silenced the band and brought the dancers broadly to a halt. A few neither noticed that she was there nor that the music had stopped and carried on doing solo acts for several seconds.

Fiona knew she had to say something and got as far as, "Well ladies and gentlemen," when Shelley appeared from nowhere like a crazed assassin and thrust an enormous bouquet of flowers at her, almost knocking her off her feet. Meanwhile from back stage came the most dreadful retching and splashing sounds, as Fiona, wanting to de-materialize thought, "Could they not at least have taken off their radio microphones before they started throwing up?"

Knowing this would probably get the best laugh of the night but cornered by fate most cruel she announced, "It would seem that the cast have been hit by a bad case of food poisoning."

She was not wrong in her prediction. Uproar. It was not so much a case of food poisoning but rather a case of wine more likely as much of the alcohol donated for the raffle never made it into the prizes. Meanwhile loud and clear from the speakers came expressions of increasing despair.

"Oh my god I want to die."

"I'm never drinking again."

"You absolute bastard. You've just been sick on my wee sister."

Running from the wing came a little girl dressed in black, (with pretty gloves), screaming in absolute horror and disgust before becoming catatonic centre stage as the contents of someone's stomach oozed from her (formerly) beautiful blond hair. The flashing lights of the emergency services now outside the school complimented the chaotic scenes to perfection as paramedics made their way into the building and quickly set up the hall like an emergency casualty ward in a disaster movie. The place was now mostly empty leaving behind pupils strewn about the floor being attended to, and a scattering of parents searching through the rubble for their loved ones.

Fiona Dalton stood silently, surrounded by Gill Paterson and a group of teachers.

"So, do you think the final show will be remembered?"

Chapter Nine

Much to his considerable discomfort John Mortimore found himself in the school office at such a time as would result in him being in crowded school corridors as he made his way back to his room for the final period of the day. He had received a phone call to say that documents required his immediate attention. As he entered the industrious work place, office staff were glancing up at him then whispering to each other, or that at least was how he perceived it. Joan Stuart who was in charge of the office approached John and said, "At last, the invisible man. Where have you been for the past several weeks? Too tied up in your work?"

"What do you mean, too tied up? What do you mean by that?" he snapped before becoming alert to his over reaction. "Oh sorry, just busy. I've just been buried in my work."

"Well clearly too busy to read your emails. It was at the beginning of last week that everyone was told to come down and check their personal records were up to date."

"Oh I'm sorry. Really..."

"It's OK, you're here now and there's not much to do really. I have to ask though, why the large tinted glasses? You just don't seem to be yourself any more," she enquired as she turned to one of her colleagues as she said this. John

Mortimore interpreted the words and glances with despairing suspicion. What did they know?

"The glasses. I am on drops that make my eyes sensitive to light so I have been advised by the consultant to wear these." This would have been a convincing impromptu answer had that been the case, but it certainly was not. Nothing in his life was impromptu any more. Everything was now carefully planned to avoid meeting people anywhere; or make direct eye contact. His routes to and from work, what time he arrived or departed, even when he went shopping to buy essential goods were thought out in advance. His movement about the school received similar attention, but this current forced digression to his avoidance strategies had left him vulnerable.

"Well all you have to do is read over the details and if nothing has changed then you simply have to sign and date it. So has your address changed; are you still a man?" Joan asked mischievously as other office staff responded with smirks.

John Mortimore was more convinced than ever that they must know something, being so overwhelmed with irrational panic that he failed to consider that perhaps they were alluding to Toni Martin, who they had actually taken to their hearts and now involved her in their social circle. John Mortimore scribbled down something vaguely resembling a signature and made his way to the door.

"Just a minute John, could you take this parcel back to your department. It looks like someone has been sending you toys." She shook it then added, "Well it doesn't sound like a rattle!"

She handed the package to Mr Mortimore who was becoming faint and dizzy with anxiety.

"Thank you petal." Joan called everyone petal, even sometimes the Head Teacher, but to John's mind every word and gesture carried a malicious passenger.

The school building signalled the beginning of the final session of the day and doors flew open flooding the corridors with pupils making their final journey before the freedom of the weekend. John was now thrown to the whim and mercy of one of his many nightmare scenarios. He tried to make his way through the enemy throng trying to be unnoticed. In truth he was all but invisible to those around him but from his view point he was being slashed to the bone by hundreds of lacerating sneers. As he approached his room it was mostly 4th year pupils making their way to who knows where. Walking with them was Miss Toni Martin chatting freely and openly with those around her. Gone was the hesitant and clumsy young teacher who made such an impression on the staff in the lecture theatre, and how also she had changed in appearance. With her hair now just that bit longer and make up complementing a face which was undergoing subtle changes brought on by oestrogen, she would not merit a second glance by strangers, or then again perhaps would but only for more conventional reasons. Her conservative professional top looked totally right and appropriate for her slender figure which was taking on very gradual redistribution. The most telling sign of someone totally at ease with themselves was the grey knee length skirt worn with casual nonchalance.

"Good afternoon Miss Ladyboy," came an anonymous voice from the crowd. Remaining incognito however did not last as many pupils' stares of disapproval singled out the perpetrator. "Sorry Miss Martin."

"Apology accepted," she responded with a warm smile which also carried an underlying message, "Yeh but don't try that twice mister!" as she walked past John Mortimore without a care in her world in complete contrast to his own acrid unforgiving turmoil. The noise in the corridor seemed to be increasing as he was being ignored by hundreds of gaping acerbic stares in the boiling tempest of bodies. Like an audio equivalent of the Rorschach test where the human brain contrives to make recognised visual forms where non exist, John Mortimore was constructing words from the incoherent noise. "Baby, Princess, dress, pink..." He eventually reached the relative tranquillity of his room, but by no stretch of reality could it ever be called sanctuary. No such place existed, especially not in the solitude of his tormented mid night hours, neither awake nor asleep. Sitting alone for now but not for long in his darkened room, closed blackout blinds being a permanent feature, he reflected bitterly on the divergent fortunes of his and Toni Martin's and tried to manufacture equivalence where he knew absolutely none existed. In the distance he could hear growing sounds and voices getting ever closer and within moments a senior class was making its way into his room in dribs and drabs. They always arrived late on Friday as this was often the norm when coming from PE and HE classes. The truth was that this actually had been one of his favourite classes before his life imploded, and a relatively calm end to the week. Now however he had become the focus of the whole world's derisive and whispering malevolence. Although the class did have Chardonnay and Madonna, they did not have an audience nor command any measure of respect in this mostly able and mature group. There was half a dozen or so who were not so academically gifted and he used to complain bitterly how impossible it was to teach split level classes. What he would give now to return to the times when that was the hub of his discontent.

With the data projector and DVD player primed for action he pressed play and slid quietly and lowly into his chair. It was becoming increasingly the case that classes watched videos in the shielding darkness or copied notes from a screen. In the class in front of him right now a few watched or pretended at least to do so while others just quietly chatted to each other. The tell tale glow on some faces was clear evidence that some had their phones out and were smiling and looking towards John Mortimore. He knew what images must have been getting projected onto their hostile retinas. It had to be him. It must be.

He became suddenly aware that the class were all looking at him with a hint of expectation. The video had finished and that should have been the cue for a teacher to start teaching.

"The video Sir. It's finished." He had misjudged or misread the time on the DVD and now found himself having to talk to a class, a wholly unwelcome situation.

"Will I put the lights on sir?"

"No!" he exclaimed in a voice of inappropriate panic. "No," he repeated much more quietly. He mumbled some words like he was in auto pilot, then fell quiet as the class responded to an empty shell standing before them. Once more he became aware that they were all looking at him.

"OK, eh yeh so if you look at the map on the wall it does look like the coasts of West Africa and South America may once have been joined."

There was of course no chance whatsoever that a wall map could be seen in this gloom. "What geological evidence is there to support this hypothesis?" Once again there was an uncomfortable silence.

"Sir, that's exactly what you just asked us already."

The concern that had been growing for the health of Mr Mortimore was becoming palpable to everyone, everyone that is apart from he himself. It had not gone unnoticed by Chardonnay either but that was of absolutely no concern to the cold heartless monster that she was.

"OK then if you would just open your books at the chapter headed Plate Tectonics and read that till the end of the period."

"Sir, you haven't given the books out yet."

"Oh right, just give me a minute," as he struggled to find them in the dark made worse with tinted glasses. Books were handed out: the wrong ones. Nobody spoke. In due course the bleeper went and the room slowly emptied, some books being brought to the front but most just left scattered in a room where order was being destroyed by layer upon layer of detritus. The room fell silent but he was not alone.

"Hi Mr Mortimore." The voice of Chardonnay left him unable even to look up. "What are Fridays without money to spend? Not the best so £300 from you right now would just make the evening so much better."

"But I've paid you this week already!" he said in feeble despair.

"Oh don't be a meansy weansy little baby to you precious Chardonnay."

"I don't have it just now."

"That's OK, bring it to the flat tonight where a few of the girls will be having a little drink."

"A few? What do you mean a few? Who have you told?"

"Don't panic. Nobody yet. It will just be another two girls and don't take on so, you know both of them," she added with mocking re-assurance. "They are also fed up with their Saturday jobs. We insist also that you attend our little gathering. It's informal let's say so you can wear some casual clothes. Something you can relax in."

Madonna looked flustered. "I thought he had to dress as a baby?"

Chardonnay could no longer be bothered explaining, then heading for the door she added, "And if you're really good we won't add anything special to your bottle."

"Drugs! Not Drugs!"

"No not at all unless you include powerful laxatives as a drug. See you later princess," and they both departed. Was that the moment perhaps Chardonnay derailed her own gravy train, or worse? Just as the girls left Fiona Dalton arrived.

"Princess?" she queried.

"Oh just an in joke. Nothing really."

The Head Teacher closed the door behind her and picking up a chair came and sat by his side. "John, I have to share some concerns with you." Seeing him immediately tense up she hastily added, "I am not here to cause you difficulties. Really. Part of my job concerns the health and well being of my staff and right now that is you."

"I'm fine honestly. It's just the new school. Getting to know my way around. You know how it is."

"And that's why you sit in the dark all the time with the blinds closed? Getting to know the school? You never leave your room other than last thing at night to go home. Have you any internal emails still unopened? Sorry this is going to sound like spying but obviously I know. It was over two hundred when I left my office to come here."

"I'll attend to that but I'm OK. I'll be back in a routine soon."

"But you're not OK and I am really worried about you. When did you ever not shave every day and what is with the dark glasses? The real problem is that pupils are reporting back to me that they are genuinely worried about you too. Do you understand? They are talking about you but really worried. They care. They like you. Always have."

John Mortimore's glasses served momentarily to hide his red eyes filling up but the tears that escaped the anonymity of the virtually opaque lenses, caught the light of the projector and served to be distress signals on his face.

Fiona Dalton put her arm around him and continued, "Parents are also starting to contact the school. I really do think you should take time off your work, and just as long as it takes. Don't take this the wrong way but the place will function perfectly without you. The school machine needs none of us in particular. Not me, not you; not anyone really. Now I'm going to arrange cover for you and do not expect to see you on Monday. Please phone in first thing in the morning to confirm you won't be in. Please do that for me. Get professional help. Trust me you would not be the only staff member who right now is having mental health issues or problems. It's nothing to be ashamed of." She pulled him more tightly to her side and wrapped her other arm around him before leaving him again to the solitude of the darkness.

"Take time off," he thought.

Chapter Ten

Hamish Jones was at a bit of a loss. It was lunchtime but his Art Department colleagues were both out of school that day so the department base was just too quiet. It was normally a place of great humour, as his fellow artists Mandy and Morag were both gifted with sharp wit and delicious sarcasm. Well, of course they were; he interviewed them; he chose them. On the day of their interviews they mentioned school ethos, teamwork, initiative, every child is special; and a whole host of in vogue buzz words and policies, but most importantly, they seemed a right good laugh. Others also pointed out that both were a cosmetic surgeon's worst nightmare, stunningly attractive without the necessity for expensive laceration therapy. Talent and good looks were not mutually exclusive he would argue. Anyway, his lunch devoured he decided to seek out the company of another department. He was not in the mood to be alone with his thoughts and judged it would be selfish not to share. His first contemplated destination was the Home Economics base and quite frequently they have some absolutely wonderful freshly made tasty treats on offer. He thought more about this option though. Much as though he got on supremely well with the riotously funny Mr Trappatoni he was clearly a big fan of his own produce, and it showed. His three colleagues clearly also shared the same enthusiasm for the end result of their own skills. It was a fairly small base and the image of trying to squeeze in with these formidable people, well prepared for an extended famine, made him think the better of it. "That is one place where the idiomatic elephant in the room may avoid instigating social discomfort," he thought and deciding that line would be going in the book he was presently writing.

"Ah the English department," he mused. "I'm sure they'll be deep in heated debate yet sprinkled with droll exchanges like Oscar Wilde and William Thackery might be, as persiflage reigned in some ethereal pub not constrained by temporal inconveniences."

In he strode to the English base and immediately knew it was not where he wanted to be. Scattered about the low table in front of him were pictures a plenty of some royal wedding or other. Being renowned as quite a vociferous republican they teasingly invited him to come share in the moment.

"I really don't think so," he remarked with melodramatic disdain. "Oliver Cromwell had the right idea. Turn that crown upside down!" as he considered that to be perhaps another line for his book. They had actually long since abandoned their interest in the glossy pictures and had turned their attention to another of his pet hates, Soaps, as they discussed last night's episodes as only aficionados and enthusiasts can; like it is real.

"I was actually looking for...."

"What, a way to get back out the room without being seen to do so?" said Claire McEwan, the Head of department. "Not a fan of soaps then?" she continued.

"What, watching grown ups play at houses? Not really, no."

"Not even the Australian ones with all those scantily clad gorgeous young girls?" added young Michelle who would not have been out of place in Hamish's Art Department.

"No I have my wife's fashion catalogues for that," he answered just too readily to go unnoticed. "Anyway, I'll leave you to continue your analysis," he said, knowing that this had not been his finest hour. His retreat could not in any way be marketed as a Dunkirk moment, but he readily composed himself and made his way to the Science department.

"The Science department. Surely a bastion of intellectual substance. Right now they will be reconciling Quantum Mechanics and General Relativity."

That simple sentence alone perhaps encapsulated Hamish. He was truly an academic and intellect of real magnitude and could have reached the highest level of anything he had selected to do. As it stood he was a more accomplished musician than anyone in the music department, spoke three languages fluently and was totally at ease with virtually any subject, if perhaps not Soaps. He would be just hateable if he was not so likeable. He didn't really expect, nor would he have wanted the Science department to be having an intellectual joust at all actually, and indeed they were not.

"TURD, BROWN TROUT!"

"FUNBAGS"

Hamish immediately discerned what was going on, sat himself down then proceeded to contribute handsomely to both tallies.

"OK," declared Matthew, "time's up and here's the result. The number of synonyms for shit is thirty nine and for boobs twenty twoooooooooo. Shit has well and truly roasted boobs!" he announced to a strangely quiet and captive audience, an audience who were kind of looking at him, but perhaps slightly beyond him. He didn't want to turn round; ever. He just wanted time frozen, but he knew he must and when he did, he acknowledged uncomfortably to himself that it was a decent attempt at the perfect score.

"So Matthew, fitting in quite well I see," said the Head Teacher, accompanied by both the Head Girl and Shelley. He opened his mouth to give the impression of imminent coherence forming in his head with a reply to follow, but it was a bluff.

"Well girls, as you can see," continued Fiona Dalton, "even during their lunch break it's just work work work."

Linda Forsyth, the Head Girl was just loving the moment with a smirk which strangely defused the situation. She was the Head Girl for all the right reasons and would surely keep this moment to herself. Yes of course she would. As for Shelley? Not a hint of emotion.

"Anyway Linda, if you can still perform the purpose of your visit?"

"Hi, we are putting together ideas for next year's school magazine and we are looking for quiz ideas." At this point Shelley thrust forth a sheet of paper which Matthew took from her frozen hand. "If you have any thoughts would you please jot them down and we will collect the sheet in a couple of weeks. Thank you."

With that, the trio departed leaving the gang to reflect upon their special moment, by reflect meaning retain a tension bursting laugh for at least a respectable few seconds. In due course they calmed themselves and turned their attention to the quiz sheet, and like bluebottles who repeatedly throw themselves in vain at a window pane, they were not to learn from previous experience however recent.

"How about getting some members of staff to sit scud naked on the photocopier and the competition could be Name That Arse?" suggested Zander.

"Talking of which, where is your esteemed Head of Department?" asked Hamish, sitting in her chair: she had her own chair. There was no love lost between them, Hamish the free spirited genius and Colette Murphy, a slave to bureaucracy, and though his IQ was somewhat higher than hers she more than compensated for this with her BMI.

"She's at an in-service training day," Zander informed Hamish.

"Doing what? Advanced sycophancy?"

"Exactly," continued Zander, going with the theme, "in preparation that perhaps one day she becomes the Head Teacher," an idea that sent a communal shudder through all who were present. "She is getting lessons from a contortionist so she can crawl up her own arse!"

This time it was Zander's turn to be caught but somehow from the expression on the face of Deputy Head Gill Paterson his outburst was of little importance.

"I am afraid I have some very very sad and tragic news. As you may know, John Mortimore from the Geography Department has not been in for a few days. As he did not call in, we felt it best to try and contact him. We have since been told that he was found dead in a flat; not his own flat. I'll spare you asking for details, and it will be common knowledge within the hour anyway so there is no need for a pretence of confidentiality. The police informed us that he was found with a nearly half empty bottle of whisky; and one of his wrists deeply slashed."

Chapter Eleven

Several days earlier and for the first time that he could recall in many months John Mortimore was light of spirit. With clarity of thought and serene conciliation he felt quite weightless with euphoria. Music filled the room, La Folia; doleful and yet not so. "Vivaldi is it?" he thought to himself, or did he perhaps actually say it out loud? There was no demarcation line between the two this particular evening, not that he was alert to anyway nor really cared. He seamlessly drifted back and forth from detached observer of his own life to deep sensual involvement. The musical progression to which he had long been drawn in its many guises served as a background this particular evening, and had been selected with purpose. As the violin and harpsichord complemented each other he took a sip of the very expensive single malt whisky that he had been keeping accordingly for a very special occasion: and there was no point keeping it for some future moment that may have proved more special than this. There would not be one. Sitting on the table beside the whisky bottle was a small pile of crisp new twenty pound notes from which he slipped one from the top. "There can be no more erotic sound," he momentarily asserted before smiling to himself that perhaps he was wrong, and that is exactly why he found himself where he was now.

Standing up he scrunched the note in his hand and carried it into the large walk-in cupboard. "Here's another one for you," he said before continuing, "Looks like you've not finished the last one yet. Is the food too rich for you? Talk about chewing thirty two times and all that! I'm thinking maybe that your eyes are bigger than your belly. My gran used to say that to me all the time. Could you imagine that? Huge big stomach sized eyes? What a weird saying eh? You've actually not said much at all recently. Has the cat got your tongue? Come to think of it that would have been a good idea. It would have left more room."

He smiled nonchalantly at his own musings then continued, "Oops, looks like you've been drooling a little bit there. I can fix that. There you go. Done! No pudding for you though!" He walked towards the door then looked back and said, "I hope the music isn't too loud for you but I'll shut the door just in case," and very quietly he did just that before silently turning the key.

"Corelli!" he exclaimed as he sat back down, "No actually I'm sticking with Vivaldi. That's my final answer. Vivaldi it is." He swirled the whisky in his glass then wondered why he always did that "Twenty year old single malt. Just what was I doing when this amber fluid began its journey to fruition? I would have been about 10 years old myself. That is when we went on our first family holiday to Spain; our first holiday abroad. Just how long did my sister and I spend in the sea? We really should have shrunk." Reminiscing evoked memories of such sensual clarity that he believed he could feel the warm water around him, taste the salt and wriggle his toes in the luxuriously soft sand beneath his feet. "I remember we got our first taste of beer. The Spanish waiters didn't care if we were 6 or 60 but they did watch us both with a mischievous glint. Jane just screwed up her face but being a boy I had to pretend I liked the nasty stuff. And just how fluent was my dad in Spanish? "Dos beerios for my sunnio and dotterrio s'il vous plait." It would have been less embarrassing if he had just said "pleasio" rather than launching into his own version of Esperanto."

John Mortimore pondered all this for a moment which then made him think back to even earlier times. He hadn't normally played with his slightly older sister even when he was only about four and for one simple reason. Girl's games were rubbish. "Could she not see that lining up soldiers then shooting them down was so much more fun than pouring fresh air from a tiny teapot into tiny cups? And what was with the strange American accent?" Now and then he recalled how he managed to persuade her to play at football when there were no boys around so she had to do; then she would get hit with the ball and run away crying. "John just hit me with the ball on purpose!" which always led to him being so unjustly dragged into the house early because he didn't do it on purpose, not always anyway. John grinned at this thought. He took another sip of his £5 a dram liquid treasure which he knew was actually wasted on him. "Peaty undertones and a hint of heather? Well having eaten neither peat nor heather in my life I will take your word for it."

The haunting music brought back another memory. "Mum I don't WANT to learn how to play the violin!"

"Well you're going to. Your dad will be starting back shifts soon and it's my bingo night. Your sister will be going with you."

"Oh mum no. Just no! That's even worse. I'll be laughed at by absolutely everybody for absolutely the rest of my life! You'd be as well sending me to school in a skirt," an idea that really had no appeal at all, then nor since.

His thoughts now focused completely on his sister Jane. He couldn't remember the last time he had spoken to her never mind seen her. "Was it her wedding? Surely not." They hadn't fallen out and had actually got on quite well before she moved to Cornwall. He had told her that it would be easier and quicker to get to New York from northern Scotland than that distant corner of England when first he found out. He was no big fan of telephones either so they just lost all communication. He couldn't even remember the name of her three children; apart from the oldest that is. "Charisma! What the hell. Charisma! Charisma Balls! What was she going to be called at school? Caress ma balls? Kiss ma balls?"

Another glance at the bottle sent him forward in time again and once more to around when he was about 10 years old at which age he started to go to the football with his dad. Such memories usually filled his eyes with tears and his heart with lead as he recalled one of God's gifts to humanity killing his hero of a father within a couple of months. Today though it was different. The memory carried no grief. He thought also how it spared his dad the pain of watching his precious wife lose all that she was, become a stranger before his very eyes; another gift from the all caring deity. He remembered his last ever visit to see her before a fatal stroke relieved his once proud and then still beautiful mum from being stripped bare of all dignity.

"You're not the queen!" she snarled at him with regal contempt.

"You are right, I'm not."

"Well don't go sitting yourself down then who ever you are. Make yourself useful and go find Her Majesty. I don't want all this food my servants have prepared going to waste!" she exclaimed gesticulating with an open hand towards nothing.

Another sip of whisky and he made a fast forward to his teaching college days where he was actually introduced to the type of music to which he was listening now by one of his first serious girl friends. "Four months I was with her," he thought. "That almost counts as married!" She ended it. He always had preferred it that way. Less drama. He still remembered the occasion with some clarity. She was delivering the standard, "It's not you it's me," and, "I need to be alone," routine. The prevailing recollection was most definitely when it appeared she may have said, "I don't think we should see each other any more," or words to that effect, and he had punched the air and shouted, "YES!" "My God she really slammed the door behind her that night. I honestly thought it was going to come off its hinges. She learned something that day. If you going to tell someone that you're going to break up with them, don't do it while the football is on."

This all just led onto more of his college memories. The booze bus, joining the football team; trying out boxing. "That was a mistake. People trying to hit me? What on Earth ever made me think that would be fun!" Deep reflection now took hold of him. "If I could could sum up my life though in one word, from early childhood through college, my family life, I know what that one word would be. Normal." He could think of nothing, no trauma, no environmental pressure that would have given him his special interest, the special interest that had brought him to where her was today; where he was in these dwindling moments of his life journey. He had been fairly relaxed at work, mainstream sexuality and never wanted for friends nor struggled to fit in socially in most scenarios. If some subliminal life event had steered him down this path then he was indeed totally oblivious to it, and also quite evidently it was a path well worn. There were clearly millions who must have travelled this same route and indulged in the same release unless all of those websites were just for him and him alone. "Not likely, I really don't think," he so softly and quietly breathed. He thought about all the clothes which so recently he had gathered up and burned but now thought to himself, "I wonder if I should have handed them into a charity shop. It was quality stuff. There must be the odd six foot baby out there; or maybe a born again Christian."

He regretted he would never get to share that line but he had had his fill of whisky and knew it was time. He picked up the scalpel that was lying on the table; lying on the table where he himself had lay many a time. "I wonder where Petra, Olga; Eva Braun, what ever the hell her name really was, is now? She did seem familiar. Just can't place her though. Anyway, I'm sure she'll turn out just fine one day," he thought surely with misplaced and over generous exoneration. Once more he looked at the glistening clean scalpel.

"I wonder if my life will pass before me? Hope not. Just done that bit. I hate repeats. Another line to remain unshared," he sighed. "Anyway, just all too much wondering going on."

With one tentative sweep of the blade he left little more than a line on his wrist which transformed rapidly to a rich red but it did not spill nor ooze. A second sweep and blood trickled down his arm. The third, "Now that's the one," he knew with a peculiar satisfaction and allowed the scalpel to fall point first to stick into the floor like an arrow, vibrating to a halt. His euphoria gently and slowly decayed to warm, comforting tranquillity, words displaced by abstract ethereal images as slowly his weakening breath became lost and consumed by sombre melody.

Chapter Twelve

Doctor Burns was a recent recruit to the Religious Education department having been moved to Highland View Secondary School as a result of being made surplus at another in the Local authority and a very sudden vacancy appearing in his new establishment. He had been reading through the assignments which he had set his senior year class a week earlier and he was nursing his rage on simmer awaiting their imminent arrival. To him it was clear that not only had his predecessor been a weak willed liberal but clearly also quite reprehensibly believed that all religions were entitled to fair and impartial scrutiny and credence. Obviously when being interviewed for teaching college Doctor Burns had made all the right noises about respect, diversity and such things. He must however have felt the flames of hell on the soles of his feet as he spoke such blasphemy in front of his four interviewers, the three lecturers from Montrieth Teaching College; and God! His interpretation of the Bible was literal and not up for negotiation.

He turned his attention back to sifting through the books and documents he had inherited from the old school awaiting demolition. "This sacrilege should have been left in the old building to be dumped with the rest of the rubble and trash," he raged as he launched book after book, text after text into his out trays he had set up at the back of the room, the out trays being large cardboard boxes destined for the skip. When he happened upon a particularity large book it was clearly from one of the many repugnant and most evil Antichrist pseudo religions, and his rage filled strength resulted in the vessel of the Devil's deceit being propelled clean out the window from his third floor room, accelerating past the science department at nine point eight meters per second squared and thumping off the baked ground outside the Home Economics Department.

Eventually he came to a batch of Bibles; illustrated bibles. "Bibles with pictures. With pictures!" A stroke seemed imminent. At least they were Bibles he thought as he managed to calm the waters of his internal sea of despair. Unfortunately the perfect storm was just moments away. For many school children an illustration is not complete unless enhanced by their own artistic skills, and with many images of someone kneeling closely in front of someone standing, there was a recurrent theme.

"One day Mr Wood will pay for his unholy negligence with more than his job."

The previous incumbent Peter Wood had indeed been forced to find another career. He had been one of those unfortunates for whom the war was long since lost and it was only a matter of time before he would spend his last day in front of a class one way or another. Not enough that many pupils made his working life unbearable, a few of his "colleagues" also derived pleasure from exacerbating and observing his torment. His final battle was with a repugnant 4th year class of really dreadful individuals. Everywhere most of this group went they caused severe trouble and spent most of their time excluded to the corridors where they could cause even more trouble. Precedent had taught them that they could do what they want. If a teacher shouts at you, shout back louder, though they may not always get away with swearing or striking out; but usually did. If you want to leave the room, just do it. If you want to throw things about the room that's OK too, and fighting with each other is fine as well. They knew the system. If you get a punishment exercise, don't do it. If it gets doubled or re-issued, still don't do it. Eventually you will be given a detention. Don't turn up, and if issued again, don't turn up again. Eventually you will be taken from your class, to sit in isolation, or to put it another way, taken out of the class you didn't want to be in from the beginning. Result! All previous sanctions are revoked so you sit in isolation for a day or two in the exclusion base. Should there be no places available, which is most of the time, you are just returned to your class to riot, as you now know you can do with impunity. The local authority thus impose their wish on despairing and impotent school management teams, so that the marauding savages do not lose out on valuable Learning and Teaching, and the rest of the class, usually those with the greatest needs, get to share the wisdom of these rioting thugs.

Mr Wood had allowed his class in first then followed them in, a class that would prove, mercifully, to be his last. The noise level was just short of the medically recognised pain threshold as they wandered and roared and pushed and shoved. Lost in this jungle of course were a half dozen or so wonderful human beings confined to the ghetto so they could, "learn at an appropriate level and at an individualized pace," a truly cynical euphemism meaning forgotten about. He tried as usual just to be heard above the nondescript roaring they used as some version of primitive language, and attempted to take the register, but was ignored; as usual.

"Be quite!" he screamed so loud that his voice broke to a high pitched squeal. This generated raucous laughter.

"Will you just shut the fuck up you moronic brain dead cunts."

The final battle was coming to an end.

"I've just had it with you shit for brains goons."

For once he had gained the attention of the class but for the wrong reasons. They knew that ultimate victory was only moments away and sharpened their weapons. When an absolute roar of laughter died down there came a nasal voice from the homogeneous fleshy sludge, "You tell them Sir," as a sneering face, resembling a human protruded from a grey tight hood.

The group of pleasant pupils long since abandoned to this menagerie were really appreciating Mr Wood's outburst; and how they shared his opinion, and wished they could conjure up a flame thrower for him. The troop looked at each other as mocking roaring laughter started to pick up again then one of them attempted to say something but before a syllable could leave his lips Mr Wood strode up to him until they were almost clashing heads and screamed, "And before you even start with your 'chillax' and your usual shit just shut your fuck'n face if you can even call it a face. More like an acne farm you fuck'n circus freak!"

His face now crimson and sweating all over he continued, "Your parents were probably morons too. You should all be locked in a building with them and torched. Do the world a favour..... If I ever meet the scummy parents who should have drowned you the moment you were born I might kill them myself before they produce any more fuckwits."

He left his room, the full consequences of his outburst rapidly starting to take form in his mind and soon he slid down a wall in uncontrollable tears of despair before being assisted to some private sanctuary by alerted teachers in other rooms. That night he got a call from the

Head Teacher telling him to stay at home until things sorted themselves out. Within a few weeks he was invited to the authority HQ where he was advised that taking early retirement was his best option as what the parents had in mind could have much more serious consequences. He signed the relevant documents then once formally released from his profession of 28 years he let the senior personnel present know first hand what he thought of the parents who had destroyed his life and what should be done to them; and his opinion of the Education Department's platitudinous Inclusion Policy.

Doctor Burns then turned his thoughts from Mr Wood to his Principal Teacher, the young and charismatic Miss Jennifer Jenson. "An atheist!" he despaired. "A head of Religious Education who is an atheist!" In truth however, in his mind, anyone who was not a member of The Free Presbyterian Church of Scotland was an atheist, and consoled himself that at least she wasn't a Catholic. Jennifer Jenson reciprocated concerns only hers were shared also by both parents and pupils as she found out from Fiona Dalton, and often pondered what the title of Doctor Burns' thesis may have been. "Bigotry. The Case For," often came to mind.

Doctor Burns was having one last incredulous scrutiny of the particular assignment that had really taken him to the edge, ensuring his flame was set to gas mark five in preparation as he read:-

John Doe: *So this is heaven? Nice? Minimalist but nice.*
God: *Yeh, I can't be doing with clutter.*
John Doe *: Love the beard.*
God *: You ain't seen anything yet. Watch this.*
John Doe *: Awesome.*
God *: Isn't it though?...... Fibre optics.*
John Doe *: Just wondering, where's JC? Is he about?*
God: *My boy? No idea. Never do.*
John Doe *: Kids eh? Just so hard to nail down.*
God *: Tell me about it!*
John Doe: *Anyway. Look, I've got to say, this universe thing you made. It's just awesome. Countless billions of galaxies, black holes, neutron stars, quasars....... It's just amazing!*
God: *Thanks. It just came to me one night.... Well when I say night, there was no sun, moon and stuff, well anyway yeh.*
John Doe *: You made some right bad stuff too. Earthquakes, plagues and things.*
God *: That wasn't me! Well OK it was. I got bored. Look, there's a limit to how long you can play at cloud shapes!*
John Doe *: Got to ask. Did you write the Old Testament?*
God *: Do I look like I do drugs? No it was a Holy ghost writer.*

John Doe: *Nice one. High five. You made me too, and everybody else. Thanks again. What can I say? It all seems a bit one way. I mean, is there anything we can do for you?*

God: *Really. Chill. You're good.*

John Doe: *Look there must be something to show our appreciation. Chocolates? Flowers? Singing Christmas card?*

God: *Well there is something but I'm frightened to ask.*

John Doe: *Hit me.*

God: *OK then. Perhaps if you ever ….*

John Doe: *Yeh? Go on...*

God: *Well, If you ever have a child would you mind awfully mutilating their genitals?*

John Doe: *Sorry what? Yes I would mind actually!*

God: *Glad to hear it. Reprehensible isn't it? Just who started that? Anyway, how about this then? Somebody picks your child up, throws water on their face and mutters something about the Holy Trinity?*

John Doe: *The Holy Trinity. What's that?*

God: *Haven't a clue. Just sounded good in my head.*

John Doe: *Who are all those folk sitting at desks writing?*

God: *Them? The naughty dead. Writing essays on why people shouldn't kill in my name?*

John Doe: *Essays? How many words?*

God: *Ten million.*

John Doe: *Harsh! Actually not really is it?*

God: *OK what else can you do? How about you grow your hair into long ringlets, wear a funny black hat and bang your head off a wall.*

John Doe: *Eh?*

God: *Just messing with you. Saw it on cable TV. Really funny. No, what you could do is have bread and wine and pretend you are eating the flesh and drinking the blood of my son.*

John Doe: *You're messing with me again. What are you like? ...... Oh, you're not messing. You're serious.*

OK. I'll see what I can do. Loved talking to you. Catch you later.

Devil: *Not if I catch you first. Ho ho ha ha ha haaaaa!*

John Doe: *Who's that?*

God: *Not exactly sure. He just follows me about a bit and does that weird theatrical laugh. Some people call him the Prince of Darkness. Calls himself Satan but he actually changed his name by deed poll. It used to be Nigel.*

John Doe: *What, Nigel the Prince of Darkness?*

God: *No that was never really going to run was it?*

John Doe: *He wears far too much blusher.*

God: *You're not wrong there. Needs a gay best friend to keep him right. Flossing wouldn't go amiss either and by* *the way don't be fooled by the horns ...... Fake.*

John Doe: *Really?*

God: *Yip. Takes them off to wash his hair..... and always wears a shower cap.*

John Doe: *Anyway it's been a blast. See you later.*

God: *Bye then; and mind the first step! …. Oh dear, best set another place for dinner.*

As the blasphemous script was being twisted in his wrathful hands the class quietly made its way in and sat down as this class tended to do. It was populated with some of the finest young minds in the school. In the class also were Andrew Cash and Dean Colt from Mr Fuck off's class. For reasons which schools with all their best efforts could not unlock, they belonged to a genre of students who just can't do exams. It wasn't exam nerves. Indeed these were two of the coolest people you would ever meet in your life not to mention comfortably articulate. Mr Munro actually said to them during one of the frequent maelstroms of screaming disorder in their Science class, "I reckon if you two went sky diving and the parachutes failed to open you would just stick music on and enjoy the final ride." The class settled quickly anticipating that Dr Durno would have an opinion to express as he held a clutch of papers in his hand.

"Never, but never before in my life have I had to endure the poisonous and disrespectful puerile nonsense I have just read. Mr Wood, your previous so called teacher," he spat out with contempt, "clearly allowed you to do and write just whatever you wanted."

He was on dangerous ground here. This class were mature and intelligent enough to appreciate that Mr Wood, when allowed was actually a very learned teacher with a sharp if eccentric sense of humour; and in their class he was allowed to be just that. They had liked him. They had also noticed that he seemed to be about the village just a bit more often now than when he actually worked in the school.

"I will go through some of these; these abominations," which he presented in peculiar deference to the ceiling, or that's how his class saw it as he perhaps endeavoured to give the gesture spiritual gravitas.

"Firstly the efforts of Jill Mackie. Identify yourself young woman." He knew the names of none of his pupils in this class or any other. Jill carried out his request and he absolutely slammed a paper onto her desk. Jill quaked with indifference.

"Just what is this? Just what is it? The assignment was what you think you may say or ask if you were given the privilege of meeting God and you write about THOR!"

"But sir, you didn't specify what God so I thought we were free to chose."

"There is only one..." He halted in frustration noting the sudden alert stares of everyone in the room. Were they going to draw first blood? To their collective disappointment he managed to put the brakes on just in time.

"Luke Newton. Who is that?" Luke duly raised his hand. "You will not be getting yours back because it's going straight to Mrs Dalton!"

"Thank you sir I'm glad you liked it. I put a lot of time into it."

"No I did not like it Sir. Not one tiny bit!" He stood almost catatonic with rage then after a few moments asked for Andrew and Dean to identify themselves.

"You two had the absolute cheek and audacity to hand in the identical homework!"

"They're not the same Sir."

"What?"

"They're not the same," the second continued. "One is called Man talking to God and the other is called God talking to Man. Two perspectives for balance and fairness. We worked on it together."

Doctor Burns was now actually beyond response. He sat down for a few moments then took to his feet again, what troubling him most being that everyone of them sat totally straight faced and silent.

"Suzie Baxter. Which one of you will admit to being her?" Suzie duly admitted to being herself.

"I will just read yours out. You know it won't take long."

He held a sheet of paper in front of himself and read out, "'Hello God.' The end."

Approaching her he repeated the parameters of the assignment seeking an explanation.

"Well sir you asked me to write what I would imagine a conversation with God to be like and that's what I did. I'm an atheist." Their stony faces nearly broke rank at this but they pulled through.

"Sarah Jenkins whoever you are elected just not to bother handing in anything at all. Explain yourself where ever you are."

The mood in the room markedly changed, suppressing laughter no longer a difficulty.

"Sarah Jenkins has not been in for a while since her dad was killed in a cycling accident.

"Oh yes. I read about that. Cycling home without a crash helmet in the dark while drunk. That was really clever."

He was met with the mortifying stare of cold narrow eyes which put out his fire and chilled the fluid flowing in his blood vessels. He would soon be excreting his vile intolerance in yet another school; and not for very long there either.

Chapter Thirteen

A fourth year Physics class was settling down in front of Zander Gordon, a class, like so many, one pupil down due to a tragic bereavement. Chris Templeton had recently lost his father to what apparently was suicide and had been absent for some time. Mr Gordon was having one final check to see if all his props were to hand. With everything in place he began to speak and the class fell quiet. That was the case with some classes especially the ones with a solid core of the type of pupils that the orange girls and knuckle dragging clones didn't like. They had come in without screaming, fighting over a chair, throwing some random object or demanding to go to the toilet immediately! Zander thought to himself that sometimes this job can be good, and more like what he had envisaged just before starting college.

"OK, a quick re-cap. Now I'm supposed to assess your understanding of the story so far with deep and searching questions but suitably structured as to be inclusive."

The class smiled. The future of cynicism and sarcasm was in safe hands. He continued, "So we have been working our way through the electromagnetic spectrum, gamma rays, X rays, ultraviolet, light and had reached infra-red which you now know is just a posh word for heat."

He reached behind his desk and brought out his first prop and put on a very large and bulky pair of goggles with criss-cross straps across his head. "Now, what do you think these do?" he asked to which an answer was immediately supplied.

"Make you look like a fanny."

There was of course an explosion of laughter as Zander Gordon reflected the merits of the reply. Could it be line of the day replacing the entry from his very different third year class that morning, "There's somebody at the door. Haha made you look," or the earlier leader in the clubhouse supplied by an anonymous voice in the corridor, "Zander the Panda."

He should of course have clicked disciplinary proceedings into gear but firstly he liked this class and secondly it's difficult to do so when you're laughing yourself. Besides, he had a caught a reflection of himself in the mirror and joking Jonathan Warwick wasn't wrong.

When things had settled down in their own good time he said, "Exactly. They are goggles which can detect infra-red radiation. Well done Jonathan, and you may have seen these used in television programs put to many uses but basically they allow you to see in the dark. Infra-red is converted to produce a light image. So, for example if a gamekeeper put these on he would be able to see poachers but the poachers would not be able to see him."

At the back of the room sat Jordan White. Academically he was well out his depth but his parents had demanded that he be put in classes that weren't war zones even if it meant he would struggle hopelessly with the course work: they had simply demanded what all teachers do with their own children in such circumstances. Unfortunately uncaring life had really dealt him an unplayable hand. There were other low ability pupils in the school but he in particular would probably suffer the least ill effect from eating ice cream too quickly. Genetics has also contrived to give him an outward appearance that mirrored his inner ability and his total lack of personal hygiene awareness was not lost on the pupils. Were he to go to the doctors with an ankle injury then at most he would wash one foot and it would probably be the wrong one; and were he to block a deadly bullet with an object in his pocket, cruel fate would fashion that object to be a hand grenade. Within his class were some stunningly beautiful intelligent pupils who were gifted with every talent ever defined. Savage nature was clearly not egalitarian. Something about the goggles however had grabbed Jordan White's attention.

The class continued with various experiments being performed and results being recorded then finally everything was cleared away leaving about ten minutes until the end of the period. "OK guys and girl guys, you will by now have been given your examination timetables so I have prepared notes for you since I know your own will be a shambles."

He wasn't wrong of course. They may have been bright teenagers but they were never the less, teenagers. He consequently handed out crisp clear new notes with colourful diagrams and not too many words then continued. "Now you are all bright and able pupils but sometimes things can go wrong, exam nerves, illness or whatever so what I have also done is include some examination tips inside the back cover."

They flicked nonchalantly to the back of the notes and began to read. At first they read in silence but this changed to sniggers and exchanging of glances until little explosions of laughter erupted throughout the room as they read:-

EXAMINATION TIPS

Always write the correct answer. If you write the wrong answer you may not be awarded full marks.

Do not point and laugh at the invigilators, and if you really must throw objects at them ensure that they are 0.1kg or less. (EQA regulation 6.1. paragraph eii, protocol E7)

If you feel sick during the examination then wipe it off your fingers and don't do it again!

If during the exam a senior citizen or pregnant woman comes into the hall, stand up and give them your seat. Do not wait to be asked!

Do not take your shoes off in the exam hall. You should have been warned about unprotected socks!

Strictly no mp3 players. The invigilators have been given permission to use tasers against offenders. However if you insist on their surreptitious use then at the very least don't sing along or play air guitar.

Should the examination hall suddenly depressurise oxygen masks will fall from above. Put your own mask on first before going to the assistance of others.

If you leave the exam hall thinking you have done very very badly then just remember the age old anagram, hiss then pap.

The same 6th year girl from months earlier came in to yet another scene of hilarity, now left in no doubt, and surely there had never been any, that Physics was more fun than Accountancy. As before she handed over a sealed envelope which Zander opened a few minutes later as his still laughing class made their departure. He read,

Would all members of staff please attend an urgent and important meeting in the lecture theatre at 4 pm. I realise that this could be a difficult and inconvenient imposition for some of you but I would really appreciate your attendance.

Thank you.

Fiona Dalton.

Chapter Fourteen

Zander Gordon made his way to the Science Base as there was still 25 minutes or so until the staff meeting in the lecture theatre. Just outside the base stood Colette Murphy. "I just saw your exam tips for the pupils. You are just as childish as they are," she said loudly, timing the moment as well as she could to ensure that both senior pupils and DHT Gill Paterson witnessed her flexing her Head of Department muscles, while endeavouring to achieve optimum humiliation. This pleased Zander. The gloves were off. Fantastic. He entered the base to be followed by Colette where the rest of the Science staff had already assembled.

"What do you think the emergency meeting is all about then?" started Christine Graham, one of the Chemistry teachers just to get the speculation ball rolling.

"you've got to think it could be something to do with the shambolic electronic control system," said Lorna Sutherland her Chemistry colleague. "I'm frightened to turn on the gas in case every light in the school suddenly goes out."

"That's why I always take a candle to the toilet," added Colette. A myriad of less than hidden glances were exchanged but everyone managed to hold it together as Colette wondered about the sudden strained silence and lip biting.

"We'll find out soon enough," said Christine, "but first there are cakes to be eaten."

"But I really mustn't," added Lorna. "My body is a temple."

"What, people take their shoes off before they enter?" enquired Zander dangerously.

"Well you won't be invited in any time soon matey!" Lorna managed to say before a meringue would make the task of speaking more difficult, but not before also scooping out some of the cream to plant on Zander's nose. Zander managed to eat the cream in a smutty manner supporting the hypothesis that male maturity is an illusion.

"Have you read about those diet supplements that so many people are trying these days that prevent fats being absorbed?" asked Christine.

"Oh God yes. They work all right but you wouldn't want to stray too far from a toilet all the same!"

"What do they call it?" asked Zander. "Shit to Fit?"

"Loose two stone and all your friends in a fortnight!" added Christine reaching for another cake. "I'll just keep the fat if it's all the same. "Adult nappies don't half ruin the line of that little black dress."

"If I put on any more weight I'm going to throw myself in front of a train,"

Colette sighed before another meringue disappeared from the table.

"And what, take hundreds of innocent lives with you?" Zander was not in the mood to be pleasant after the "childish" comment in the corridor.

Not to be drawn Colette changed the subject rapidly.

"Mrs Dalton has not had her troubles to seek what with the electronics difficulties not to mention that Tony Martin nonsense. I don't even know what toilet he is supposed to use!" she laughed to discover no-one else joining in.

"She uses the Women's toilets, and besides everybody has always liked Toni. Don't you? She is just so friendly and sincere," Lorna felt compelled to say, more than just a bit annoyed.

"And very pretty too. I don't know what she's been doing or taking for the past few months but what a change. So stylish and elegant. I might ask for some of her pills or whatever she uses," added Christine to continue the theme, and with targeted purpose.

"Well I don't know about you two but every time I'm in the toilet and the door opens, my heart is in my mouth in case it's him!" Colette added but with increasing disgust.

"Wow, that must look weird, like you were giving the invisible man a blow job," which Zander then mimicked for increased impact.

"It's just wrong and against the bible," growled Colette under her breath managing to turn even the Christians against her.

"But what if she's not religious?" added Zander feeling compelled to get involved. "Not everybody is a soot head."

Seeing the confused look on Matthew's face Lorna enlightened him. "The heathen is alluding to Ash Wednesday," she said before playfully hammering down a heavy book on Zander's head.

"The heretic has no idea what you're talking about Lorna," added Christine. "Nice shot though. That sounded really painful."

"I most certainly do know all about Ash Wednesday," protested Zander with theatrical indignation while rubbing his head from the spirited blow. "It dates back to when the Catholics beat the Jews at cricket."

Somewhat annoyed by the flippant direction the conversation had taken Colette Murphy endeavoured to re-stablish appropriate reverence. "Well I've always said, better safe than sorry. It's better to say you believe just in case."

"What? Your God would be so naïve as to welcome the hypocritical fodder of Pascal's Wager? Seriously?"

The silent opinion in the room was that Colette had absolutely no understanding of what Matthew McKenzie had just enquired with Matthew himself still particularly angry at the comments she made earlier about Toni for a reason soon to become apparent.

After a pause she repeated, "Better safe than sorry." The silent opinion was confirmed.

"Maybe it's about the PE teacher who was running the lunchtime club," speculated Lorna with some excitement.

The new female PE teacher had just finished a short and spectacular career in teaching about which she would probably be given the opportunity to write a book from a prison cell. She was unnecessarily gorgeous. Even one hundred percent heterosexual woman would have to recognise that she was devastatingly beautiful. Not far short of 6 feet tall with long blond hair, the face of a cover girl and a figure that was simply flawless and captivating, the 25 year old goddess had proved to be a huge attraction to the lunchtime club which she had set up for the 5th and 6th year boys to whom she gave individual tuition, her speciality subject being the joys of sex.

"Absolutely disgraceful," snarled Colette. "These young boys, some of them only 15 will be damaged and traumatized for the rest of their lives."

"Seriously?" Exclaimed Zander. "The only ones traumatized will be the ones who didn't know about the club!"

"What you are saying is that under age sex is OK? It's totally acceptable for a teacher to be a paedophile, and you a teacher! Should you really be in this job?"

Zander volleyed back, "OK that's the straw man fallacy out of the way. What's next from your repertoire of incoherent nonsense?"

"Well I just find it totally unthinkable that I could ever run such a club." No one disagreed.

"Dear God," Colette spat, "we have a teacher having sex with babies and another ladyboy freak being allowed to take classes!"

This was too much for Matthew McKenzie. "For your information Miss Murphy, ladyboy freak and I have been going out with each other for the past few weeks." Matthew was momentarily taken aback by his own candour and then just as suddenly felt relieved of a burden which inspired him to continue, "and if you are thinking of spreading mischievous gossip about me then let me make it quite clear. No, I am not gay!"

The silence was only short lived before Zander wrapped his arms round Matthew and said, "Congratulations young man. Proud of you mate," soon to be followed by hugs and kisses from Christine and Lorna.

"That is just so wonderful. Fantastic."

Once more Colette endeavoured to change the course of discussion. "Can I just remind everyone that we are supposed to be in the lecture theatre in the next few minutes." Having momentarily caught most of the staff's partial attention she continued, "and I think it is painfully obvious what the purpose of the meeting is all about; and I fully intend sharing my thoughts and observations with appropriate personnel."

This caught Lorna's attention. "You can't just leave it at that. What do you know? Spill the beans detective Murphy."

"I can just see you in a deerstalker with magnifying glass to hand," said Christine Graham now becoming slightly intrigued herself.

Having attained her much coveted place in the spotlight she elaborated but chose her words carefully. "You are right. I have been doing a bit of Shylock Holmes work." Once again direct eye contact had to be avoided. "It's more what I've seen with my own eyes. When I was in Brogan's DIY store I was buying cat litter."

"I don't know why you bother," interrupted Zander, "they just shit in it anyway."

Waiting for the exasperated silence to calm down much to Zander's annoyance Colette continued, "As I was saying, when I was in the store buying the cat litter there was someone else you all know who was buying rat poison."

"Well lots of people buy rat poison. That's not much to go on, but who was it anyway?" Laura asked.

"I'll keep that to myself for now but this same person has been seen all over the village recently staring at houses, taking pictures and scribbling notes down."

"It's still not much to go on," said Christine Graham.

"Well perhaps not," Colette answered pausing for theatrical impact, "but once you add motive?"

Sensing that nothing more was going to be volunteered the momentary diversion was soon replaced by a return of congratulatory outpourings, and plans already being made to have a night out, with suggested bridesmaid options being proposed with much self interest. Colette had already left the base by this time to scuttle down to the lecture theatre and take up her position. Matthew then dared to ask, "How did she ever manage to become Head of Faculty?"

"That my friend is the 8th wonder of the world which has spawned much speculation."

"No other candidates perhaps?" Christine reminded everyone of a previous often aired suggestion.

"Or she turned the other candidates into toads?" Lorna supplied.

"No," said Zander, "I think she slept her way to the top," a suggestion and image which produced a communal grimace combined with sounds of disgust as everyone's knees partially buckled beneath them as the posse of Scientists made their way down to the lecture theatre.

Chapter Fifteen

Staff were wandering into the lecture theatre with many already seated. At each entrance stood a uniformed police officer and a janitor. The science department chose to sit together near the back of the theatre apart from Matthew who made his way towards a smiling Toni Martin sitting closer to the front. Waiting to address them were Head Teacher Fiona Dalton and Detective Inspector Buchanan. There had been a great deal of speculation before arriving at the theatre but the high visibility police presence effected an immediate dismissal of many hypotheses. Clearly it was not going to be about the somewhat disastrous electronic control system. This led to some disappointment as it had been hoped that due to Health and Safety issues the school would have to be closed for a while. School closure was often to the forefront of teachers' minds as they waited so often for a letter to be sent around the school from the Head Teacher if there was a momentary blizzard, strong winds, a 30 second power cut or a shortage of toilet roll.

"Surely the health and safety of the children comes first?" they would often voice in desperation as falling snow outside would maliciously refuse to stop melting. Most staff however suspected that the theme of the meeting would be something somewhat more sombre and in a few moments they would be proved correct.

Fiona took to her feet first to begin proceedings. "First of all I would like to thank everyone for attending this meeting in your own time though to be honest most of you dedicated professionals don't leave the car park most nights till long after the end of the school day anyway."

"Yeh, that's because the gates won't let us out." Hamish didn't like to miss an opportunity.

"Yes the automatic barriers can be quite an exciting end to the day, and yes again, all the cars driven by staff that were modified by the stripped executioner from above have had the costs met by the local authority. However that is not the theme of the day as you have all probably deduced by now and to that end I will shortly invite Detective Inspector Buchanan to take over proceedings. Before that there is some news which I must share and have been given the go-ahead by the Inspector as it is probably already common knowledge out with these four walls."

She paused to take a breath and continued. "You perhaps may not have noticed but Mr Drysdale from the Maths Department is not with us. Most of you will know that his wife left him a while back and made no contact with him or anyone else in all that time. Well his wife has been found."

Only a few were naïve enough to smile at the news. "Her body was brought aboard in the nets of a fishing boat in the firth. At this moment Mr Drysdale is at the station helping police with their enquiries. Now to the real matter in hand. As you must all be aware, in recent months this school, this community has been hit with a series and a strikingly high number of sad and tragic events; to which you can now add yet another. This has not gone unnoticed by the public in general but neither by the national press. Theories and rumours are flying about but it is the purpose of this meeting to demonstrate that there is nothing sinister or mysterious going on and that is the message that must be taken away by everyone here in the hall. There will also be a meeting tomorrow night in the Civic Hall to which you are all invited to attend but it will essentially just be a repetition of what you are about to hear just now. Detective Inspector Buchanan."

Fiona Dalton surrendered the floor to the Inspector who stood up to a smattering of uncomfortable applause which quickly subsided as the perpetrators sweated an uncomfortable moment.

"OK ladies and gents, let me introduce myself. I am Inspector Buchanan but not the usual kind of inspector who visits your school from time to time though I believe your last report was absolutely glowing."

There was a self satisfied look spreading throughout the staff. "I'm guessing they didn't mention the school show then?" There was no option but to laugh. "I actually made a secret recording of the entire performance the only copy of which I am willing to sell. Can we start the bidding at five thousand pounds? Do I hear five thousand?" Quite bizarrely no one wanted to meet his stare lest they twitch or blink.

"OK, I'll get to the point. There have been several fatalities of late in the area with the school, fairly or not, being perceived as a particular focal point. The purpose of this meeting is, as Mrs Dalton said, to put conspiracy theories, serial killer hypotheses and other such things to bed and to make a statement to the broader public and press that the series of awful events is not a police matter."

"Perhaps a lower Police profile would have been advisable then," interrupted a nervous young supply teacher possibly wanting to make an impression during his probation years.

"And that is exactly why we have masked out the word Police on the cars outside."

"Really?" he replied. The sniggering throughout the hall probably ensured he would never raise a point in public again throughout his career.

"My apologies. That was a cheap remark to a valid point," Inspector Buchanan generously responded seeing his discomfort but the damage was done, and now one of tomorrow's bright young stars heated the theatre with his dripping scarlet face, his now drenched white shirt transparent with cruel hot sweat.

"OK, without talking in riddles, there have been a number of deaths in the past few month which I am going to go through individually and show that foul play was not involved in any of the grievous events of late. I am not going to go through them in chronological order either to avoid implying a pattern by default. You must be aware that the school has been given a few new names."

"Highland View Cemetery," and "Body Count Academy," were contributions volunteered by some staff in unison, these names and more actually doing the rounds.

"I am familiar with these and others," continued Inspector Buchanan, "and it is such things that we must endeavour to dampen especially for the sanity of the office staff who are at the forefront of fielding the concerns." The office staff nodded in agreement.

"OK to the first tragic death, and in fact this was indeed the first, and before I begin, everything I am going to say this evening has been cleared by next of kin. They too want an end to the speculation and the invasion of their privacy by reporters who seem to be lurking ready to pounce in every aspect of their personal life, even just going for a coffee."

The Inspector recomposed himself to begin proper proceedings. "Joseph Hanley and his wife Claire were found alone at home, both fatally overcome with Carbon

Monoxide fumes from their gas fire. Their windows were found to be taped shut probably due to the excessively cold winter we had endured before the summer months arrived. Unfortunately also the flue to the outside wall, fitted after the chimney had been sealed off many years earlier, was found to be totally blocked with leaves. They had a Carbon Monoxide detector fitted with a working battery. Unfortunately it had been inserted the wrong way round. Both front and back doors were locked although the front door key did hang from a string. Obviously we would advise against such a practice but none the less we have no reason to believe that it was anything more than a dreadful accident."

Lisa Muldoon and Jacky Forster whispered to each other that they didn't think Joe and Claire were the sort of people who would not throw open their windows in the summer. They were not alone in finding that out of character with two such walking and hill climbing enthusiasts who greeted the spring with the enthusiasm of Pagans. Noticing this Inspector Buchanan invited anyone at any stage who had concerns to air them at any time in the interest of why the meeting had been called in the first place.

"Now moving on. Most of you will be familiar with Sarah Jenkins in the 6th year. Absolutely lovely girl from all accounts I have heard. The body of her father was found at the side of a road leading to his country home. What we found at the scene was Mr Jenkins lying at the foot of a tree with what transpired to be a fatal head injury. There was still blood on the trunk of the tree. In his pocket was a shattered half bottle of whisky still partially held together by the label. Tests at the scene indicated that there was very little whisky in the bottle when it was broken. There was the smell of whisky from his mouth and on a rock in the grass against which it's assumed the bottle broke. It would seem he was cycling home on Wednesday as he frequently did after being at the village pub."

The look on Hamish Jones' face was sufficient to invite a query from Inspector Buchanan. "Something seems to be bothering you Mr Eh Mr....."

"Jones," Fiona Dalton assisted.

"Thank you, Mr Jones."

"Wednesday night is quiz night and though not a regular attender whenever I did attend Mr Jenkins was always there. He would have couple of half pints of real ale which he would nurse for the duration of the quiz then head home. I never ever saw him have a whisky or any spirit for that matter."

"That could well be the case and I don't doubt you but it is becoming increasingly more common that people top up so to speak to make evenings just a bit cheaper. A pub measure is a pricey business as you might know. At police functions there would be a panic if suddenly our pockets and handbags got searched trust me!"

There was a laugh of recognition but reluctantly so given the nature of the meeting.

"What we are doing is presenting the various scenes and incidents as we found them and yet again there was nothing to suggest third party involvement, deliberate or otherwise. OK I know your time is precious so I will press on, and please don't see this as inappropriate haste. Twenty years has not hardened me to tragedy but only served to develop strategies to conceal my emotions. The next case is horribly common I'm afraid. Well to me it seems that way anyway. Perhaps it's just the nature of my job and two decades of experience which makes it seem so. In this case I will not be going into unnecessary detail. Again we are dealing with another sad case of a fine young pupil being bereaved, Chris Templeton. His father was found by his mother slumped in a chair with a half empty bottle of whisky and an empty bottle of sleep aid tablets, non prescription which can be bought from any pharmacy over the counter. In addition, most horrifically his wife was faced with the horror of the consequences of both his wrists deeply slashed, the knife sitting by his side. It would seem he was deeply depressed but like so many men was reluctant to share. It only came to light when a series of melancholy and disturbing comments were found on his social network page."

"What! I mean sorry what?" Grant Cameron spluttered out in an involuntary outburst.

There is something you want to say I'm guessing?" said the Inspector.

"Bob Templeton was a friend of mine and had been for years since we met at school. Social network? He couldn't send a text and never even wanted to try. It's something we joked about all the time. He was cajoled into using the internet once and never tried again because he thought he had broken it!"

"Well when we carried out our investigations he was signed up to a network and made a few posts...."

"No no no. Sorry just no." Grant gradually fell to a murmured conversation with himself while shaking his head.

Detective Inspector Buchanan was beginning to feel that the foundations of his presentation were not just as solid as when he began but pressed on with the next case. "Can I point out that your input will not go unrecorded and I should have and meant to point out the police officer who is taking notes at the back of the theatre. Feel free to approach him when I have said my bit if there are issues about which you are just a shade ill at ease let's say." Once more he paused.

"Quite dreadfully the next incident involves yet another pupil Pamela Swanson. Mrs Dalton has already informed me that the school roll is already beginning to fall as parents are starting to take their sons and daughters to other schools believing that foul play is behind the deaths, and some have shared their opinion that the school is cursed." This induced the despairing shaking of heads from the majority while a few of the less rational exchanged knowing glances.

"I know time is getting on so I will be as brief as possible without being too sketchy. Please remember that the purpose of this meeting is to assure you that every one of the horribly tragic incidents can be fully explained without any reason to speculate upon foul play." As he said these words he knew that his audience was becoming increasingly troubled by traces of incongruent detail but he pressed on. "Pamela Swanson's mother Julie was found by her partner Diane Frew. Pamela's father left the family home years earlier when Julie's sexuality came to light. She was found in her bath, the room lit only by some very exotic candles with animal prints on the side."

"Those sound like the candles I donated to the raffle," said Jacky Forster. "Those plus floating rose petals."

"Yes those were found too."

"Oh my God did those kill her? Were they toxic or the candles gave of fumes or explode or something?"

"Oh no no. Not at all. They played no part in this death," he rapidly moved to reassure. "Mrs Swanson was clearly trying to set up a relaxing atmosphere as the CD she had chosen to play was the kind of sounds and music you may hear in perhaps a Beauty salon."

This caused most to look directly at the Inspector. He stroked both hands gently down his face and said. "Such fine features don't come cheaply you know." Gentle laughter momentarily escaped the tight grasp of grudging conscience. He continued. "The music system she was using, was attached to the mains."

He paused knowing that the reality was he had no need to continue but for completeness did so. "The CD player must have fallen into the bath and electrocuted her."

"Now to the final fatality, thankfully. It is only as I'm describing each sad misfortune one after the other in such a short time is the scale of events really starting to sink in. It has been a devastating and disturbing few months." The inspector stalled. Taking stock had suddenly impacted upon him.

"We return to one of your colleagues. As you probably know already Mr Mortimore was found dead having consumed a large quantity of alcohol and with his wrist slashed."

"Snap!" shouted out Hamish Jones perhaps louder than he really intended.

"Sorry what?"

"My apologies. That could come over as a bit insensitive and callous," he admitted then continued," but so far every murder. Murder? Sorry where did that come from?

Anyway every awful death so far has been different until now. Though they all have one thing in common. Cliché."

Everyone in the theatre knew what he meant if perhaps not Colette Murphy who ironically would struggle to speak if denied their use.

"I recognize what you're saying. Yes they do smack of the stuff of melodrama and theatre. Now, going back to the circumstances of Mr Mortimore's suicide. Let's just be open and use the word. There is perhaps more that you don't know but soon you will. Trust me on that via the internet, newspapers television you will find out soon so you may as well find out now. Mr Mortimore had a rather different, but as it happens far from unique but rare way of relaxing at the weekend you may say. It would appear from images in our possession that he liked to be restrained in a bed, OK a cot and dressed, how can I put this, appropriate to his confinement. I will leave it at that. The staff started to murmur certain words with "Princess" being the most frequent.

"It would seem that perhaps discordant fragments may be starting to take on a form. To continue as we are well beyond our time schedule. These images were compiled by, and in the hands of hostile young individuals and Mr Mortimore was being blackmailed dry as his bank account and credit cards revealed. Topped out to the max. A girl is helping us with our enquiries."

Once more the same words were being murmured though somewhat louder than before, but this time a palpable rage and anger accompanied the names Chardonnay McPhee and Madonna Graham. They also wondered why only one girl was being questioned. Vague and quite unbelievable rumours embellished by others which were just malicious fabrications were reaching the staff from overheard classroom snippets albeit notoriously unreliable sources, the same sources which talked of bottles being hidden by teachers just before classes arrived when a few of the teachers cited had never actually drunk alcohol in their lives.

DI Buchanan continued. "Despite what you may be thinking I have not yet disclosed the complete story which is probably as I speak making its way into the public domain. The girl we are questioning revealed nothing. Every question she was asked she replied, no comment. She had clearly been coached by someone else should the police ever get involved. Even when asked, do you want a cup of tea, she replied no comment with a self satisfied look on her face."

Madonna was the name now volunteered with some confidence.

"You may have noticed that Chardonnay McPhee has been absent from school for some time. What we suspected was that she saw the other girl being apprehended by the police and did a runner. Sadly," and he gave the impression that he was not being entirely sincere, "this was not the case. Now you may not know this but Mr Mortimore had a second flat just outside the village. We came upon this intelligence and went to investigate the property."

Here he paused again for a very long time. "What we discovered in the flat in addition to the body of Mr Mortimore was a second body, that of a girl who fitted the description of Chardonnay McPhee locked in a cupboard. Her hands and feet were bound. There was cotton wool inserted in her nostrils and her mouth was taped shut. When the tape was removed we discovered her mouth to be stuffed full of bank notes."

One staff member spontaneously held up two clenched fists and said, "Yes!" before becoming immediately concerned about how his action would be received. He need not have been concerned in the slightest with others wishing they had done exactly that. There was most definitely a look on most faces that said, "Good. Hell mend her."

"To sum up then," Inspector Buchanan said with less conviction than when he had begun only an hour or so earlier, "What I hope I have done is demonstrate that other than the body of the young girl found in the flat, every other heartbreaking event was either suicide or death by misadventure, and we do not intend carrying out further investigations in any of the cases discussed this afternoon other than of course that of Mr Drysdale's wife. Well thankfully that brings proceedings to an end and hopefully put you more at ease."

What only so recently had seemed like an appropriate and credible closing remark now rang strangely hollow in everyone's minds including his own. As he was about to ask if anyone had any questions but desperately hoping they didn't, the fire alarm ensured that none would be asked and he was grateful for the unexpected and welcome reprieve.

Fiona Dalton took to the floor and said, "Well it looks like perhaps a car must have left the car park at the same time as someone switched on a kettle," and everyone slowly made their way from the building assuming as usual and correctly that the alarm was yet again crying wolf. It was clearly the case from the murmurings of the departing audience that no one had been re-assured or put at ease about anything but in reality the flames of suspicion had been fuelled by inconsistencies.

Last to leave the hall were DI Buchanan and the other police officers who had been ambushed by Colette Murphy. She did much talking and gesticulating while periodically thrusting the screen of her phone towards her captives.

Chapter Sixteen

Matthew McKenzie was having a bad moment to himself. It was nothing serious or of any great importance but just the realization that yet again he had forgotten about the extra mini period which had been added on to the end of period 2 every day, so instead of heading off for a short break and a coffee he had to endure this latest initiative called Pastoral Time. This plague of a concept that was spreading from school to school was most probably spawned by some individual seeking promotion to at least Deputy Head Teacher status and as a consequence of his interview party piece, every school in the local authority was now being subjected to the latest burdensome educational fashion accessory. It was structured such that pupils from all year groups would be formed into classes for the purpose of providing first line guidance; or at least that was the rationale. The reality was that the pupils hated it because they got separated from their peers and the staff hated it because an extra class had surreptitiously been slipped into the school day. The staff seeking promotion themselves just loved it of course like they did every trendy imposition. There was the assurance that absolutely no preparation time would be required, but when this was quickly exposed to be ludicrous deception, preparation time was mangled into the school day.

"Oh dear God, what are they supposed to be doing today, I haven't even checked the file?" Matthew thought to himself in amber alert panic as his group started to trickle in. He clicked on an icon and a list of topics filled the screen from which he frantically identified that the week's topic was Bullying. A further click brought him to a set of instructions. The room was now full and to get the registration part out the way he shouted, "OK, if you are absent put your hand up."

"You say that every day Sir," said a third year girl wearily without even looking up.

His next short cut was to count the heads which told him that someone was absent. "Right, look about your little social groups. Who is missing. One person is absent."

"Sir, it's Beth like it is every day. Remember she moved to Australia about a month ago?" a second enthusiast advised, once more without raising her head in the slightest.

"Of course. Yes. Anyway, those who forgot to bring in absence notes today, bring them in tomorrow. Now on to Pastoral Party time. Yesssssss," cheered Matthew in sarcastic joy. "OK get into your pastoral groups." Nobody moved. "Come on now. Pastoral groups now. Rouse!"

" I wasn't here that day," said a fifth year boy, while not looking up from his desk; well of course not.

"Pastoral groups; now! Remember, you all had to choose club names and design a badge for your groups?"

"Is that those groups we went into when we thought the school was going to get inspected?" said one of the Prefects, Jamie.

"That's the ones, yes."

"You should have said then," and at this they all slowly wandered about and settled around tables.

"Now before we start we have to give ourselves a quick reminder about the Five Point Star." There was silence. Mr McKenzie tried again. "What are the five Pupil Potentials written around the PASS, the Pupil Aspirational ...... S,S. Somebody tell me what they stand for."

"Do you know Sir?"

"Of course. Look, just one of the points. Effective contributors and all that stuff."

The pupils could recognize bluff when they see it and Matthew McKenzie knew this fine well. "Well for tomorrow you could all refresh yourself on the Pastoral Star thing." He paused for breath knowing what lay ahead.

"Right, the focus this week is on Bullying and the first group activity for the week is to randomly select a group member who is to be subjected to bullying."

"Will we just chose the gingers then?" asked Jamie again.

"No randomly I said. I'll leave it to you lot to come up with someone." Eventually victims were chosen. "Next bit. The one you have chosen to bully has to start speaking about anything, or even just start counting. It doesn't matter. Next, each group has to do one of two things. When the victim tries to speak you have all either to turn your back on him or her and fold your arms and say nothing, or face them and just start saying blah blah blah when they try to talk."

"Sir, are you trying to take the piss?"

"No I'm not trying to....Don't use that word. Look just do it in case a real grown up comes in. Just humour me OK?" Dutifully much arm folding and blah blah blahing ensued. After five minutes Matthew McKenzie shouted out, "Right, time to move on to the next stage. On the whiteboard come out in turns, one from each group and write on the board what type of pupils may be bullied."

In little time they had produced quite a handsome list starting with gingers then moving on to height, weight, race and religion and eventually a sixth year girl wrote, sexuality. "That's plenty, fine and quite a diverse list."

"Sir see those who have sex changes, do you think they get bullied?" said Jamie pointedly who had clearly elected to take on a leading roll today. He did of course generate immediate interest and now suddenly every eye was trained on Mr McKenzie. It was no longer a secret that he and Miss Martin were an "item".

"I'm sure, in fact I know that they do."

At this point, Tracy, one of the sixth year girls said, "Sir, I saw you down at the village pond sitting close beside Miss Martin feeding the ducks."

"You may well have done. Why?"

"Well sir, it's such a cliché. Do you also run together in slow motion through long grass, holding hands and laughing at just everything and nothing as well?"

"We try, but it's the staying in mid air that's the tricky part." There were laughs from all year groups and suddenly Pastoral time was doing what it was meant to do.

"Don't you find people starring at you and saying things when you are out together?" asked Jamie mischievously.

Taken just slightly aback by Jamie's boldness Matthew asked, "And what do you think they might be saying?"

"Well I think they might be saying things like, "He must have loads of money," because Miss Martin is really pretty; a real catch, and well, no offence but look at you!"

Matthew turned to Jamie and said, "Hook, line and sinker you little..."

"Shit sir?"

There was still about five minutes to go and the class started to wander into social groups. One of the groups near the front of the room was clearly starting to discuss the unusually large number of deaths and tragedies of recent months and they moved to include their teacher in the discussion.

"Mr McKenzie, do you think all these deaths have just been accidents or do you think there might be a murderer in the village?" asked Linda Forsyth, the Head Girl.

"I have no reason to think that it is anything other than just a series of dreadful tragedies."

"Well Miss Murphy told her class that she thought there was someone behind it and even told her Pastoral class who she thought it was," continued Linda.

Matthew already had a rapidly declining respect for his new boss of only a few months but he refused to believe that even she could be so stupid as to say something so potentially slanderous, especially not to pupils. "I have to say Linda I find that just a bit difficult to believe."

"But it's true!" added Christine Clelland who, like Linda, was not the type of pupil to talk or spread silly gossip or rumour. "She didn't come out with a name directly but just said to her class when asked, 'What are trees made of, that's all I'll say.' When her class suggested she meant Mr Wood she just smiled back at them."

Before the conversation could go any further, Jamie, looking out the window said, "Look! There's Mr Wood outside the school fence across the road."

This resulted in the whole class moving to the back of the room to look out the window.

"A police car has stopped beside him!" said Linda. Two police officers got out of the car and approached Mr Wood. Within a few moments he was in the car and it drove away.

"Mr Wood has just been arrested by the police!" shouted Linda Forsyth in excitement, and two rooms further down the corridor the exact same scene was being played out in Colette Murphy's room.

The buzzer sounded, everyone made their way out the room and there was only one topic of conversation. As the last one left Zander Gordon came in. "What's all the talk of Mr Wood getting arrested? My room faces the other way."

"I can only tell you what I saw. Mr Wood was on the pavement looking towards houses when a police car arrived and he was taken away in it. But there is something else. Have you heard about our glorious leader telling her class that she thinks he's involved in the recent spate of deaths?"

"Please tell me you are joking. Not even she could be that stupid!"

"That was almost my exact thought," said Matthew who went on to describe what he had just heard. In due course they accepted that they were both wrong: she could be that stupid. Matthew then turned to the subject of Pastoral Time and said, "Pastoral time. God that was weird. Who thinks up the stuff we have to do? I don't think I'll forget Bullying any time soon!"

"Bullying? That's next week. You are supposed to be doing The Holocaust this week."

"Oh Jesus Christ, no wonder Mrs Dalton was giving me strange looks when she glanced through the window. Shit shit shit! What's worse I had actually totally forgotten about the Pastoral period again. At half past three I'll be racing the pupils out the door."

"Oops, I think you have maybe forgotten something else. The Open Night straight after school?"

"Oh fuck, just shoot me where I stand."

Chapter Seventeen

The final buzzer of the day went which normally signalled also the official end of the working day at least, but as had been brought to Matthew McKenzie's attention, in two hours time the school would start to fill up with parents but worse, all the most detestable pupils. It was just one of those strange phenomena. The pupils who go to such efforts to point out just how much they despise school are always the ones who come back to the place in their own time when they don't have to. What makes them particularly objectionable is having to be inappropriately civil to them on such nights.

Matthew thought things could not get any worse and at least he was off timetable period five. That was until Gill Paterson appeared with a little pink slip asking if he would cover a wild and repugnant fourth year Spanish class instead because the supply teacher had to go home terrified. The science staff were assembling around a table in the base.

"Right," began Colette, "What show are we going to put on for the parents this year?"

"Show? Sorry what?" enquired a bemused and still thoroughly tired and disgruntled Matthew. "It's an open night. The parents wander round the various departments to get a look at our resources and how we cover the curriculum. They want to get a feel for a typical and normal day at school for their children so it should just be a few books on desks and some software on display, yes?"

"No no no. Not at all," said Zander as everyone else shook their heads while breathing in loudly through clenched teeth. "So young, so naïve."

"But I'm not wrong. That's what an open night is supposed to be."

"Yes, and inspectors are supposed to see a normal few days at a school," said Christine Graham," "just like people's houses are always immaculate for expected visitors who are then greeted with, "You'll just have to take me as you find me.""

"So we invite the parents in to lie to them?"

"Exactly!" said Zander. "That's that cleared up."

Christine then endeavoured to supply a quick explanation of how things came to be how they are now.

"Matthew, you are absolutely right of course but in recent years we have created a monster. The problem started when staff started to have a wander to see what other departments were doing. Home Economics perhaps gave birth to the creature by having a French theme and turning the department into a Parisian type café with pupils dressed as waiters and waitresses."

"After that the PE department put on a gymnastic show and hired a professional goalkeeper for a penalty shoot out competition," added Lorna from Chemistry.

"And after that Drama started putting on plays followed by the English department trying to put on better plays etc. etc. That is how we got to where we are today."

"OK then," asked a reluctant Matthew expecting the worst, "What do we do?" It became clear to him that his "worst" was not even close, culminating in Matthew adamantly asserting, "No I will not be wearing a fuck'n costume!"

"Oh go on," pleaded Christine, "Stephen Munro was always a great Albert Einstein."

Time was running out and they only had about an hour to turn the department into an inter-active Science Museum. In a darkened room a Van Der Graaf generator sat sparking away for no good reason and a hologram had been set up utilising a split laser beam. Once again Health and Safety had been put on hold. A variety of animal skulls were on display, and chemical reactions never seen in a normal class were set to effervesce, change colour, glow in the dark and so much more. Various other bits of equipment pinged, beeped and flashed while in another room a murder scene had been set up, with the white chalked outline of the body ready to be investigated by various forensic techniques. Although it was thought perhaps to be in bad taste this year, it was thought also that to abandon their renowned detective extravaganza would be to admit there was an element of suspicion regarding the recent fatalities. With space running out and the doors about to be opened it was decided to clear away text books and other such irrelevant distractions and set up more toys and games.

"Half past six. In two hours it will all be over for another year," said Zander to Matthew trying to drag him from the gloom of a day he wished had already finished some time ago.

"Do you know who I hate the most?" said Christine, "The smart arsed dads who try to catch you out with the very latest snippet from a Science Magazine they have just read. You know the kind, "What do you make of the theory that the speed of light is thought no longer to be an absolute as the universe expands and has started in fact to slow down time?""

"Well it certainly slows down talking to boring old bastards like you," said Lorna, completing the scene. "You are so right though. The smart assed dads," she concurred.

Soon the building was filled with parents and visitors, plus of course the wholly unwelcome wild obnoxious pupils. There were also pleasant pupils specially selected to help out for the evening. Among the parents the management team also did their rounds and Fiona Dalton arrived on the scene. "What no Albert Einstein this year?" Everyone looked at Matthew. "How disappointing."

"As soon as she was gone Zander and Lorna shook their heads and said, "How disappointing." They then looked at Matthew and decided not to pursue this line of amusement any further.

Colette Murphy appeared on the scene and spoke to a few of the parents as they made their way around the Science Fair. One of them asked Colette, "And do you use books at all?" It was meant as a light hearted joke by a parent but with Colette such straight faced humour does not resonate in the slightest. What further unsettled her was not knowing who the woman was. She may after all be a Head Teacher from another school for all she knew and could not take that chance.

"Yes indeed we have the very latest publications written specifically to meet the skills and outcomes of the latest educational initiative, Excellence in Education for All which I really thought I had put on display. Someone must have cleared them. I will get them now."

The woman who actually had no connection with Education at all was then going to ask, "How can everyone be excellent?" but thought the better of it. Meantime however Colette was now having second thoughts about having no books on display and set off to remedy the situation.

"Is everything going OK so far?" Colette asked Christine.

"So far so good. There have been no awkward questions and the pupils are keeping everything running smoothly."

"Well if there are any problems I'll be back soon."

At this Colette made her way to her own room at the end of the corridor which had not been used for any of the exhibits as confidential information was kept in many of the filing cabinets. She unlocked the door and went into the darkened room choosing not to put on the lights as it may attract parents or pupils. She made her way into a small store at the far side of the lab and then to the far end where the text books were that she had decided should go on display. She had a good idea where they were so she selected torch mode on her phone which she felt would be enough. She searched as quietly as she could, wary of attracting any attention at all while she selected a sample of books which were still in delivery packaging so would be in mint condition.

While she was doing this she was completely unaware of the classroom door being opened then very carefully and quietly closed. Without a sound the intruder was stealthily moving towards the store room. This door was opened; then closed just as silently as the first. Colette, on her knees was facing the far wall looking down at books oblivious to her situation. The dark figure stood silently against the door, saying nothing, making not a sound and just watched Colette choose books while gently whispering words to herself. She stood up then turned around and froze solid at the image in front of her. She could neither move nor speak. Her body ached with fear as she stood petrified. Before her vision could adjust to the light to make out any detail of what stood before her a light was shone in her eyes. It was a dim light but enough to ensure that she would see nothing other than that light trained on her face.

The figure between her and the closed door, behind which was an empty black room and yet another closed door, did not speak but began to breath slowly and heavily. Colette was by now close to collapsing in terror but still the figure chose not to utter a word; not just yet, and then, "So you decided to report me to the police?"

Colette made an attempt to say something but no words were really in her mind; any thoughts displaced by all consuming fear and panic. A twisted squeak emerged from her tight dry throat. "Do not speak. I do not want you to speak."

The figure fell silent again, the figure as Colette Murphy now knew was Mr Wood. There was not a sound from either of them. There was not a sound to be heard. It was perfect silence; a silence to be repeated terrifyingly often.

"So what are you thinking right now Colette? Do you hope you were wrong; or do you fear you were right?"

Silence reigned once more. How skilful was her torturer? She was now left alone with her own thoughts and fears. Had he been wrongly accused what might he now do?

Had she been right? Once more the silence was broken.

"What do you think the police may have said to me? Am I still under suspicion? Am I out on bail?"

Once more Colette was abandoned to her lonely silent torment. The pattern continued.

"Do you know what it's like to have the Police go through every file in your computer; every message; every search? Do you know how it feels to have your phone taken from you: and your laptop? To be held in a police station knowing that someone is going through every drawer in your home, every item of clothing that you own? Having your absolute soul laid bare to the preying searching eyes of some people you don't know; and worse; some people you do?"

The lacerating silence returned. "My memories of teaching are not fond memories you know. They could have been made better but for some help; but my cries were ignored. Some people actually enjoyed watching me struggle from day to day. People who could have made my life better but took pleasure from making it worse. Can you think of anyone like that? Someone who could be so nasty and evil?"

Suddenly every moment that Colette had ridiculed Mr Wood, in front of other teachers, in front of pupils when he had been abandoned to cover baying and screaming science classes were recalled with chilling clarity. How when things were getting totally out of hand and the sweat was pouring from his face in despair she would chose her moment to wander into the room grinning to the pupils and saying, "Is everything under control Mr Wood?" All the many times when she had taken such sadistic pleasure at his distress were now as vivid as the days she had helped to engineer them.

Silence was resumed though this time it seemed to Colette that it would never end, but as always it did.

"So now I am unemployed and my source of income has been replaced by a pension not a quarter that you will get; if you get it."

Once more a long silent pause ensued; long enough for Colette to process to what he might just have alluded.

"My life is now harsh. It is so hard. Do I even want to continue it? Do you want to know more than you deserve to know? I will tell you. With the modest sum of money I had at my disposal I thought about buying a property I could let out to try and earn at least enough to get by. So yes, I was looking at houses and I was taking pictures and writing notes. The thing is though that with so little money at my disposal I would only have been able to buy properties in very poor condition. Oh yes, and one more thing. Infested with rats."

Mr Wood elected to have another silence. It was time for Colette once again to be tortured by the fear of what retribution may lie ahead. She knew that no one would come looking for her. She hadn't even said where she was going. She was totally at the mercy of someone in whom she had taken pleasure from inflicting pain for years: at the mercy of someone she told the police she believed to be a murderer. He gave the impression that he did not care himself whether he lived or died so why would he care in the slightest about sparing her?

"Is that a cross you are wearing around your neck? So you are pretending to be a Christian? What are you going to tell God when you see him?"

This sent the chill in her veins falling to an uncharted new depth. What did he mean? Was this to be soon?

"Can I suggest what you may say? Try something like this. "I do not have a single fibre of Christianity in me; neither in my body nor in my soul but I follow the rituals to meaningless perfection." Now it is time. I want you to return to the position you were in on the floor before you knew I was standing behind you. It looked a bit like you were praying. DO IT," he demanded when she looked like she may beg to make a desperate utterance.

"Now think of a prayer and start saying it, softly, so softly; and really mean it."

Collete's body was now uncontrollably shaking with terror as words hissed from her lips in alarmed and broken despair.

Now she knew how it felt to be powerless and humiliated.

"Zander have you seen Colette recently?" asked Lorna

"No not for ages."

"I have."

"Peter it is so great to see you. How have you been since you retired?"

"I've just been telling Colette all about it actually. I saw her going into her room so we had a bit of a catch up. She was in the store when I left a few moments ago."

Chapter Eighteen

It was Friday evening and as was often the case there was a gathering of a close knit group of senior students who had mostly known each other from primary school. The gathering place was in the loft of Luke Newton's house or rather that of his parents. Far from just tolerating his friends' frequent visits, they actively encouraged it, enjoying the company of each and every one of them. Their house was a large and very old two storey detached building with an attic which for a long time had just been a space for dumping rubbish they could not bring themselves to throw out. His dad in particular was just terrible for attaching sentimental value to some of the most outlandish items.

"That was Luke's first ever football," he would plead when his exasperated wife even hinted at having a clear out. It was indeed Luke's first football; and his last. He hated the game. The museum of oddities grew year upon year until they came to an agreement at least to pack the bits and pieces of clutter; or treasure depending on perspective, neatly away and free up the loft to be converted to a space for Luke and his friends when they became young teenagers.

The space was quite cavernous and after proper flooring and wall panels were put in place then lighting and wall sockets fitted it was left to the gang to make it their own. The most recent rule put in place by Luke's parents now that they were all around 16 was that should they drink alcohol, they did not want to know!

The loft was beginning to fill up as more and more arrived. Long gone were the days that they ever knocked on the back door. As they came in, they shouted, "Hi Luke's mum and dad," left their shoes at the door and made their way to the loft via narrow stairs behind a door. It was a wonderfully interesting and quirky old building; and haunted, well of course.

As late comers arrived there was already dark but ironically comforting music playing in the background. Recent events had dulled their desire to crank up the volume. The room was dimly lit as they preferred it with flickering artificial candles giving the place a welcoming warmth. They had previously used real candles until Luke's Parents discovered this whereupon another bye-law was urgently proposed and seconded by his legal guardians.

For once the entire team was present, all sprawled about on beanbag chairs, and cushions, no two remotely alike. Around them they were looked down upon by music icons of the fifties and sixties, interspersed by demons, vampires and various other creatures from parallel worlds. Scattered about the floor were rugs of opulent thickness which probably contained many colonies of planet Earth's smallest co-habitants. An ultraviolet lamp finished off the sinister but cosy world they treasured.

Amelia Rosenberg was wearing a long black dress with just hints of purple in the fabric which made full use of the ultraviolet giving the garment an almost mystical look. Her long dark brown hair was tastefully decorated by a garland of the most delicate small white and lilac flowers. Held in her arm tucked low by her side was Chris Templeton. He was still deeply grieving the loss of his father but still liked to come here for comfort though he always felt so guilty about ever leaving his mum alone at home. He asked that everyone act normally which they endeavoured to do but of course they couldn't. Tonight though there would be great laughter ahead. Chris, like all the boys present wore jeans and shirts which were an extension of the wall décor. They sported a selection of hair styles, non shaven, and all mostly fashioned by nature.

Jill was also dressed like the boys but in no way did she look like one; and the boys were becoming increasingly aware that she did not look like one either. Occasionally they were caught out as their fleeting glimpses of what made her different were not quite fleeting enough. Wendy, on the other hand was unashamedly girly. She too was wearing jeans but clearly the fit and style were very carefully selected. The gypsy top she wore, again was a bold and beautiful statement about femininity and it was stylishly complemented by gold and diamond jewellery, or as far as the boys knew at least, were diamonds. Her bright red lipstick and nail varnish matched her red shoes: they were actually chosen to match her shoes. She was still totally accepted though as a one hundred percent paid up member of the gang. It wasn't her fault after all they thought.

There was no real focus at the moment and everyone was for the most part alone with their own thoughts, tuning or plucking idly at guitars that were always about the place, or just sketching away at something. A few phones were out but soon got put away. Everyone in their world that they knew was here in this escape. Everyone also of course had a beer in their hand or sitting close by. A full fridge and a couple of crates ensured that they would not run short.

Conversation surreptitiously crept up upon them and suddenly they were all engaged in reliving the latest episode with Doctor Burns but all acutely aware that they must not encroach upon the latter moments of the session in the present company given the recent bereavement suffered by Chris.

"So what did Mrs Dalton say about the play you wrote? What happened?" enquired Jill. Not everyone in the loft was at the RE class but everyone had by now certainly read the play.

"She thought the play was absolutely hilarious and the pathetic old sad loser should get a life!" Amelia stared at Luke and said nothing. Words were not necessary.

"OK, they weren't her exact words but clearly that's what she meant." Luke was perhaps partially correct. She had found some of it quite amusing but her exact words included disrespectful, final warning and isolation base.

"It was quite well written," Amelia joined in, "and all your own work too."

"Well actually, here's the thing. It wasn't." This revelation grabbed the attention of everyone. Had the literary maverick genius in their midst just called upon the assistance of the internet; was he a shameless plagiarist and simply copied the obscure work of another?

"Who helped you then?" Amelia enquired.

"I'll let you be the judge. I had been writing some of it in Mr Jones' room but at the end of the period I forgot to pick it up. Well the next morning I went back to collect it hoping he hadn't really paid it particular attention. No such luck. He was already at his desk and said, "I think you might be looking for this." Well it wasn't until I was on my own that I discovered some of it had been scored out and changed, with completely new bits added." The jury had already returned its verdict and Mr Jones, almost impossibly now enjoyed even more respect that before.

"Jill, you came oh so close to getting a kill." "There is only one G.......""

"I know." Jill replied to Luke, "We could have had him hung drawn and quartered but for the completion of one more tiny little word. And what about you two chancers handing in the same homework!"

"It most certainly was not!" exclaimed Andrew Cash in mock protestation, while Dean Colt in the background looked similarly offended, his years studying Drama now serving good purpose. Everyone's attention now fell upon Suzie Baxter.

"That was just inspirational," applauded Luke. "I spent hours on my masterpiece and you trumped it with a couple of words."

He reminded everyone of her somewhat concise submission for the benefit of those who weren't there but Suzie was quite uncomfortable with the adulation. She was quite a modest girl who actually shied away from attention. "Hi God.....The end." This time they could release the laughter which they had so painfully but admirably kept bottled up behind their deadpan faces that glorious day.

Andrew and Dean then recounted the Mr Munro story for the 100th time before his celebrated departure. If there was ever a story that did not need gilded or enhanced this was the one and it would be a long time before anyone in this company would tire of hearing about neds being sworn at: they did not share an affinity with that particular alternative sub culture.

Wendy Croft went to the fridge for another beer and asked, "Anyone else need a refill while I'm up?" Amelia was first to raise her hand followed by a few others then Chris said, "Just make sure you don't tumble down the stairs Wendy."

Everyone laughed when reminded of Wendy's school show performance when she crashed off the stage, but there was also a feeling of relief for Chris that he felt he could now get involved in the exchanges. Perhaps the start of the healing process was just possible in the coming months or years.

"I tripped!" she complained with a smile on her face.

"How much did you all drink back stage?" asked Suzie.

"God how should I know," she smirked before swallowing a handsome measure of lager in one go.

"What made you want to be in the school show anyway?" continued Suzie.

"What? I've been in the school show every year! You mean you've never noticed me!" she exclaimed in a totally insulted manner, totally not insulted.

"The first year I was dressed all in black running about the stage with 50 others. The next show I was all in black running about.... Maybe you've got a point."

"Did anyone hear about Jordan White?" enquired The Josh in his usual quite and laid back manner. Absolutely no-one in the world knew why David Green was called The

Josh, not his parents his friends or even The Josh himself.

"Well," he breathed in a relaxed manner to his attentive audience. Combined with his story telling ability and the gang's eventual need to hear something new, the floor was his. He didn't elaborate his tales, he just told them in an engaging way with perfect timing. "Well," he repeated. "it seems that he was at a Physics class when the electromagnetic spectrum was getting discussed."

"Eh, that would mean a lot to him!" interrupted Dean. Everyone knew what he meant.

"So anyway it seems he may at one point have inadvertently woken up to hear Mr Gordon describe the use of infra-red goggles and how if gamekeepers wore them they could see the poachers but the poachers couldn't see them."

The gang were getting a feeling for the flavour of what might come next but eagerly awaited the details. "It would appear that he managed to sneak the goggles out of the Physics lab without being noticed for his own personal project let's say."

If ever there was a moment that a teenager needed to pause and take a draw from his pipe for effect this was it. He didn't have a pipe so he just pretended, right down to packing tobacco into it and opening the side of his mouth while lighting it. He had no idea why pipe smokers actually did that but that was of no importance.

"Christ watch where you put the match!" said Andrew carefully picking it up and blowing it out before putting it carefully in an invisible ashtray, while Jill shook her head and stared at him sternly and waved the naughty finger at him. This was no gang but a colony of beautiful symbiotic sentient beings. It was one of lives' inevitable tragedies that one day this group would all go their separate ways.

"Apologies for my carelessness. Let me continue. Well he headed up to the shops in the village centre and was going right up close to girls and staring at their boobs."

They all now just knew how this would conclude, especially Jill who was nearly subjected to Jordan's special scrutiny.

"As you will no doubt have figured out for yourself he thought that wearing the goggles made him invisible." The laughter shook the walls and they literally cried until they were absolutely exhausted and hurting.

Keith Jack abandoned his doodling for a moment and said, "Remember that snippet he shared about his holiday, quote, it was great having a swimming pool. It meant you didn't have to worry about there being toilet paper!" The hysterical revulsion had everyone reaching to cover their mouths.

In the same theme Wendy continued, "Remember when he was asked if he always washed his hands when he had been to the toilet and he said, no but I always dry them." More groans ensued. "Honestly, I think if he brushed his teeth he would lose about two pounds!"

"Enough!" begged Dean. "Please, no more!"

"Who else was there?" Jill was asked by Amelia, grateful that she herself wasn't.

"Mr Wood. He really has been about the village much more than when he worked in the school." Jill answered, continuing, "He seems to be looking closely at houses and writing things down." This observation received nods of agreement.

"And Shelley."

"Well of course Shelley was there. Shelley is everywhere!" said Luke to be joined in harmony by everyone.

"Its true though," said Jill. "She is everywhere and always going somewhere or just coming back from somewhere."

"Maybe she is one of twins or triplets?" suggested The Josh.

"Or maybe she makes clones of herself in her laboratory," added Dean in an outrageously slow and bold mad scientist voice, while behind him Andrew did a visual impression of her that was just too good. Meanwhile Keith was drawing achingly cruel caricatures of her. Amelia was of course uneasy with this. She was never comfortable with people being singled out and ridiculed. She had to admit though that despite her best efforts to talk to Shelley, only cold mechanical words were returned.

"Where was Shelley?" asked Amelia.

"She was coming down the front path from Mr Munro's house."

Everyone was immediately alerted to the alarmed expression on Amelia's face. For some reason this one piece of information was the trigger for subconscious disparate fragments to take soul chilling grip of Amelia. She struggled to her feet still faint with realization. "I have to go. I have to go now!"

"Where? Why? Can someone come with you?" asked startled and concerned voices from all directions.

"No I'll be fine. I just have to go," and she disappeared down the loft stairs, grabbed her shoes and made a hurried exit from the house. Amelia made her way expeditiously to where she knew Mr Stewart lived. Even in haste however she moved with grace and elegance, the way she delicately lifted the hem of her full length dress above her shoes making her look strangely theatrical and anachronistic.

In the time it took her to arrive she was able to gather her thoughts into some kind of coherent order. It was not a normal thing to go disturbing a teacher well into Friday evening. Having reached the path to his house she stopped to compose herself then opened the large creaking gate which surely must have announced her probably most unwelcome intrusion she feared. It was clear that no-one was going to come to the door so she rang the door bell which chimed with the grandeur appropriate to a much larger house. Mr Stewart came to the door dressed not unlike the boys she had left behind with music coming from somewhere not unlike what they would have listened to. With a beer in hand he would have fitted in seamlessly and she wondered to herself what she had actually expected to greet her at the door. A figure with a nightcap and a candle perhaps?

"Amelia, this is a surprise. What can I do for you? Is there a problem?" He was joined at the door by his wife or partner she presumed. "You best come in."

The three of them went through to the source of the music which was promptly lowered and they sat together. His wife, as she turned out to be, contemplated leaving the room to give them privacy but in the circumstances, a school girl alone with a teacher on a Friday night, could generate future difficulties with those who seek to make mischief. Quite soon it became apparent that what she had to say went well beyond the remit of a Guidance Teacher so they set the wheels in motion to assemble the appropriate personnel.

Chapter Nineteen

Richard and Barbara Rosenberg were as usual on a Friday having a night out in the only Indian restaurant in the area for many miles. The Bombay Tandoori advertised itself as the finest Indian restaurant in the area. Simple maths ensured that couldn't be argued. Fortunately however it was, in the opinion of everyone who used it, absolutely superb. The truth was that it was owned by a Pakistani family who had settled in the UK over 70 years earlier. Richard had actually asked the owner and oldest member of the family, Mr Bhatti about this knowing that India and Pakistan had a bit of a history. He informed him that they once had a restaurant marketed as Pakistani which was struggling a bit. They gave it a make over, re-launched it as an Indian Restaurant but with exactly the same chef and family recipes, and consequently more than doubled their profit to rave reviews, his enduring quote being, "What do I think first thing in the morning, Kashmir or cash register?"

Richard and Barbara had just finished their Vegetable Pakora served with a fragrant chilli dip and spiced onions. It was as always just heavenly. Their weekly fix was partially satisfied. Their next addiction would be their usual main course, Lamb Tikka. They, like so many customers often wondered if perhaps there was literally some addictive agent present in the food. Something else they often used to puzzle over was how they could supply such generous portions of expensive cuts of meat for such competitive prices. Some of course took it further and offered wild speculations about what they were really consuming. Had the recent spate of deaths also included missing persons then there is no doubt the speculation would have been taken to a whole new distasteful and macabre level. The subject of the cluster of deaths was never far from the conversation anywhere just now with three often repeated salient points, small village, four months, seven dead and this didn't include the three almost forgotten poor souls who had just passed on in the normal cycle of nature.

Richard and Barbara had arrived by taxi as both enjoyed a drink with their meals. For Richard it was a plentiful supply of genuine Indian lager all the way from Birmingham while Barbara's preference was Pinot Grigio served in glasses the size of which, a couple of decades earlier would have been considered closer to resembling a decanter. In a flurry two waiters appeared together and filled the table with dishes of hot sauce, rice and a naan of extraordinary proportions, light and fluffy with beautiful well fired edges.

"Lots of people say naan bread," Richard said to Barbara. He continued, oblivious to her expression, "but naan actually means bread. That's like saying bread

bread." There was a silence. "I've mentioned that before huh?"

"Well yes, just a few hundred times, and please spare me the 3D sequel, Pin Number!" They were clearly still very much in love. In the distance they could hear approaching the sound they had come to know that promised so much. Within moments a hissing spitting mountain of delicious red and gorgeous Lamb Tikka arrived heaped with a garnish of onions, unashamedly glowing with artificial colouring, filling the surrounding area with a thick savoury smoke, momentarily giving the restaurant the appearance of Victorian London.

"If this had been about in the time of Rabbie Burns we wouldn't be piping in a haggis every January," Richard said almost dizzy with expectation. "His poetic gift would have turned to immortalize this ambrosia," words and sentiments which combined a peculiar and diverse collection of cultures and traditions. The extraordinary fact was that the issue had once been debated at the esteemed University of Glasgow no less.

For the next half hour or so they savoured their feast rarely exchanging a word: they were allowed to do this as they were married, and then chose to finish the evening with coffee, the mints promptly despatched into a handbag of course.

As the bill was laid on the table, Barbara looked across the restaurant and said, "Look I think that's Mr McKenzie, Amelia's new Physics teacher."

"What the one who replaced Mr Fu...,"

"Yes," interrupted Barbara who was not really comfortable with the renowned nick name."

"He's with that girl in the teal dress?"

"How can you tell what it's made of from here?"

"Teal is a colour ya daftie."

"Why do women need so many colours? Men get by with about six while you lot need a hundred!"

"Yes, 10 for each of your imaginary inches." Richard knew he had just been insulted but he wasn't quite sure how. "Looks like they are coming to sit at that table next to us."

"Hello Mr and Mrs Rosenberg How are you? How was your meal?"

"Please, Richard and Barbara will do. We're not at school now, and by the way I'm Richard and she's Barbara. Things aren't just as straight forward as they used to be eh?" There was a distinct lack of reaction which made Richard think that maybe it wasn't quite comic genius but even Christmas cracker jokes get some kind of forced response.

"Aren't you going to introduce us?" asked Barbara.

"We need no introduction we have met several times before." This drew blank expressions. "At parent's evenings? I have been Amelia's Maths teacher for the past three years?" Puzzled looks turned to stark realization.

"Oh of course, Miss Martin. Amelia has spoken of you." Richard began staring what Barbara considered rather inappropriately and it didn't go unnoticed by anyone. Barbara moved to break the tension and observed that Miss Martin was wearing a rather striking diamond pendant. "I think Richard is just admiring you gems." That didn't help at all. "They are quite large. Are they real?" and that really didn't help either.

Miss Martin replied calmly with a hint of a self satisfied smile, "Whatever he is looking at the answer is yes."

"Anyway, we must be going as we have ordered a taxi. It could be there already actually," rushed Richard as they said their good byes and headed briskly for the door, unknown to them leaving behind Matthew and Toni tortured with suppressed laughter.

"I think we handled that fairly well," said Richard. They both looked at each other and smirked childishly. "We best phone that taxi then that we've already ordered."

A police car was parked just outside the restaurant from which came an extremely young policewoman who was immediately recognised as Amelia's former babysitter. "I hope you had a good meal?" PC Isobel Tennent enquired with disguised purpose. It is not the gambit of someone about to deliver serious or tragic news, and Mr and Mrs Rosenberg were no strangers to tragedy as she knew, thinking back to the loss of their younger daughter.

"Are you here to pick up something for yourself Isobel?" enquired Barbara.

"Well no to be honest, I'm here to pick up you."

"Oh dear what has she been up to?"

"I'm here for both of you actually."

"I was framed!" Richard protested but clearly wanted to know what was really going on.

"Now first of all let me assure you that nothing at all has happened that you need be in the slightest bit concerned regarding your daughter Amelia, but she believes she has information which she judges to be of real importance so at the moment she is at the police station."

"What? Why? Why?" Barbara asked with a level of anxiety.

"I will explain on the way there but honestly she is absolutely fine and has done nothing wrong. We just didn't want to proceed without both of you being in attendance."

"Richard, now quite relaxed, noticed his next door neighbour approaching for whom he didn't have a great deal of time to put it mildly. He often in fact used very descriptive terms for him but felt now was perhaps not the moment. He allowed just sufficient time for the neighbour to recognise him before concealing his own identity with his jacket by the familiar method then guiding his head into the back of the police car with his own hand in a surprisingly convincing manner.

"Richard, grow up!" up Barbara said, both knowing full well that she never wanted that to happen ever.

Meanwhile Detective Constable Watt found himself outside a riotously noisy bar with all the key words from his check-list from hell shouting in his face, Karaoke, Bingo, Quiz and Tribute Act. Why had he been sent to find Inspector Buchanan he found himself asking. What had he done that was so horribly wrong in a former life?

The door flew open and the racket got louder then closed but it didn't get quieter. The poster didn't even identify the act to whom the performers wanted to pay tribute. Had a part of the sign been removed by the rain and wind or was it perhaps kept vague deliberately? It would be difficult to say a tribute act was bad if you were never told who they were meant to be in the first place. Could he just get away with saying he tried but couldn't find him? That was a non starter. He would be interrogated and found out at the station. That was their job after all.

He steeled himself to enter then pushed on the swing door. The door was promptly pushed back on him with interest. He was still outside. Fortunately someone came out which meant that theoretically there should be space for someone else to squeeze in. He seized the moment and found himself in a nightmare beyond his worst fears. Everyone appeared to be screaming at everyone else. A throng of heaving bodies were packed and merged together as one with a layer of about ten feet of the homogeneous flesh endeavouring possibly to be served at the bar but it was hard to differentiate them from the rest of the humanoid sardines.

The place was so gloomy and dark other than the lights on the stage where four blue and white latex clad individuals performed their thing barely heard but unfortunately still could be. There was also a spotlight trained on someone else, a giant of a man with an eighties style mullet getting primed to launch an unprovoked attack of bingo or whatever.

Detective Watt looked about but in all directions he could see little further than the end of his own nose. "How can it possibly be getting louder?" he said to himself in growing despair. He felt he could throw a stun grenade and it would go unnoticed. Reluctantly he accepted that he may have to start asking about. He chose someone at random, tapped his shoulder then screamed into his ear. The chosen one pointed to his ear and shook his head. Watt had no idea what this meant. Was he deaf? He had no choice but to shout again only louder. This time he was summonsed to crouch down a bit so his own ear in turn could be screamed at. "Ten o'clock" He made out. "What," he puzzled to himself, "Inspector Buchanan is at ten o'clock. Is this guy a former fighter pilot or something?"

The man pointed to a sign on the wall. Watt became, quite impossibly, even more exasperated. How could, "Have you seen Inspector Buchanan," possible sound at all like, "When does the bingo start?"

He had no option but to start twisting and wriggling through the heaving crowd as a cocktail of sprays and splashes left samples on his outdoor jacket. He was tempted to put up his hood. For reasons unknown the noise level dropped momentarily. Perhaps some had suffocated. Once more he selected a random stranger to scream at but this time the random stranger pointed to a group standing near the stage and said something which sounded vaguely like second from the left.

He made his way to this group like an explorer fighting his way through the thickest jungle and got within site of his target. None of them looked even remotely like Inspector Buchanan. He was on the point of giving up when it dawned on him that it was not those in front of the stage who were being pointed out but those actually on it, and true enough Detective Inspector Buchanan was the one second from the left. He caught the attention of a surprised then clearly not amused Inspector and they fought their way out a side entrance.

"This better be important. I'm about to do my big signature solo. Why do you think everyone is here?" DC Watt briefly explained the situation and they made their way to the Detective's car.

Fiona Dalton was having a night at home with a close friend and ex-colleague who used to be one of her Deputy Head Teachers but got promoted to Head Teacher in one of the large schools in the city. As she now lived far enough away for a drive to be inconvenient, Elizabeth Law would be spending the night in Fiona's rather grand accommodation. Finding a spare room would not be a problem. Given what they had planned to drink the police may have had something to say about driving home also. Both Fiona and Elizabeth had already eaten before they met up so the evening would be dedicated to drinking and grazing, with much to graze upon as was the norm. Both were dressed for comfort which was basically jeans and a top. Elizabeth was wearing a New Zealand All Blacks rugby top which had been given to her by a visiting relative from Glasgow. She never queried it. Fiona was wearing a T shirt from a theme park proclaiming the name of roller coaster ride she had survived. She was actually a roller coaster enthusiast.

"Pinot Grigio OK with you Liz?"

"Absolutely fine. I thought you were more of a Chardonnay person if I remember correctly."

"I've kind of gone off Chardonnay recently."

"Why? Of course yes. I'm a bit slow tonight. Not had enough to drink. I actually taught that evil creature when she was still in first year. Even then you could tell that she was a horrible wee cow."

Although the model professional, Elizabeth enjoyed the freedom to express herself without constraint or fear when not in work mode.

"I wouldn't argue. What I found so unsettling was how she re-acted to compliments. 'How fuck'n dare you say something nice to me you horrible bitch!' her expression used to say." Fiona too liked the full freedom of language when allowed.

"I'm not suggesting for a minute that I'm pleased about what happened to her," Elizabeth feeling a touch guilty that she did not embraced fully what she had just said. She judged however that she was no great loss to society at large.

"Poor John definitely brought the dreadful events upon himself, though perhaps there should actually be some in-service training for all staff to that end."

"What, if you're going to get tied up dressed as a baby girl, don't get caught!"

They both laughed and no further clarification was required, both understanding that even the tiniest indiscretion can be your undoing in the hands of a determined and malicious foe.

"Did you ever see the pictures?"

"Yes unfortunately I did and so wish I hadn't. Remember these were not pictures taken in harmless moments of pleasure, albeit not quite mainstream. No there was terror and abject humiliation in his eyes. Horrible actually."

"How are you coping with the whole death thing anyway? Are you getting pestered with the press?"

"That's the thing. It's hard to tell who the press even are. Would you believe a new 6th year pupil enrolled a few weeks ago who was actually in the payroll of a particularly sleazy rag?"

"That is just shocking. Scum!"

"It's when I think back to whom I may have spoken before I became a bit more savvy. But no it is hard. I actually keep my funeral outfit in my office now. Seriously. Every time I see some tall guy in a hood I think it's the Grim Reaper."

"I was going to have a little moanfest myself but my difficulties are just so boring and mundane by comparison."

"A surprising difficulty is just getting flowers. With the eight school related incidents plus three run of the mill deaths, you know, grow old, die like it's meant to be, it's hard even to find flowers anywhere. They are so often sold out."

Elizabeth went to speak but before she could Fiona suddenly and out of the blue shouted," Petrol!"

"What?"

"Oh sorry I've just made sense of something Hamish Jones said when I told him I was going to the florists to buy flowers. He said, "Remember to buy some petrol for your man."" Elizabeth was puzzled momentarily then it suddenly made sense.

"I think his ambition is to be so obscure and subtle that nobody actually knows what he's talking about. He did the same to me. One day when I was with him and looked down to discover my tights were torn and he said. "Don't worry just use the fan belt from your car. I was halfway home before I figured out what he was talking about."

"Another time," Fiona now found herself triggered to recall, "I was with him in the music room. He picked up a microphone and said, "I wonder how many people when they are alone in their bedroom with one of these brush their hair with it?"

"Oh my God. I understood that. I'm starting to think like Hamish Jones!"

"More wine?" Elizabeth returned a look that just said, "And you need to ask?"

It's quite good having the place to myself now and then, though I'm not a big fan of being alone in such a huge house."

"Where is Charles anyway?"

"He's away on a skiing trip with the boys. Yes, what snow you're thinking. There never is on their annual event but it doesn't seem to be an issue. Actually he frequently works late on a Friday."

"A Friday? That's just weird."

"Well actually he says he likes to be fully prepared for Monday."

"Yeh, I suppose that makes sense." They smiled at each other and shook their heads to imply quite the opposite. "I hear Mr Martin is now Miss Martin. I only knew him for a few months before I left. What a brave young woman. Honestly. Especially in a school of all places." Fiona pulled an expression which wrongly suggested annoyance.

"What, you don't approve?" asked Elizabeth a bit surprised but none the less fully expecting an acceptable explanation.

"Oh Liz, no. I don't have a problem in the slightest. Honestly. She's just so bloody beautiful. It's not fair!" They both laughed, but they also both really thought it wasn't fair.

"I hear you've been landed with Doctor Burns in the RE department. What an absolute prize winning screw ball he is. I met him once. What a total fruit loop."

"Well firstly you can drop the Doctor and secondly he is gone. PhD? He has never been inside a university in his life!"

"What? So how did he beat the system?"

"Don't know. Don't care. It came to light when he tried working in a different authority. For once a problem is the problem of someone else," to which she raised her glass and took a healthy volume of wine.

"Quite right, so then, apart from six deaths, seven? one bogus doctor, a sex change, a sex club and a school building with malicious intent is everything else OK?"

"Well setting aside the murdered wife of Mr Drysdale the wife murderer, and a battered and abused runaway parent? Colette!"

"What?"

"Colette Murphy."

"Ah right. Still paying social calls then."

"Honestly, I wish I could change my office every day so that I'm harder to find!"

"What is irking her these days?"

"The usual. Her staff. Credit where credit's due. She is being very fair minded. Doesn't like any of them."

"What's the problem now?"

"The same as it's always been. They stubbornly refuse to be passive replicants of herself."

"Ah well at least you have that wonderful new modern hi tech school. Is it really as bad as you have told me? Surely not!"

"Seriously. I was ready for jumping in front of the demolition ball to stop them knocking the old school down!"

"That bad, really?"

"Really. Honestly I'm frightened to use the phone in case it turns the sprinklers on or guard dogs get released into the corridors from secret panels.... Was that the doorbell? I think it was. Excuse me for a sec."

Fiona returned with a police officer. "I'm sorry Elizabeth, I'm going to have to go to the police station. Something has come up. I hope you'll be OK on your own for a bit."

"To be honest, I'd have been disappointed if there hadn't been a bit of police action while I was here. I'll be fine. I know where the chocolates are and I've brought some glossy magazines"

"Well just remember," said Fiona, "that we are heading off early tomorrow to those shops in town just bulging with stuff we don't need."

Turning to the police officer she said, "I'm a bit informal, will I do?"

"Oh trust me on that one. You'll be fine," he said with a smile.

Chapter Twenty

Amelia was sitting in a large office with her guidance teacher. It was similar in layout to the boardroom in the school where she had attended groups regarding fund raising and such things. Scattered on the substantial table surrounded by about a dozen office style armchairs were little bundles of leaflets to do with knife crime, home security, drug abuse, drink driving and much more. On the walls were posters with similar themes, and all served to heighten Amelia's cold feeling of misplaced culpability. It was very brightly illuminated, brighter than made Amelia comfortable but in truth she only ever felt at ease in subdued lighting and she was most definitely not a sun worshipper. She was torturing herself with illogical thoughts of liability. Even with her considerable intellect at her disposal and knowing that her feeling of guilt was totally unfounded she had somehow temporarily been stripped of rational thought.

David Stewart sat quietly on a chair roughly opposite her. He had long since run out of things to say and it was obvious also that Amelia did not seek small talk. He looked at the clock as if by doing so he could speed it up and bring all the participants to the table. He heard noises outside, the door opened and a policewoman showed in Amelia's parents.

Amelia looked up at them and smiled but did not speak then they took up seats either side of her. Both sensing that she was not in the mood for idle talk or indeed any kind of conversation they turned their attention to David Stewart.

"So this is where you spend your Friday night's then is it?" asked Richard for no other reason than just to be saying something, and for exactly the same reason David replied,

"Well it's warm, and it's and a roof over my head. Can't complain."

"You've got it looking nice," joined in Barbara and they all smiled limply but knew there was little mileage in this exchange and they fell quiet. Fortunately the tense silence was not required to stretch any tighter as the door opened again and in came DC Watt followed by DI Buchanan. Suddenly there was no tension at all. A senior police officer wearing huge blue and white flared trousers and a top with sleeves and simply huge collar to match has that affect.

"Hello everyone, I got here as quickly as I could when I was told about the hypothesis of our young sleuth here." Amelia smiled and for the moment at least her undeserved burden lifted, temporarily. DI Buchanan, obviously alert to everyone quite understandably looking at him added, "I was working undercover."

"Yip," joined in DC Watt, "He managed to infiltrate a drugs ring." There was certainly no tension now. Moments later Fiona Dalton was shown in.

"Well it looks like I'm the last guest to arrive," and looking at DI Buchanan said, "Ah yes. I now see what the policeman who collected me meant." She seated herself across from Amelia and smiling, reached out and touched her hand. DI Buchanan began to speak.

"Well clearly when the invitation said, fancy dress optional I was the only one who made the effort. Now I'm sure you have all been briefed about the purpose of this meeting, and at this stage let me make that perfectly clear. This is not an enquiry nor investigation so we will neither be recording nor writing down every last detail of what is said."

"Slow down sir, you're talking too quickly. I can't keep up," said DC Watt holding a pencil to his notebook.

"Every class has its clown. Isn't that right Amelia? Anyway before we get started I have ordered some snacks and sandwiches. Is coffee all right for everyone?"

"Could I just have water please?" asked Amelia.

"Of course you can. Coffee's not everybody's cup of tea." He picked up a phone and modified the order. "Being a Friday night most of us could probably be doing with a cup of coffee. Amelia is probably the only one of us fit to drive?" Amelia's sheepish look was noted and the point not pursued. No one in this room had ever touched a drop of alcohol until their eighteenth birthday was the communal thought shared by none.

He turned to Amelia knowing that sooner or later the joking must end and the purpose of the gathering initiated. Her sketched thoughts with which everyone in the room had been made familiar to different extents carried sufficient substance to have gathered so many together late on a Friday night.

"OK, firstly I would really like to thank everyone for coming here though I suspect you all know that Amelia may well have a theory worthy of our attention. Mr Stewart. Thank you. Clearly you are quite closely involved although I must add quite oblivious to what may have been unfolding."

"Not a problem and it will make interesting listening as Amelia puts it all together for us. Can I just say that I believe Amelia has the skills and intellectual wherewithal to do this without my assistance."

"My apologies again. Mr and Mrs Rosenberg I really should have come to you first and I hope the policewoman who picked you up didn't alarm you in any way."

"Not in the slightest," said Barbara. "When I think back about it she played it so well."

"Agreed," added Richard, "She must have put quite some thought into it."

"Mrs Dalton, I always assured you that you would be kept in the loop should anything arise. I hope you weren't dragged away from something important?"

"No just busily working away like everyone else here," she said doing the internationally recognised drinking gesture with her hand then remembering Amelia's presence immediately wished she hadn't.

"Now to the most important of us all." All eyes turned on Amelia. "Would you please in your own time share your thoughts with us and trust you are not going to be quizzed or cross examined in any way."

At that moment the door opened and soon the table was covered in trays of sandwiches, sausage rolls, crisps, tea, coffee, water and to Amelia's relief, fizzy drinks and not the diet versions. Coffee was enthusiastically poured and Amelia lifted a can. Not just a drink but also a sugar rush was much needed. One more time DI Buchanan said, "Amelia, when you are ready."

For some time she had been rehearsing in her head for this moment but now it seemed so much more difficult putting it together, or more exactly, starting off, but with one more sip from the can she began.

"Last year I went to Mr Stewart's room to ask about the possibility of doing a Modern Studies course a year later. When I went in Mr Stewart didn't notice me and was saying to himself how he would like to kill some of the pupils, and was swearing in the process."

She looked at Mr Stewart with an air of discomfort who said, "Just tell it like it is Amelia. Don't worry about me. These details are important."

She continued. "He apologised then said that there must be a few pupils in the school I wouldn't mind too much being executed and I said that since he was more experienced than me I would let him choose." At this point Amelia paused and looked around at all the faces trained on her. "We were just joking and having a laugh."

Amelia's mum put her arm around her and said, "You really don't have to explain," then looking around said, "Honestly she's never killed anyone before has she Richard?"

"Well not that she's shared with me anyway," he replied.

"Look Amelia, you are doing just fine," said Fiona Dalton. "You are carrying out a rather daunting task here."

Amelia continued. "Mr Stewart then pointed to a newspaper pinned on the wall and said that he blamed the parents anyway referring to the Headline. At this point we realized we were not alone, Shelley was standing inside the doorway and had been for one minute fifteen seconds." This brought strange looks from everyone. "One minute fifteen seconds is exactly what she said and indicated that she had been looking at the clock."

Amelia stopped and took another drink. "The next part is about the school show. As always Mr Stewart drew the raffle tickets and this year Shelley delivered the prizes to the winners insisting that everyone show their raffle ticket. At the time everyone found this really funny." Amelia stopped to take another drink then continued but now her voice was broken and hesitant. "Tonight when I was with my friends someone mentioned that they had seen Shelley come out from Mr Munro's front path who I remembered had won a prize but had given the ticket to his daughter; and that is when everything for some reason occurred to me. Everyone who has died has been directly connected with winning prizes in the raffle."

Amelia's voice had been reduced to short hurried breaths. Pulling it all together; articulating it had rekindled her glowing embers of guilt into a roaring flame. She was responsible for all these deaths. Only two hours earlier she had been holding Chris Templeton to her side to comfort him but she was responsible for asking someone to select who should be murdered and Chris's dad was one of them. She might as well have killed him with her own guilty hands. No-one actually knew or would even understand the self inflicted torment being suffered by Amelia and thought only that the enormity of what she was disclosing had taken its toll, and she was simply emotionally exhausted.

"That's fine that's fine," DI Buchanan said taking over. "I think our young detective has done a wonderful job and really given us something to take further."

Everyone nodded in agreement and said words to that end. "Please Amelia, allow me to summarize what you have said, but be warned, and everyone else, I am going to be coldly succinct and precise. Shelley heard Amelia tell Mr Stewart that she would let him chose who to kill. He then said he blamed the parents. He chose the victims via the raffle and Shelley killed the parents or in one case the grandparents."

Only once put in such blunt terms did everyone suddenly appreciate Amelia's distress which had now manifest itself as a motionless silence.

There was substance and coherence to Amelia's interpretation of events and it was clear that there were sufficient grounds for apprehending Shelley immediately. "Police officers are on their way to the foster home of Shelley as we speak," DC Watt updated DI Buchanan.

"Mr Munro right now will lying in the sunshine thousands of miles away somewhere, a drink in his hand with absolutely no idea just how lucky he has been," said DI Buchanan.

"Sorry Sir, but just to be clear. Mr Munro is Mr fuck off yes?"

"Well yes I think everybody and their dog know that. Why Do you ask?"

"He isn't a couple of thousand miles away. Very recently I saw him step out of a taxi with whom I presume to be his wife and daughter!"

Chapter Twenty One

A few days earlier Moira Munro had been lying in a beauty parlour getting extravagantly expensive oil rubbed into her skin that 72% of women from a sample of 45 said hadn't done them any harm. (The laboratory animals were never surveyed.) She was holding a glass of champagne reflecting on the fact that many months later she still did not miss standing in a cold factory gutting fish. Her husband Stephen had always said that it wasn't totally necessary as they could have got by on his salary. Getting by though was not really part of Moira's psyche. She reminded him often back in Abercorrie that Aphrodite's Temple of Beauty was not a charity, and beauty therapy was not one of life's luxuries but a vital part of the respiratory system.

The life changing millions that had come their way from a lottery win would keep them in luxury, not wanting for anything for the rest of their lives despite Moira and their daughter's best efforts. Stephen was by no means tight fisted, indeed he was very generous and giving but he did not like waste nor money to be squandered. It was largely for this reason that they were going back to Scotland. There were still matters to be sorted out including the sale of their house which should bring in a hundred thousand pounds or so. That, he thought should buy a considerable quantity and array of totally ineffective beauty products.

"So how was the Caribbean cruise then?" said the beautician Tracy.

"It was just wonderful but sitting at the captain's table a few times really meant I needed to have something different to wear every night."

"But Moira, you just look fantastic no matter what you wear," fawned Tracy who recognised a money cow when she saw one. It was actually something like that she called Moira in more private moments. "And where is Stephen today?"

"Well I'm taking a wild guess here but I suspect it will be the Irish Bar down at the front. Paddy's Bar."

"Paddy's Bar. I wonder how many stressed nights the owners had before coming up with that quite original name? Does he go there often then?"

"He should have a season ticket. I don't know why he keeps going to the same place all the time. I thought he would want to do the circuit so he could tell even more people his wonderful story."

"Ah yes, that story. His last day at school. Well at least you know he won't be exaggerating it. I mean how could you?"

"He tries, trust me."

"Anyway, thanks as always. You are a life saver. I'm just away to meet him now. We have a bit of packing to do for tomorrow."

"Oh of course, your trip home to tidy up loose ends. Ah well enjoy the flight and

213

I'll see you next week. Thank you very much Moira, you really are too generous," she gushed as she received a huge wad of notes in her hand, so substantial that counting it out would not really be essential. "We'll not talk about you while you're away."

"My ears will burn if you do."

Moira made her way down the long floral archway to the sea front then the short walk to Paddy's Bar where Stephen was surrounded by cheery faces primed for hilarity having had a plentiful supply of free beer, "and then the rest of the class started shouting, tell me to fuck off tell me...Oh Hi Moira I was just telling them....."

"Let me guess now. Was it the story about your last day at school?"

"You haven't lost you psychic powers doll." Stephen had never called his wife doll in all his life. Beer and a testosterone party can have strange consequences.

"Well doll," Moira continued with the theme, "we are meeting up with Michelle in the hotel bar soon so drink up, say, 'The End,' and let's go," knowing soon they would be in the bar and Michelle would be late. They made their departure and sauntered hand in hand back to the hotel.

"That's half an hour now. Any idea where she is?"

"She said she was going to meet up with Fernando," Moira replied.

"What that really tall thin guy?"

"No the other Fernando."

"The wee blond waiter?"

"No that's Guillermo."

"Dear God never mind. I hope her boy friends don't want to wave her good bye at the airport. We'll need to hire a fleet of taxis, or that big long pink Limo. The Tramp Trolley is it they call it?"

"Shoosh here she's coming. You're a bit late. Well I suppose for you, not really? Anyway we have a flight time for quite late tomorrow and you will just need hand luggage OK?"

"You are kidding me on!"

"No I am not kidding you on. We fly in, get a taxi to our old house, get the personal things we really want, get some paperwork then early the next morning it's back in the taxi to the airport. What could you possibly need to take with you?" asked Moira as if craving sarcasm.

"And remember we are really just trying to kind of sneak in and away again. It's a secret journey. There could even be reporters about if people get wind of us coming back," added Stephen.

"OK, if I'm going to have to look like a total tramp I'll just tell Mandy that we won't be able to meet up after all." She stopped, realising what she had just said.

"Her parents just looked at each other then Stephen turned to his daughter. "Secret, Secret! I'm guessing you never got round to writing that one down in your word book at school?"

"Dear God Michelle who knows how many people she might have told."

"But she won't have. Honest. I told her it was a big sec..," She was to embarrassed to finish her own sentence. "I'm actually chatting to her now."

"Well here's an idea since you are talking to her. Get her to go round to our house and put the heating on, buy coffee and fill the fridge with drinks, snacks and whatever. That would be useful. Remind her that the key is under the big blue flower pot in the garage. We'll pay her. Tell her to send us her bank details."

Michelle tapped away at keys while Moira ordered up drinks and a bar lunch. A few moments later, Michelle said, "You're not going to like this. Mandy has sent back her bank details. I'll just read it out. "It's a big red building with two windows either side of a blue glass door.""

When the three of them had recomposed themselves and dried their tears, Michelle made her instructions a bit clearer and took care of the bank transfer. That is something at which she was becoming very proficient with their recent millions.

"How much did you send her?" Stephen asked his daughter.

"Four hundred pounds."

"Four what? Jesus Christ is she going to Brazil for the coffee?"

The following evening arrived. Michelle hugged and said good bye to Gustavo, Hernando and Javier then they bundled into a taxi and within a few hours they were settled into their first class seats flying back to Scotland.

Stephen and Moira had still not become blasé about travelling in such style and they fully appreciated the opulent luxury. However the food and drink were somewhat wasted on Michelle who had weight issues bordering on pathological. American size zero was her Holy Grail.

She picked up a packaged food item and studied it carefully.

"Dad, how many calories is twenty?"

Stephen Munro was rarely stuck for an answer to any question about anything but this one? He rattled thoughts about his head but formulating anything of any substance failed to happen. He just steeled himself for a slap of teenage sarcasm. "Twenty I would say."

"Thanks dad," then she sat the package down. "Dad says twenty." He looked at her beyond puzzlement and tried to imagine what it would be like to see the world through her eyes and remembered reading how Albert Einstein had imagined sitting on a photon while compiling his Theory of Relativity, then wondered what the celebrated genius would have found the more difficult to imagine? He duly abandoned that for Einstein to decide and had another single malt whisky instead while debating if parting with well over a thousand pounds for extra leg room and free drink was really worth it. There was little point, he knew all too well, asking for his wife's opinion on that one.

When the flight landed it wasn't long again until they were in another taxi for the hour long drive back to Abercorrie. They entered the house and memories just came flooding back. Suddenly everything was special, so special that they reconsidered if they actually wanted to sell it at all. They really did not need the money from a sale. They closed the blinds and curtains and didn't put on any more light than necessary then explored their old home. It just felt so exciting to open a cupboard and find a book, an old toy; anything. It was a treasure chest of spine tingling memories. This house would not be getting sold any time soon.

There were things that needed done, documents that needed found and gathered but eventually they were all sitting together staring at the coal effect gas fire and making use of the plentiful supply of provisions which Mandy had left. Without being asked, Mandy had actually replaced the bed sheets so they were fresh and inviting which prompted Moira to say to Stephen, "Four hundred pounds well spent," and he began to laugh but quickly noticed his mirth was a solo act. Moira was clearly becoming comfortable with wealth.

Later in the evening Stephen and Moira had each noticed the other momentarily drifting off to sleep and decided that it was time for bed, joking that it was jet lag though knowing it was just a four hour flight and not even a different time zone.

Michelle was texting Alonso, Quito and Jose but soon she fell asleep where she sat; then silently the back door swung open.

Chapter Twenty Two

DI Buchanan pulled off his theatrical clothes and just pulled on what came to hand and also a thick jacket belonging to someone. They wouldn't miss it for a bit. He then headed towards the police car park with DC Watt where they found that a layer of deep snow had been laid down while they had all been in the station, and it was continuing to fall heavily. Steep hills lay in most directions from the police station and already there were cars stuck and slipping with volunteers and passers by trying to keep the traffic moving. They had already been informed that Shelley was not to be found in her foster home and a search was already in progress. The police cars were fitted with weather appropriate tyres but the obvious weakness in such foresight is that all other vehicles on the road must have them also or their value is very much diminished.

Driving from the car park was not too difficult and once on the road their destination was Mr Munro's hurriedly abandoned house. He could have been anywhere and being a millionaire with his spectacular departure, they reasoned he would want to keep a fairly low profile. He would probably therefore be staying the night in a quality hotel somewhere rather than a long since abandoned small house so the task was on to make enquiries in all the hotels in the vicinity. They still wanted to check out his house however just to ensure he wasn't there but also to investigate what Shelley may have been doing there recently. Within moments though it was obvious that the car was going nowhere as already the village streets had ground to a halt, and as reports came in it became further obvious that all police cars were being abandoned where they sat. Even snow tyres were defeated.

"It's no good, the wheels are all torque and no traction. We are going to have to walk," said DI Buchanan. "It's only about half a mile or so, no more."

In these conditions though half a mile was going to be a challenge. The snow was driving into their faces like little ice bullets as they struggled to see where they were going. There were only about another 4 police officers in the village and all on foot. The others who lived in surrounding areas would have no possibility of road travel. On they trudged further, the wind starting to really pick up. When within about a hundred yards of Mr Munro's house the village fell into total darkness.

"Oh great, the storm has taken the power lines down or something." They pulled out their flash lights and approached the abandoned house or so it looked, but with the whole village in the grip of a power cut it was no different at all from the rest. They made their way around the perimeter, first checking the doorways and windows. All were shut and locked. The two detectives met up at the back of the house trying to communicate with each other but being heard at all was now nearly impossible due to the roaring gale. DI Buchanan pointed to a garage and they both made there way to it. They found a side entrance door which they pushed open and went inside where it was still freezing but at least in shelter. It looked like it had been stripped bare of any tools which may have been here in the past.

"There doesn't appear to be anyone inside," said DC Watt.

"I didn't think there would be but it was best to check," said DI Buchanan who then radioed Shelley's foster home where a policewoman had been stationed in case she returned. PC Tennent informed them that there was no sign of her.

"Well she doesn't know we are looking for her and surely this weather will drive her home. From what I'm led to understand she is not liable to be at a friend's house either," said DI Buchanan. As it was Shelley did know, or at least reasoned correctly, that soon the police would be coming for her: just as she had hoped. She had been watching those arriving at the police station and from the composition of the group deduced that they had completed the jigsaw.

"I fancy giving the place one last check. I'm going to look in the windows again," said DI Buchanan and he made his way back into the blizzard. He attempted to shine his torch through the windows but the snow was covering the glass as quickly as it could be cleared. DI Buchanan then started shouting Mr Munro's name through the letterbox but as expected there was no reply or sign of life. It would seem that there was no-one inside the building as they had always expected. Outside the house however was DI Buchanan, DC Watt; and Shelley. She had been watching them since they arrived and judging now was the time, took out her phone, pressed a couple of keys and inside the house a tiny little flame was born. What Shelley's phone had also done in this blackest nights of all nights was to act like a beacon and with DC Watt's eyes now adjusted to extremely low light the illumination from her screen was enough to identify her position buried partially by branches. She immediately knew she had been spotted and moved as if to effect an escape but DC Watt caught her in seconds with surprising ease and brought her round to the front.

"I've got Shelley," DC Watt screamed at DI Buchanan through the worsening storm. DI Buchanan pointed to the garage again and they made their way back inside with their captive.

Once inside she smiled, "You are too late. Welcome to hell."

"Too late for what?" enquired DC Watt not really expecting an answer.

"Radio to call off the search and get anyone out there to come to this location.

She isn't here for nothing. I'm going back for another look and make sure she goes no-where."

DI Buchanan made his way back to the front door but this time as he passed a window there was definitely a glimmer of light. He swept aside the snow again and could now clearly see a flame starting to take hold. He rushed back to the garage and shouted, "Get the fire-service, just anybody."

There was no chance the fire engine could get near this place but he abandoned that particular problem to someone else and searched about for any kind of tool in the garage but it was stripped bare of anything that could be useful. He went back to the front door and tried to kick it open but it was not going to move. Looking about desperately he saw an edging stone for paths propped against the wall which he managed to carry towards the door. It had rough edges and his numb hands were starting to bleed. He picked it up in both hands and slammed it against the door beside the key hole but it sliced back through his hands causing more severe lacerations to his seeping fingers. He took off his jacket, wrapped it about the concrete border stone and drove it into the door again and again and again...... The door burst open.

The flames were moving rapidly towards the bottom of the stair and the heat was already picking up. He put back on his cold and soaked jacked for protection and ran up the stairs guided by the beam from his torch competing with the smoke but fighting a losing battle.

He made his way into one room and found two people lying on a bed. A quick search in the other two rooms revealed a third person. One look back and it was already obvious that escape via the stairs would be impossible and all he could do was buy time. By now breathing was becoming difficult and his eyes were burning agonisingly. His next move was to drag the daughter, he assumed, into the room with whom he further assumed were Mr and Mrs Munro. This he did at great speed slamming the floor, doorways and much else with the limp and unnaturally light body.

With them all in one room he headed into the upstairs bathroom to try and source then gather water by any means. The water was off and the tanks were drained dry so he headed back to the room where all three still unconscious bodies were, one of them now almost certainly sporting fractures from his rough and hurried dragging of it across the hallway, and closed the door. Sheets and pillows were stuffed around and under the door to try and block the fumes then he tried to open a window but they were all locked. He thumped at the toughened glass though knowing that it would be a waste of time. His next and last desperate bid was to find a hard heavy object that might smash the window but there was nothing. Absolutely nothing.

No heavy objects! No water! "Welcome to hell!" came back Shelley's words.

DI Buchanan, with his throat and nostrils scorched and raw, and his eyes swimming in acid, sat his flash light on the window as a despairing beacon to the world, dragged Mr and Mrs Munro to the floor and covered everyone's heads with sheets then his own and lay still beside them; said his good byes to his wife and waited to die. He knew it was the last futile effort of a desperate human clinging on to life. As he passed out, the roar of the both the flames and the storm were battling for supremacy.

"Richard, Richard can you hear me? Richard wake up. Please wake up?"

DI Buchanan was in a dark and cold place of fleeting hazy images. There was noise, lots of noise but a voice. Richard. Nobody called him Richard apart from his wife. The voice became more distinct and he moved from a semi conscious state to one of waking bewilderment as his eyes flickered painfully. There were two faces looking down on him, a stranger holding a mask to his face and his wife.

"Richard, Richard. His eyes are opened," shouted his wife.

DI Buchanan tried speaking but it was excruciatingly painful and a waste of time. Around him he became aware of others kneeling beside people then there was a roar of a powerful engine above as he made out what could only be a helicopter passing above them. He slipped back into unconsciousness as the helicopter made its way to land in the school playing fields. The difficulty of getting four unconscious people half a mile through the snow was not his concern.

Chapter Twenty Three

Amelia Rosenberg and David Stewart were making their way across a bleak desolate windswept landscape, their destination Moorland High Secure Hospital. They were on their way to observe Sarah Jane Primrose being questioned by a Psychiatrist after she had been sent there, without limit of time, following a Not Guilty verdict in the High Court for reason of insanity.

Months had passed but the same damaging thought lay siege to Amelia's conscience. She had asked Mr Stewart to select for her the parents' of pupils to be killed and now they were dead. To her, that was an accurate précis of events. Still fresh in her mind was how she snuggled Chris Templeton to her side to comfort him, now knowing that she herself had essentially selected his father to be murdered. She was a monster created by Shelley. Some of her closest friends had lowered their dead parents heartbreakingly into the ground. She had witnessed all of them break down in uncontrollable anguish and tears; and she was responsible. All her friends had assured her personally she was not. Psychiatrists had also tried and failed to exorcise the unwarranted guilt that had imprisoned her soul. For this reason she was being taken to witness Primrose's treatment session. It was most certainly not a unanimously held belief that this was an advisable course of action. No-one however could actually bring themselves to voice the chilling feeling many feared, that without something being done for her, the residents of the small village may yet again be gathering in the bleak hillside cemetery to wave farewell to a young unfulfilled life. Shelley was gone; Shelley never existed. It was an alter ego created for her own macabre purpose by Sarah Jane Primrose herself. Now, in the village, throughout the country and beyond she was simply the instigator of The Primrose Murders.

David Stewart also felt compelled to observe the interview. He felt uneasy, not about the actual string of events in which unwittingly he was involved, leaving the name Abercorrie for ever synonymous with mass murder, but how he could have read Sarah Jane Primrose so wrongly? Certainly there must have been environmental impact in shaping what she had become, but court scrutiny and evidence strongly indicated that the substance of her evil was innate. He took his guidance remit very seriously but now doubted his suitability to continue if he could be so completely deceived. He was however troubled further. To play him so well she must have built up a psychological profile of him. Just how much did she know? This deeply troubled him as there was very much to know.

The visit would not be happening had it not been for the disturbingly enthusiastic approval of Primrose herself. She had been far from responsive in her sessions with the hospital psychiatrists to date and simply toyed with them. Indeed it was she who had suggested that the detectives should come along also. An audience was required and demanded before Sarah Jane Primrose would perform. The fact was though that the detectives would have been in attendance anyway because her confinement had not resulted in an end to yet more suspicious deaths.

DI Buchanan was still beyond gratitude that he was alive to attend the interview at all but also disturbed by a combination of guilt and anger. His memories were still sketchy. Passing out in the fire ravaged house was a blurred and stretched moment in time but waking to hear his wife then see her face was now the most special; the most cherished moment of his life. His recovery in hospital from damage to his lungs was fairly short and painless but that is where he was informed of the two fire fighters who were still facing disciplinary action for not adhering to procedure. With the fire engines snowed in and blocked like every other vehicle in the village two of the local fire fighters had made their way quickly to the fire station and grabbed a minimum of equipment and clothing then made their way to the blaze, managing to rescue all four trapped by the flames. They had been suspended since and their case was imminent. "Surely fire fighters would not be found guilty of fighting a fire and saving four lives? Surely not?"

The police car made its way along a narrow winding tree lined road from which they emerged to a featureless expanse of cultivated lawn. A tall wire perimeter fence with a central gate divided the lawn and through the fence sat a large building of no beauty but clear purpose. The two police officers in the car, Amelia and David Stewart had to present the ID which they had been instructed to bring. Once scrutinized and returned, the gates slowly opened and the vehicle made its way to the front entrance of the building in which there was another gate, tall wide and solid. Amelia and David Stewart were suddenly prisoners of irrational fear and panic. This was a one way portal. The ID routine was repeated and the vehicle made its way into a large courtyard. Only when the gate closed behind them did the police officers exit the car and release their passengers. All four walked towards a further entrance.

They all had their ID to hand by this stage which was duly checked again. Once inside they were instructed to place what little hand held items they had which were then scanned by x ray. All four then went through a metal detector after which the computer randomly selected Amelia for a further rub down body search. From there they were taken to another room and photographed, and within a few minutes were issued with ID badges which they were instructed to put on immediately before being taken through to a waiting room.

"If you would just wait here please until DI Buchanan and DC Watt arrive. I believe they are already at the outer gate," said an employee of the hospital. She had an ID badge but it was unclear who or what position she held and she herself did not volunteer the information.

"You would think they would have better security in place," said David Stewart trying to lift the oppressive atmosphere.

Amelia smiled briefly acknowledging his transparent effort.

"It is so quiet," she returned. "I have never known such silence."

"As quiet as a ned speaking his mind eh?" Amelia had exhausted her limited supply of courteous facial acknowledgements and David Stewart felt foolish at trying to make a near 18 year old girl of maturity and intellectual solidity feel at ease with such inane comments. It was not long however before DI Buchanan and DC Watt were shown in whereupon everyone was informed that Dr Galloway would be along shortly.

"Quite nice here isn't it?" said DI Buchanan for broadly the same reasons that the David Stewart had previously spoken. It was the first time the Inspector had been in Moorland Hospital but not his first opportunity. A relative of his had worked here for years and frequently invited him for a tour of the premises. It did not quite have the same appeal as the tour of a distillery he thought and quite remarkably always had to decline the offer because of appointments elsewhere, his most recent being, "Sorry I'll need to give you a rain check.("What does that even mean," he thought to himself.) I'm already booked for a tour of an abattoir followed by lunch." He recognised that was probably his weakest and most unbelievable excuse ever; and not surprisingly was never asked again.

"Yes beautiful surroundings. Quite a lovely place really to be....." DC Watt added, unable to finish his own sentence. He actually new exactly how to finish it but, "locked up," did not quite convey the essence of his original intent to put Amelia at ease.

"It is just so extraordinarily quiet," DI Buchanan said sharing Amelia's observation, "considering the residents who stay here," taking it in quite a different direction.

There was the sound of footsteps at the door and a quiet conversation taking place then in walked a man perhaps in his early thirties at most accompanied by another man of considerable size and weight almost entirely composed of well developed muscle. He was a man with whom anyone in their right mind would avoid conflict, a group with which not everyone in this establishment could claim unquestioned membership. Both sat down to complete the small group of six around a low coffee table on which sat nothing at all, matching the walls on which there were no pictures, posters or anything else. Clearly drawing pins, paper clips etc. were not something they welcomed being available in a holding area.

"Well good afternoon everyone, let me first introduce myself and my colleague. Firstly Charge Nurse Murdo McQueen. He will be with me in the interview room as I interview Miss Primrose in fifteen minutes or so."

"I would imagine you would be of great assistance from time to time," said DC Watt with a smile, so obviously alluding to his physical attributes in time of need.

"Indeed yes," replied Doctor Galloway who had yet to introduce himself. "Having someone by my side with a 1st Class Honours Degree in Psychiatric Nursing and a Doctorate in Mental Health can often be useful."

If DC Watt felt small beside him when he came in he now felt minuscule and hated himself for saying anything quite so crass.

"Now to me. I am Doctor Galloway and Miss Primrose has been my patient since her arrival. Now before we come to the case in hand and the purpose or actually the many purposes of this interview today I would like to let Charge Nurse McQueen, or if you prefer, Doctor McQueen speak briefly to you about security issues." DC Watt cringed one more time after a further twist of the knife hoping that their thirst for humiliation had been quenched.

"Yes, right now Murdo will do fine actually. OK you can't help but have noticed that to get this far security has been quite tight. Please don't feel picked on. Everyone of us every day go through exactly the same procedure and I have been here for more than 10 years or so. Now I don't want to alarm anyone here and you are in no danger if a few guide lines are followed. It would be negligent of me however to understate the real dangers that exist within this establishment. Approximately one hundred poor innocent people have met their death at the hands of those who reside here. Firstly, the name badges around your neck. Please keep them on at all times and do not remove them until told to do so. Just on a practical side, it could delay your exit for a long time should it go missing prior to your departure at too early a stage. Now please don't put this to the test but if you tugged at the badge at all firmly the cord would readily snap."

DI Buchanan wanted to say, "Can't you afford decent ones?" but having his colleague take the hit moments earlier that would surely have come his way had he been a split second faster he chose to keep his silence.

"Now soon we will be moving as a group to our destination. Can I point out we will be returning as a group also, or at least that's the plan." This led to some uneasy but welcome light laughter. "Seriously though. Start as a group, avoid looking in windows or what ever and most obviously, but I will say it anyway, do not wander off on your own. Thank you."

"Thanks Murdo. Now to the matter in hand. Miss Primrose has been playing with us since she arrived. I could try and dress it up in more technically appropriate language but really, that sums it up best. She answers in questions, talks in riddles but we have found out very little other than she has an intellectual ability of a truly extraordinary level; and she is very very dangerous."

Dave Stewart interrupted here. "Trust me we are all aware that she was a very able pupil."

"I don't think you are quite grasping what I am saying here. She has a simply extraordinary intelligence. She deliberately camouflaged her abilities just to get run of the mill A grades. She could have written a thesis in any subject of her choosing. You may even actually struggle to recognise her at first. Her very appearance contrived to deceive. It was all a calculated callous act. Had this particular series of tragic events not unfolded, another path of ruthless cold blooded murders would have been followed, just waiting for a cue or catalyst in her evil mind to start the process. I'm sure you appreciate that evil is not really a word I would ever choose to use in a public domain."

"I don't feel quite so bad then, though not exactly good either, how I have been so totally deluded by her." Quite soon Mr Stewart would know the full extent of the delusion but that would most certainly be the least of his worries.

"Only the two of us will be in the interview room with her," Doctor Galloway resumed. "The four of you will be behind a one way mirror. She has consented to this. In the viewing room with you will be a further two staff nurses. Now I know you all have different reasons for being here but our first priority is the health and well being of the patient bizarre and understandably distasteful and unwelcome as that may sound."

DI Buchanan felt moved to ask, knowing the heartache that this one patient alone had produced back in Abercorrie. "So if someone with a history of a similar nature to our Miss Primrose has a medical emergency you are never even tempted, how can I put it, just to let nature take its course?"

"The Hippocratic oath, I'm sure you are familiar with it Detective."

"Yes, the mantra of all doctors. Measure twice, cut once. Just before we go however, can I share some more intelligence that has recently come to light?" said DI Buchanan. "You will be aware that Mr Drysdale had been helping us with our enquiries following the tragic re-appearance of his wife in a fishing net." He paused. "Amelia, my apologies. I sometimes forget you are here."

"And I think you are all forgetting that I am now eighteen years old and no longer at school. I am alert to all of you trying to be protective and evasive but it really isn't necessary, and may serve to cloud important issues," said Amelia trying to get her point over without offence.

"Point taken. My apologies. OK, back to the murder. Mr Drysdale never thought there was the slightest chance his wife's body would be recovered so he was a bit sloppy let's say from a forensic perspective and consequently gave a full confession. His wife had stumbled upon him having an affair. An affair, OK sex, with a school girl and he decided that his wife had to be silenced. And the school girl? None other than our own Sarah Jane Primrose."

"But why though?" asked Doctor Galloway before answering his own question. "She probably considered him to be a useful tool to add to her collection." This induced involuntary smirking.

"And there is more. You may remember the vivacious young PE teacher who ran a lunch time club for the senior boys. It seems that a girl took offence that her special tuition was not open to a wider clientèle. Yet again of course that girl was Miss Primrose. Had our young teacher just consented to a bit of girl on girl action she would probably still be in a job, and the year group photograph displaying somewhat bigger smiles than all the previous generations."

"I would have thought that Sarah Jane would have had a use for the PE teacher, well other than for leisure. I wonder why she just decided to spill the beans?"

"Will we ever know?"

Doctor Galloway smiled and said, "OK let's go," and Charge Nurse McQueen led the way with Doctor Galloway falling to the back of the group. They came to a door where they were stopped and every ID badge was examined very carefully before a code was punched into a key pad and the group proceeded into another corridor. They followed the L shaped corridor lined with rooms for the first time hearing voices but as instructed just stayed focussed on following the charge nurse until they arrived at another door where the corridor ended, a sign above which read, High Dependency Unit. IDs were inspected of course and more keys were pressed. At this point Amelia was alert to a very specific heavy perfume in the air, a smell with which she was familiar. It was sweet to the point of being sickly and had a heavy overpowering scent of vanilla. She suddenly recalled from where she had noticed it before. It was in the court room in which Sarah Jane Primrose had been on trial. She must be close or have passed this way very recently. It induced a moment of panic and fearful recollections. It didn't go unnoticed.

"Are you OK Amelia?" asked DI Buchanan.

"I'm fine honestly." It was not the case however. Amelia knew also that there was another occasion when she had sensed that same perfume. Just where though and just when proved elusive; for now.

The door was shut behind them where they walked into a closed chamber and where also they exited after the charge nurse punched in yet more codes. Almost immediately they came to a door which for once just opened and in they went to a very low lit room with a row of ten comfortable seats either end of which sat a staff nurse and ahead of them a large dark window which was the full size of the wall. The doctor and nurse left them to sit themselves down then departed. A minute or so later the dark window suddenly flicked into action revealing a room in which there was a large desk with two chairs backing towards the window and a further chair facing them from the other side of the desk. The image in front of them was so sharp and clear it felt like there was no glass between them and the room at all. Immediately Amelia wanted to touch the glass for re-assurance but was frozen in her chair.

A door at the side of the room opened and in walked Doctor Galloway who sat down furthest from the door and Charge Nurse McQueen took the other. Moments later between two staff nurses walked Sarah Jane Primrose. The nurses departed as she sat down and looked straight through the glass seeming to focus on each one of them personally in the eye and said, "Oh good, the entertainment has arrived. Let us prey."

Chapter Twenty Four

"Good afternoon Sarah, you know Charge Nurse McQueen?" Primrose remained silent. She hadn't been asked a question but Doctor Galloway was not going to take the bait.

"OK Sarah, just to make absolutely clear, you know that you were made aware that others would be observing our conversation today. Are you still giving your permission for this to proceed?"

"Permission granted doc. But can I just make clear that my name is Sarah Jane, and don't be imagining that nasty little hyphen thing in your head either. Sarah minus Jane? What ever does that mean?"

"My apologies Miss Sarah Jane Primrose."

"Just Sarah Jane. Capiche?"

"Sarah Jane, do I have your permission?"

"Can I just confirm though who is in there munching their popcorn and slurping a bucket of cola? Do we have Detective Inspector Buchanan?"

"Yes he is here, as is...,"

"No no no. Don't rush me. Good afternoon Detective Inspector Buchanan. I'm sure you have some burning questions you would like answered."

Already by her demeanour alone it was clear to everyone that Shelley never existed at all. What a long and convincing performance of consummate deceit she had delivered. Here sat a teenage girl; an attractive teenage girl of style and elegance. Everything about her from her hair to what she was wearing, and how she chose to wear it was a master-class in assuredness who spoke with relaxed composure. However was this the real Sarah Jane Primrose or just a different manifestation of the detached monster? Was there a real one at all?

"Detective Constable Watt. I haven't seen as much of you lately." She paused. "Why the puzzled unsettled look? You don't remember having ever really seen me at all until that dark night when you grabbed me in the bush." Every word she uttered was chosen with purpose and menace. "And you would be right. Doctor Galloway can I trust you will tell me if anyone I mention couldn't make it today? I know there has been a terrible bout of death doing the rounds."

"Both detectives are here Sarah Jane."

"Splendid, let's move on to my Guidance Teacher, dear and caring Mr Stewart. Isn't it so ironic Mr Stewart that you were meant to have built an extensive knowledge profile about me and yet it is the other way round? By the way, don't feel alone. We all have our little weaknesses." David Stewart was beginning to feel troubled by what had been said already and she had not even answered a single question.

"Amelia. The lovely lovely simply perfect Amelia, "With your considerable experience I would let you choose,"" Sarah Jane said, mimicking Amelia to perfection, her now charged and emotive words to Mr

Stewart all those many months ago, repeated with mischief for the benefit of the assembled group. It was already becoming apparent that if closure was the hope for Amelia, it already seemed a wholly unlikely outcome. Her unhealing ulcerous wounds had just been doused with acid; and Sarah Jane wasn't finished with her yet.

"Thank you for drawing those not so lucky numbers for me at the school raffle Mr Stewart. Decreasing numbers perhaps? What do you think? Amelia?"

The calculated process of everyone of them becoming focused inwardly on themselves by Primrose's transfixing dark magic just as she had planned was under way. Even being apprehended with such ease on the night of the fire was contrived. She wanted this moment.

"I can't wait until we meet up some time soon Amelia. I'm sure we could be best friends for life. I could come over to your house for a sleepover. We could have milk and cookies and tell each other ghost stories, plait each other's hair. Wouldn't that be fun?"

Doctor Galloway saw this as an opportunity to ask a question, his first question since already Sarah Jane had taken control of proceedings. "Sarah Jane...." but he was interrupted again.

"Not so fast. Is their anybody else in Cinema One other than the invited guests?"

"There are two nurses who..."

She interrupted again with a dismissive wave of her hand. "OK then, you may continue."

"I was just going to ask, what makes you think that you will be seeing Amelia some time soon? You know what judgement was given in the court."

"The judgement passed after I was put before my peers?" she sneered. "Oh that's not important. Books are a wonderful thing. Do you know what I was diagnosed with? Don't answer. It was rhetorical. Something curable. That's what. I will get better. Isn't that just wonderful news?" she mocked knowing the implications of this. "Without limit of time? Well perhaps not necessarily eh? Now what genre of books might I read while I'm one of your celebrity guests? I think perhaps Law. Yes Law and maybe Mental Health."

Primrose paused, then continued. "It's always important to have a plan B don't you think so if plan A is mischievously sabotaged then I'll just leave. Security isn't exactly the best in this place is it now?" and she brought out a mobile phone and sat it on the desk.

"Ooh, I'm not meant to have that am I? What about this then?" and she brought out a narrow leather strap about 2 yards long. "Some people in here could get up to a little bit of self harm with that don't you think?" Charge Nurse McQueen slowly reached out and slid the items to the far end of the desk.

"I've saved the best till last though," and she sat her closed fist down on the desk palm up. In the split second that everyone was distracted by her hand a long sharp plastic object was thrust into Doctor Galloway's chest aimed for his heart just piercing his skin. The chair prevented him from moving back. The charge nurse could not intervene. In one swift movement she could have driven it home. She opened the other hand and there was nothing.

"There was actually a white mouse in my hand but I made it disappear. Thank you folks, I'm here all week.... maybe."

She released the long sharp plastic object and dropped it casually on the desk. The charge nurse immediately moved to restrain her. "Oh and not a moment to soon Captain Wonderful," she smiled at McQueen, "and what a handsome figure of a man you are. You really must work out day after day; and with your illness too. That makes it just all the more commendable. Oh sorry I hope I didn't put my big fat, or actually rather dainty size four foot in it? The syringes I saw you taking, they were for medicinal purposes I assume. Pernicious Anaemia perhaps? Wait a minute. I'm thinking one and one is two. Super developed physique; syringes? Oh nurse please don't tell me you take performance enhancing drugs? Not anabolic steroids! Who on earth would prescribe them for you? Maybe that should be investigated doctor? Inspector? Oh by the way nurse they don't enhance every performance." At this she held up a crooked pinky.

"I think we need to bring this to a halt right now Doctor Galloway."

"No, no, let's continue. I'm fine." Doctor Galloway may have pretended to be fine but Charge Nurse McQueen most certainly now was not. They did continue but they moved her seat to the back wall to put distance between them and Primrose and brought in one of the staff nurses to be ready to intervene.

"Everybody can relax now, don't worry. This alcoholic old retard will keep you all safe."

The interview continued. Doctor Galloway was shaken but in truth was now totally engrossed in proceedings. He wanted this to continue oblivious to the gentle trickle of blood meandering down his white shirt.

The place fell silent. Primrose had stopped speaking and Doctor Galloway was rather taken by surprise but quickly established that her silence was her granting him permission to take control; of sorts.

"Well Sarah Jane first and foremost this is a hospital and it is our aim to get to the source of your problems and perhaps an effective therapy. We all want what is best for you."

She remained silent. Doctor Galloway was aware that this session had multiple purpose. Back in the village, people were still dying: back in the village fear pervaded the community. There was therapeutic intent but embedded in the interrogation was crucial input from DI Buchanan.

"OK Sarah Jane, could we begin with you just telling me in your own words what happened at the home of Joseph Hanlon and his wife Claire?"

"They died." She paused. "Oh you want more detail? OK then pull up a chair. Oh, you're ahead of me. This lovely couple were creatures of habit. What time they ate and what they had each particular day. Even what they watched on the television which wasn't much. They preferred to read, knit, care for the plants. They lived on the edge. Even when they had tea they had a routine. Boil the kettle, pour water into the teapot and then leave it at an open window to cool for 4 minutes. That's when the sleeping pills got popped into the pot. Back came Mrs Hanlon for the pot and closed the window."

"Sarah Jane, where did you get access to sleeping pills? Doctors are extremely reluctant to prescribe them to Minors. If I remember correctly you were still just 15 at the time."

"Yes, that was a problem I identified while still only 14 actually. I plan ahead. Let me demonstrate how I got round that little problem." Sarah Jane positioned herself not unlike an actor in readiness to perform. "PLEASE PLEASE MAKE IT STOP. NO MORE BLOOD NO MORE BLOOD!" Everyone jolted in their seats at the volume and intensity of the harrowing screams, but just as quickly as she started, she stopped.

"Could you imagine that two or three times a night every night?" she smiled.

"My foster parents, bless their simple souls, didn't have to imagine it. I had always to ensure I wasn't laughing when they came into my bedroom grey and shattered to comfort me. Anyway, one night when I judged their sanity was slipping away I told them that if only I could get sleeping pills I knew that would help. I also explained it could be difficult to get pills prescribed for me. Actually I told them it would be impossible. Doctors would have none of it. As I said, simple people. My foster mum managed to get them prescribed regularly for herself and I never woke up screaming again." She paused with a theatrical look of puzzlement on her face indicating that she had not yet finished speaking for the moment.

"Foster parents giving non prescribed powerful medication to the children in their care to make them sleep? That can't be right can it? Can it Inspector? Doctor? Are they really fit to be doing what they do?" Before that day was out two heartbroken dedicated and caring foster parents would be foster parents no more.

"Back to the house. I chose a cold night. It had to be cold to be credible. Soon they were asleep and I was in the house. Hanging a key from a string? Really now! By the way the prescribed dose is way too cautious as I found out with pets."

"Pets? From what I remember many pets were found brutally killed and mutilated," interrupted the doctor.

"From what you remember? From what you fuck'n remember? Yes because that's what doctors do in their spare time after all; read about dead pets from a village 50 miles away. You briefed him well Inspector," she smiled looking at him through the mirror. They all wondered uneasily how she seemed to know where everyone was seated. Was it just luck?

"I think it would have merited a bit of investigation had lots of cats and dogs just been found drugged so I had to dress them up a bit let's say. Little boys can be so nasty. Anyway it let me practice other techniques. I'm boring you all. To the point. I shut the windows and sealed them, turned the gas up full and pulled the door shut behind me." Looking through the glass and pausing again she said, "Oh Inspector, you look puzzled."

Anyone who looked at him would concur that he did look puzzled but there was also growing concern that she could actually see them. Had they got the lighting wrong in the observation room or something?

"You are thinking that there was a draught excluder which had clearly been pushed back by the door. I bet your beautiful young assistant noticed that when he arrived." Again, they wondered how she could know such detail? Was she actually watching them; listening to them as they carried out their briefest of investigations?

"OK class. Pay attention. Put the draught excluder on a rug. Close the door. Pull the rug under the door et voilà, the door is sealed. Do you know that the draught excluder was actually made by one of the grandchildren? Isn't that sweet? By the way, it was me who knocked the wool off her lap. It just made it a more poignant image for whoever was first on the scene, and it was me who turned the battery the wrong way round also in the CO detector."

Doctor Galloway, sensing she was finished began. "You know that Monica lost her parents to a car crash when she was younger don't you?"

"Yes. I'm just guessing here but let's fly this kite anyway, pull the flag up the pole and all that stuff. Maybe you are thinking why would I be so cruel?"

"Well then, why?"

"Why what?"

There was no emotion; no more words but eventually continued. "I knew she would be first on the scene. I mean really in a hotbed of activity like that place where she lived who else would it be? Hotbed. Sorry, how insensitive of me Inspector. I knew also that she would not be back till late. She always got a taxi back from town. Last buses are long gone by the time she stops partying."

Doctor Galloway moved on and thought he would try a word which had been skipped around and avoided. "To the next murder. Mrs Swanson. She was found dead in her bath."

"Murder! Honestly what a vulgar word. I prefer to think of it as suicide by proxy." Sarah Jane Primrose did not allow the doctor the luxury of expanding upon his few words. "Oh by the way, and I hope you are not disappointed but there are going to be a couple of recurring themes. Sleeping pills and windows. Sleeping pills work. They do the job fine. Don't fix what ain't broken eh?" she said breaking seamlessly into a theatrical American accent. "Yes sleeping people can be oh so compliant and co-operative can't they? You'll know that Inspector when you have sex with your wife. Ah yes next. Windows."

The Inspector sat awkwardly. On this occasion she was bluffing but what difference did that really make?

"Windows. A much undervalued surveillance tool, and they're large screen, high definition 3D. Just love them. Who needs television, and no adverts either."

There was now a growing feeling of considerable unease among everyone. What was she going to say next?

"Well inspector, I never saw you as the novelty underwear type. But then again? Anyway all those cartoon animals. Do you have a favourite? I have to say however, when it comes to underwear what about your wife? She doesn't skimp on material does she? Oh my God who makes the fabric? NASA? When she eventually manages to roll it off her lardy frame she just about doubles in size! Now, Detective Watt. Young energetic Detective Watt. It would seem you definitely want to start a family."

Now it was his turn to want proceedings to come to an abrupt ending as he writhed in discomfort at the thought of Sarah Jane Primrose leering in the window at him and his wife together in their bedroom. As it happened it was not the case but again what did it matter? Damage was inflicted.

"Yes I think you would make a great father. I can see you taking your son to the football or pulling your daughter about on a sledge in the snow, building snowmen and having snowball fights; and tucking them into bed last thing at night, their little angelic faces looking up as you tell them a bed time story. You would be just a terrific dad. Yes you would." She drew breath and sighed, "It's just such a dreadful pity that your wife doesn't want any children." Pausing only for malicious effect she continued, "Maybe I'm wrong though. Maybe those pills she takes and hides in a box on top of the wardrobe are just paracetamol. I don't know. The thing is though when I looked through your bin." Sarah Jane paused again. Her mastery of pregnant pauses amplified damage.

"Don't upset yourselves everyone. I wasn't looking for scraps of food. Your community consciences can remain clear. No when I looked in the bin I found an empty foil for holding pills. Do paracetamol have the days of the week written on them? I'm just young. I don't know everything. I'm sure you and your wife can talk this through detective. Trust is everything in a marriage don't you think?" From this moment on Sarah Jane Primrose could have been reading out cake recipes for all Detective Watt would have noticed. He had been eliminated from events. He wouldn't be the last.

"I have never been on the pill. Mr Dalton always took precautions." Now Sarah Jane had taken proceedings to a different level. The damage was not going to be limited to those in attendance.

"He often worked late on a Friday Mrs Dalton was always telling people, while shopping, while in the school; while at home. I am quite insulted actually. Work am I indeed? Work! Anyway I never wanted for pocket money so I suppose it was work of sorts. I prefer to think of it however as a magical romantic clandestine affair with benefits; yeh OK, pocket money. You have to admire Charles, my dear precious Charles who clearly had my interests at heart. He knows how difficult and demanding it can be for teenage mums, especially one who is still at school and only fourteen years old, so he always took precautions." Again she paused. "I've earned a lot of pocket money."

Sarah Jane had made a slow look about the room and at those behind the glass, deliberately failing to conceal her smirk.

"I'm not sensing universal appreciation for Mr Dalton's compassion and altruism. He was very careless with the protection he used however and what compelling forensic evidence it would be if only you could lay your hands on one of these discarded little things Inspector. What do you think? Don't look at your fellow detective. He's not listening any more, trust me. Charles only needed little things by the way. Wait a minute. Maybe, just maybe if you go into my bedroom back in my foster home and look under a floorboard near the window you might find a sealed plastic bag in an air tight tin that may be of interest."

If anyone thought that Sarah Jane could not become any darker, more pernicious and sadistic they were about discover they were wrong.

"I've left a little something for you also Amelia if you would care to look under the carpet at the window in your simply gorgeous bedroom."

Amelia was now beyond damage: catatonic. Now she recalled exactly where and exactly when she had noticed that pungent vanilla perfume.

"Yes, a gorgeous room. A bit single themed all the same. If you've seen one skull or whatever, you've seen them all. I hope you like your little gift. I perhaps flatter myself to believe that I know the things that you like. Do you know something, even in your sleep you are simply adorable. Your gentle breathing is the music of a fairy princess. Honestly you looked good enough to eat. Well I could have made Amelia. See what I did there? Huh? What not even a smile? My god you are a difficult audience!"

Doctor Galloway knew that he had to get back on schedule. From a Psychiatric perspective he had much to take back to discuss with his colleagues but from DI Buchanan's position very little had been achieved. "Sarah Jane, would you please get back to Mrs Swanson?"

"Of course. You know what? I had totally forgotten about her. I was thinking about Charles again. He was actually quite good. Made the best of what he had. I'll tell you something. Some of the staff in this place would put him to shame though. Oh my goodness me yes!" She stopped to make some erotic groans.

"Mrs Swanson. She invited me in. Wasn't that nice?" Sarah Jane put on the sweetest smile and said in a high velvety voice. "Good morning. I hope I'm not disturbing you. I am from Highland View Secondary School and we are hoping to start a coffee morning to raise funds to buy new books for the library. We are carrying out a survey to see who would be interested." Returning to what was for now her normal voice, she continued, "Once I told her I wasn't really sure how to make a cup of coffee as I wasn't allowed it by my parents she just took me through to the kitchen to show me."

Nobody really needed to be told what happened next, nobody that is who was still listening and not consumed by the personal black vortex destroying their own individual lives born of Sarah Jane's psychological sorcery. Even one of the nurses in the viewing room was now sitting uncomfortably.

"Now I bet you all know what happened next. Detective Watt, pay attention!" She turned to Doctor Galloway and in a lowered voice mocked, "He's just young. Maybe needs a nap."

Sarah Jane continued "Well yes of course she had a quite delicious cup of coffee with me then the effort of it all must have crept up on her because all of a sudden she fell fast asleep. I pinged her nose a few times. You can't be too careful eh, then dragged her through to her bathroom. Thank goodness it was down stairs, that's all I can say. My God what an effort that took! You know what? Abercorrie really does need a health and fitness club. Anyway I started to run a nice hot bath while I stripped her naked and put all her clothing in a neat little pile. I know it's what she would have wanted. What she also wanted was a bath believe me! You know what I'm saying here!" Sarah Jane wafted her hand under her nose. "She was a bit whiffy I'll tell you. Anyway I managed to fold her into the water. I hope it wasn't too hot for her.

It soon would be by the way. Anyway once in the bath I surrounded it in candles, lit them and added the petals to the water. I knew she had these things and where to find them just like the little CD player she had. Well of course I knew where they were! Anyway I inserted the CD I had bought for fifty pence, Soothing Music To Die To or whatever it was called, and everything was in place. Guess what happened next though? She began to wake up. At first I thought, oh no but then it became a strangely welcoming occurrence. Initially she seemed confused. Well who wouldn't be? You last remember making a cup of coffee and now you are naked in a dark room surrounded by candles with a wicked looking school girl staring down at you. I can do wicked. Want to see? No? OK then. Suddenly there was panic in her eyes as she saw me poised with the music system and she slipped about trying to get out of the bath then, splash! You know what? I had kind of hoped for sparks like you see in the movies but the look on her twitching straining face and her arching body more than made up for it until she fell still and silent."

Doctor Galloway was by now struggling to continue. Academic interest was being overwhelmed by pure repulsion. It wasn't just the murders but the callous humour. He had though to go on. The death toll could have increased as they sat there for all they knew.

"Mr Jenkins. He had a cycling accident. What can you tell us about that?"

"To be honest there isn't much to this one. It was still fun though. Mr Jenkins had a routine. I hope you are all realising by now that routines are more dangerous than smoking. Anyway he cycled to the pub on the same night every week. The time he arrived, the time he departed. He was pretty regular. Anyway I had chosen my spot and lay in wait for him; again. Yes again! The previous week a car past at just the wrong moment. I was livid. Can you imagine me livid? Want to see me do livid? Another no it is then. You lot really don't give me much encouragement. I heard his bike approach and timed it right just to smash him across the face with a solid heavy branch. Thwack! Honestly, Babe Ruth would have been impressed. What a sound it made. It was a branch from the tree against which his body would be found close. Attention to detail is important. Well actually not but I'll come to that. I had to be fast and dragged him off the road into the woods and grabbed his bike moments later. Next I grabbed him again and pulled him towards the guilty tree. I could see he was actually still alive and starting to come around. That didn't last long. I grabbed his head solidly in both hands and absolutely hammered his head into the tree. There was this fantastic cracking sound and yet the tree wasn't damaged at all. What could that sound have been? I took out the half bottle of whisky

I had in my pocket. Imagine I had been caught with that eh and only sixteen years old. Boy would I have been in big big trouble? It was only about a quarter full as planned and I poured some of it into the cap and let it trickle into his mouth. I put the cap back on, put the bottle in his pocket and smashed it with a stone. I then rubbed some of the whisky oozing from his pocket onto a large nearby rock. But here's the thing. There is just no way his pocket could have smashed against the rock. As I said, attention to detail not always necessary, not when the investigating officers have a game of snooker to finish back at the station. I positioned his bike kind of carefully but not that carefully and headed off."

Those who were still paying her any attention were starting to become numb to the atrocities that were being shared with them. It was becoming a horror film, a television show: somehow not real. Just how could it be? A visit to the village Graveyard however would confirm the macabre reality.

Doctor Galloway was so acutely aware that only one murder remained. He no longer wanted to be in her presence. He wasn't sure if he would ever want to be again. As usual she just fell silent between tales of sickening savagery told with such levity.

"Sarah Jane we are nearly there but we must press on. There are still a couple of incidents for which I would like some information, just to seek out or discern an underlying problem which resulted in such tragic events in your life," Doctor Galloway added suddenly remembering his own remit and objectives. "Mr Templeton was found at home...."

"Mr Templeton," she interrupted. You know it makes me so angry just thinking about that. There is me trying to make every death different then babyman cuts his wrists."

"Snap!" thought DI Buchanan. "That's what Mr Jones, Head of Art had said. Oh God yes. Now it makes more sense."

"You know, I could have killed him. Honestly, I was livid." For the first time Sarah Jane Primrose looked genuinely annoyed, the joke, wholly unintentional and unnoticed by her. She continued, "It was a mistake passing that gig onto Chardonnay. Why did she have to get so greedy?" Looking where she somehow knew the detectives to be she said, "I'm sensing shock here. Do I really have to explain? I guess I must. When I intercepted Mr Mortimore accessing, who's a naughty baby dot perv or what ever the site was called then observed him multi tasking let's say as the computer screen lit up his excited little face I thought to myself, "You know what Sarah Jane I think Mr Mortimore and I could maybe set up a little symbiotic relationship here," and thus the mysterious Eastern European nanny was born. It was a nice little earner but I thought I would increase the financial return just a bit. However when my naughty little charge got a bit uppity and had clearly being pursuing my false trail I decided it was time to quit and pass the franchise on; with a little bit of retribution as well for his cheek." Turning her attention to Doctor Galloway.

"I used to sit in the same class as Chardonnay and Madonna. Well let me tell you, Mr Mortimore was so sarcastic to those two. Quite cruel sometimes." With the indignant voice of a slighted parent she added, "Surely Doctor that does not bring the best out in pupils? What harsh revenge might they seek if given half a chance? Anyway I gave them that chance, they got greedy, blah blah blah." She sighed, "Could he not have jumped off a cliff or something though rather than slashing his wrist?"

She fell quiet again but for the first time not for effect. "Mr Templeton? OK back to him. You know, it's hard work making every murder look like suicide or an accident. It will be different the next time." That should have been both a chilling and shocking statement in itself but emotions were becoming paralysed with exhaustion.

"Right from the start it was going to be difficult with this guy. God was he transported from the nineteenth century?" Sarah Jane was recovering her swagger. "His computer. Really. Just to make it fit and able to communicate with the web was a challenge but I have to say, and credit where credit is due, Abercorrie Academy taught me well in so many skills that I could put to good use, or at least pointed me in the right direction," she just had to add. "Anyway I created an account for him, some imaginary friends, you know, just like religious people have, and wrote a couple of "what's the point of life?" type messages. You know the kind that people post in the small hours of the morning. I couldn't be too blatant though. Just to make it easy for the boys in blue I put his username and password on a label stuck to the keyboard. You wouldn't believe the number of people who actually do that! Well luckily for me he did like a good drink, so when the moment was right I popped in the magic pills. I knew what night his wife would be out. I told you. Routines are a serious health issue. How did I get in and out of his house so easily? They kept a key under a flower pot. Honestly, Abercorrie is homicide heaven. How did I get the pills in his drink? He goes to the bathroom and by the time he comes back; ta dah! Anyway, he went to sleep, I slashed his wrist, spurty spurt, he was dead. Kind of boring really but still fun."

Once more, the silent signal. Quite mechanically Doctor Galloway, now drained, invited Sarah Jane to move on to the final incident. It would not be long until his focus would suddenly be brought back to sharp relief. Would she be so co-operative though this time Doctor Galloway was thinking to himself since after all no one had died?

"After this we will bring things to a close. It has been a long afternoon for all of us. So the fire at Mr Munro's house." The psychiatrist was beyond constructing and articulating a question, and hoped she would just take the initiative as she had done so enthusiastically so far.

"The fire. Yes, DI Buchanan. What a hero. Breaking in so you could die beside the sleeping family. I hoped someone would try that and I got lucky. Can't deny it. You see, I was actually getting a bit bored, and with babyman topping himself? It just wasted everything. Well I just couldn't be bothered making it look like an accident or whatever any more but to make up for it I would try and expand the joy; and thank you for that Inspector. I have to say I was quite angry with Detective Watt. How unlucky was I? A power cut! That wasn't part of the plan, though it suited my needs quite nicely. Anyway I could have killed him if I'd wanted to." Once more a pause. "You do know what I'm saying here don't you? Sorry that I sound like I'm talking about him like he's not here, but he isn't really with us any more is he? I digress. Back to the house fire. I chose my moment carefully and selected dial a flame on my phone. I ensured it would be difficult to get in, no tools in the garage or about the garden just to give the flames time to take hold a bit.

By the time he had stumbled up the stairs in the smoke filled darkness and found the sleeping beauties the flames had made sure that going down was not an option especially with the water being switched off and the tanks drained; and oh yes a tiny bit of accelerant added to the stair carpet. Not too much. I knew he would then take everyone into the same room, seal out the smoke then try and break a window, as they were all locked of course, but there was just nothing in any of the rooms that could be used to smash the toughened glass. How unlucky was that?"

Sarah Jane Primrose fell silent again but Doctor Galloway was still suitably alert to realize that there were some unanswered questions, and questions to which he knew DI Buchanan would want answers.

"There are some aspects of this that I can't quite pull together Sarah Jane. There are two issues in particular that trouble me. They were all found upstairs in a deep state of unconsciousness. I can't think how you managed to do that, but also, how did you know they would be back at the house?"

"Good questions. Well done. As I said I got lucky that night. God had obviously decided that before the sun rises or the cock crows three times and all that kind of thing, that three of his lambs would be drugged by a deranged teenager and left to burn in their own home. His followers aren't wrong you know. He really does move in mysterious ways. By the way, how are their burns?" Sarah Jane looked through the glass towards DI Buchanan in that uncanny way she had done for the entire interview. "But how, but how, but how you are asking yourself Inspector aren't you. OK, just for you. The fridge was full of food and drink for them arriving and the heating was also on. This had been done by one of Michelle's friends. This of course gave me plenty opportunity to add generous quantities of my favourite little crushed pills where ever I could." Sarah Jane stopped again. "What puzzles you this time Doctor?" she said in mock exasperation.

"This is what puzzles me. There is a limit to what these pills can achieve. How could you possibly have got Mr Munro up the stairs on your own never mind not waken him? Apart from that all three were in a very deep state of unconsciousness I would imagine for a long time."

"Remember what I said about God and luck. Mr and Mrs Munro both decided that exhaustion was kicking in and took themselves up stairs. Look, I think you have to understand that if they had just stayed down stairs I would have torched them as they sat. It was no big deal really. Anyway it was sometime before Michelle the skeleton passed out so I gave her the booster shot and dragged her up stairs, the same one I had already given her parents." She paused again. "OK, go on then. Ask."

"The booster shot. Just what was this? I can think what it could be but there is no possibility it could be prescribed to your foster mother."

"Correct again. Here's the thing. If a married man with a promising career has sex with a school girl it is amazing just how responsive they can be to requests. This particular married man just happened to work in a hospital. He kept pleading that he couldn't possibly get away with taking some samples, but you know what? He managed. Some people really do lack confidence in themselves."

Doctor Buchanan interrupted. "Sarah Jane, you know that DI Buchanan would like to know who supplied you with the powerful and dangerous anaesthetics and syringes."

"I'm quite sure he would but I'm not finished with him yet. I'm sure he can be put to good use again when I'm out of here." The matter of fact way she repeatedly alluded to being beyond the confines of the State Hospital served always to heighten the fear and alarm as intended.

"I also had my emergency anaesthetic to hand. A claw hammer I think you'd call it Detective. I know you are such an enthusiast for gardening and DIY. It certainly worked on the cats and dogs I practised on."

Although all but depleted of energy and motivation to continue the "assessment," he reminded himself that it was, but also now reflecting with sudden clarity how it could have ended for him in a bloody and swift manner less than an hour earlier, he could not help but be impressed by how the noxious abomination in front of him persistently managed to attach destructive function to most every utterance. He was soon to find out from a personal perspective just how destructive.

"You were seen by a few people coming out of Mr Munro's garden. Wasn't that a bit careless of you?"

"Of course it wasn't careless. I actually came up the pathway a few times to ensure that one of Amelia's disciples would see me and report back to their leader. You see Amelia is a clever little girl. I knew she would figure it out; if given enough prompts. I bet right now, little Amelia is protesting internally that she is not the leader of the twilight gang. Trust me they all simply adore her. I bet she is the last thing on the boys' minds when they lie alone in bed thinking. Don't you just love euphemisms? One of the girls too actually. Maybe it's just a phase." Sarah Jane flashed her eyes seductively towards Amelia.

"You are still wondering how I managed to collect my intelligence. Well for sometime now I have been monitoring the social network exchanges between Michelle and her fellow intellectual leviathan Mandy Airhead. Oh dear God it hasn't been easy. "I've found a new way to cook lettuce to reduce the calories." "My nail varnish is taking too long to dry; I hate my life!" Trust me here. MENSA isn't about to get two new members any time soon. Well one day Michelle mentioned the family were coming home on a secret visit to sort out some things. Fortunately, Michelle doesn't fully understand the meaning of secret; nor most things actually. Doctor, I can see that you still want to ask me something. Don't be shy."

"Getting access to the girl's exchanges. How did you manage to do that?"

"Well let me just tell you. Wifi is the nosey neighbour's best friend, especially if that neighbour knows a few tricks. Want to know the difference between bad encryption and good encryption? Thirty seconds! I actually did a bit of roaming about the village just having a little check on people's online activity. Just for their own safety you understand. As I said, Detective Buchanan, gardening and DIY really are your thing. How crushingly boring that was. I got excited when you started shopping for binoculars, then soon found out you were interested in bird watching as well. Fortunately some people's online searches are much more interesting." Mortified may be an over used word but in this situation it applied perfectly if perhaps not literally to David Stewart, the Guidance Teacher. He was trapped in a prison awaiting the inevitable; and he did not have to wait long.

"Mr Stewart. Mr Guidance Teacher Stewart. I'll tell you something, you certainly like your girls big don't you?" At this she held her hands under her own ample breasts and gave them a slight lift. Oh yes. Something else. You like them quite young as well don't you?" She grabbed her hair and held it in two bunches, looked down but turned her eyes up, fluttered her lashes and looking straight at him through the glass said in a mocking babyish voice, "Oh I wish I had a wowee pop. Do you have a wowee pop I could suck Mr Stewart?"

She regained her original aloof pose and said. "Do you know something Mr Stewart, I'm not sure those girls were all over sixteen. Maybe you should check that out. Were some of those sites even legal? Actually ask Inspector Buchanan to help you. The police are very good at that kind of thing."

Behind the window now sat a teacher perhaps facing prison but certainly never stepping foot inside a school again and visibly shaking with despair. It had never actually occurred to him that some of the girls on his favoured sites may be under 16. His earlier fear of exposure fell short of a reality somewhat worse. Beside him was a detective sitting silent and still wondering if his marriage was savable but coming up with the same heartbreaking answer every time. One distraught nurse knew that it was only a matter of time until an investigation would see him at least struck off the register and possibly so much worse. He did not even want to think about it but found he could think of nothing else. In the midst of the emotional carnage sat Amelia. The intention of a salving outcome which would destroy her demons was more than a lost cause. Crushing guilt now had to share its home with hideous imagery of a most heinous violation. She had retreated to the inner most dark corner of her own mind; but a mind in which a faint ember in the darkness had been born and was slowly growing and evolving. Beside Sarah Jane stood a nurse who thankfully had only been humiliated about his alcohol addiction and across from her both the towering frame and intellectual magnitude of Charge Nurse McQueen were now deflated and beaten.

Doctor Galloway was hesitantly grateful that he had survived the lacerating tongue of this pestilential teenage genius. He still wanted to ask her two final questions, the first really on behalf of Inspector Buchanan, and the second in an attempt to find out anything at all about her other than she had an IQ of, in her case, a literally terrifying magnitude.

"Perhaps you are not aware of this but since you were first held in custody there has been another tragedy. Two people died and another two suffered internal organ failure as a result of paracetamol poisoning. It is not yet clear if they will survive. Do you know anything about this?"

"I might," she smiled meaning I do. She remembered reading fondly of tens of thousands of pounds of food being dumped as a panic swept the village. She knew it was all fine. That just made it that bit more satisfying.

"Do you know if there might be more incidents?" This time her smile emitted a cryogenic wave that no words in existence could have made any more disturbing. Only she knew, for now at least, about the electrically live microphones in the school waiting to be touched, the slow release poison in water tanks, cut throat wires across sparsely used cycle paths, car brake lines cut, petrol mowers waiting to burst into flames, bad wiring in houses just waiting to ignite, spikes in hidden traps in the woods; just so many sweet surprises. In most cases fatalities would just be an unexpected bonus but in every case the terror and fear would grow and grow. Sarah Jane was aware that she was frequently spoken about as always going somewhere; coming back from somewhere, well now they would all begin to know where.

"Well, that's for me to know but remember Mr Stewart when all the teachers were asked to think about quiz ideas for the school magazine? Well that could be the quiz idea. You could call it, "Guess the body count!" What do you think?"

"Sarah Jane, can I ask did each murder get easier after the first one? Did it give you more or less of a thrill?"

"And can I ask, what murder did you think was the first?"

"Joseph and Claire Hanlon."

"The Hanlons? No they weren't the first." Doctor Galloway in some way now regretted having asked but Inspector Buchanan became once more sharply alert.

"That cold dark morning I arrived at the school covered in my mother's blood? Oh that was her blood all right. Trust me."

The sardonic smirk on her face could have been the devil himself and froze everyone in a second. Those who thought she had reached the depths of revulsion now were achingly aware that there was no bottom to her satanic pit. This dragged everyone out from their private ferment.

"I heard that my father committed suicide recently. Now that blood has to be on your hands Inspector. Another game of snooker that couldn't wait yes? What do you guys and gals down the police station actually do?" DI Buchanan was starting to wonder that himself. An investigation had since been opened; he would liked to have thought re-opened into the disappearance of Primrose's mother but that would have been of little consolation. Sarah Jane was right. That blood was on his hands.

Doctor Galloway had one last question which just had to be asked. "Sarah Jane, can I ask you why? Just why?"

She looked blankly at him. He wondered if the question even meant anything. "Oh my goodness, don't you think it's getting hot in here? Is it just me? Really?" At this she undid the top two buttons of her blouse partially revealing her breasts. She looked towards Doctor Galloway with a teasing sneer and said, "Oh Doctor, I hope I'm not embarrassing you, or perhaps even getting you excited just a bit? Oh, what am I thinking? It can't possibly be that since we both know you're gay. It's OK, it's our little secret. Shhhhhhh," and she held her finger up to her mouth.

"I'm guessing your wife knows as well yes? Surely she must. I mean how many headaches can a man have? Oh by the way I looked at that website you quite often visit." Doctor Galloway slumped lower in his seat and put his face in his hands. "Oh don't you go panicking there. It's a legal site. Consenting adults can do what they like and my goodness don't they just? Those images! Do you do that stuff? You must be quite the athlete if you do. Men's bodies eh? They really are just biological amusement arcades are they not?"

She pointed to the phone still sitting on the desk and continued, "I've passed on the name of the website to a few people. Pete's Pink Playground by the way. Pete's Pink Playground! How are you ever going to dispel the stereotypes with a name like that? Honestly. And something else, I also circulated your username and password."

By now Doctor Galloway was beyond listening and was just another carcass on the communal grave, but Sarah Jane wasn't finished. "I really have to take issue with you by the way regarding your user name. Loony Repairman! How do you think that makes me feel? I'm really quite hurt, and I'm sure all those patients with whom you have developed a close and working relationship won't be too impressed either!"

She buttoned her blouse up again. It had played its part. "I am actually getting just a bit tired now." She turned to the nurse who had earlier been assigned to stand with her and said, "Chaperone would you please escort me back to my private suite if you would my good man; if you can actually walk you pathetic old drunk."

Her final words were for Amelia. "Good bye for now sweet Amelia. I'm sure we'll have a catch up soon but not in this horrid old place. By the way I noticed among your ghosts and vampires you also had pictures of some fine young men. That's a pity because I really thought we could get a bit closer if you know what I mean. Anyway you don't know if you like something till you've tried it, I say."

As a final chilling gesture she moved closer to the window and breathed seductively, "Au revoire Amelia," blew her a kiss and she was gone.

The party who had made their way in now made the reverse journey but not a word was spoken. Door after door, search after search they finally arrived at the point where their ID badges could be returned and they could drive through that final exit, but most would be returning to a world far colder than the one they left behind only two hours earlier.

DI Buchanan collected the phone he was required to leave at reception and turned it on. There was a message From Fiona Dalton. "Please fill me in on details at first opportunity." He also got in touch with the Police Station to have Mr Stewart's laptop and much else confiscated for investigation. Mr Stewart was totally compliant about leaving with Detective Watt and another police officer, the young detective choosing not to drive, and DI Buchanan left with Amelia. They both knew that the other did not want to speak, Amelia seeking out the seclusion of the back seat. There were so many thoughts and images in her mind but the one slowly gaining prominence was that off Sarah Jane Primrose looking down upon her as she slept. She tried but failed to avoid thinking about how close she had been: close enough to feel her breath? Did she touch her; kiss her even? Subconsciously however, deep within her troubled spirit was an emerging nemesis. Richard Buchanan meanwhile reflected on the many lives now sabotaged and blighted, with no little guilt that he from most everyone involved in the orchestrated slaughter had come through mostly unscathed, the Chamber of Horrors mercifully shrinking in his rear view mirror.

What is yet unknown is yet to be, inner warmth holds tenure; the dead are still living. Richard Buchanan would soon be entering the family home: Richard Buchanan would soon know. Warmth extinguished. For now chilling grief and heartache are merely delayed.

Chapter Twenty Five

The sun had been promising to rise for some time as Jack Proctor made his way across the stark frosted moors in the middle of which several miles ahead sat the incongruous and quite alien transplanted woodlands which incarcerated Moorland High Secure Hospital. No other trees grew in this unending expanse of bleached white grassland interspersed by black clumps of protruding heather and unforgiving grey rock. At over 2000 feet this plateau of biting wind swept hostility discouraged the company of any life or beauty. The narrow road lay flush with the landscape on either side inviting the stinging gusts to whistle their deathly strain. Frequently and without warning streams of twisting mist would swiftly dart across the road hugging the surface before dispersing like menacing spectres.

Driving to work had never exactly been a joy for Jack Proctor. It was a job. It paid his bills but he could never escape its hold whether at home, on holiday thousands of miles away or alone with his thoughts in the night. This was the case for most staff at the hospital. Strangely it wasn't because of the sights and sounds which they had encountered in their lives, disturbing as much of it was. It was always the thought of what might happen, what could happen; what awaited. Though none admitted it to the others they always checked the back seat of their cars before getting in; and many feared ever looking in the rear view mirror during their vulnerable solitude miles from nowhere chilled at the thought of what may be looking back. Recent events however had added a quite deeper level of darkness and torment and sorrow.

Jack was now driving along the final stretch of his journey, winding his way through the tree lined track. The sun had failed to keep its promise and his headlights cast a shadowy animation of evasive glimpsed figures and transient faces in his peripheral vision. There must have been days when he arrived in the sunshine but he could not recall them. The fence, the surrounding lawn and that place in the middle was an unchanging image; and the routine to gain access a menacing reminder of what lay ahead. One thing had changed however and that was the personnel. Many had been eliminated following the "Primrose Day Massacre." Just how many lives lay lacerated and destroyed by the unrelenting onslaught of verbal razors and venom? Those who most reluctantly replaced the victims were warned in the most severe manner about the pernicious consequences of allowing Sarah Jane Primrose access to their soul or actually inviting her in as many had done to their demise. Had Jack's integrity remained undiminished? Today he seemed particularly alert to protocol.

"Morning Jack. I'll have a cup of tea ready for your return from your tour of Loony World."

"You'll becoming with me I assume Nurse Purdom as described in the Inspection procedure?"

"Warning! Warning! Call security. Staff Nurse Proctor has been possessed by the spirit of Lance Corporal Bureaucrat," mocked Bob Trent peering now curiously over the top of his newspaper.

"Since when did we ever do the twilight head count in pairs, and what's with the Nurse Purdom routine?"

"Exactly Jack," continued Bob on the same theme," I mean Doctor Proctor. You really should have been a doctor eh; or change your surname to Purse? Seriously though, what gives?"

Jack Proctor knew that his sudden adherence to code of practice would not go unnoticed. The only people more cynical about such things other than these two was Jack himself and he knew it. He continued however. "Look guys it was only a couple of months ago that it was laid on really thick how we must conform rigidly to rules and regulations following the slaughtering inflicted upon us at the hands of the bitch genius, Miss S J Primrose, and not only that there would be spot checks and unannounced audits and such stuff."

"How could we forget Jack. Instant suspension focusses the mind somewhat," said Craig Purdom, "but come on, there are only the three of us here right now."

"Unless," interjected Bob, "you think one of the patients might be a plant."

"Quite a few of them are plants Bob." Jack was becoming uneasy but fortunately they would soon be complying without much further interrogation. Craig wasn't just quite finished though.

"Are you thinking maybe its a bit like those secret shoppers in super markets and that's why the checkout staff have to ask you if you need help to pack when all you bought was a packet of chewing gum? "Sorry to keep you waiting," they apologise after the threat of deep vein thrombosis from queuing for 1 nanosecond."

"Are you saying Craig that down in the farm we might have, a secret psycho?"

Both sensed Jack's unease so Craig said, "OK Nurse Proctor, let's go. Nurse Trent you are on tea duty, and don't forget protocol 5 Section 4e part 2. Bring the pot to the kettle not the kettle to the pot."

Jack's torture was over and they made their way down to the wards; well not quite over. "Should we do the security dance just in case? OK I'm finished. Promise."

Eventually they gained access to the doors behind which lay some very dangerous individuals and whenever they looked in through the small but robust one way mirrors measuring little more than one square foot or so the joking always stopped. Only once when they totally believed they had identified someone lying in a bed would they venture to put their eyes close to the glass. The sudden appearance of a wild screaming face a few centimetres away was a lesson none ever forgot but also an experience of which no new start was ever pre-warned. It was a rather sick rite of passage.

"Well everything seems in order Jack eh Nurse Proctor. Just one to go." No name was exchanged; no exchange was needed. There was one further level of security to clear before gaining access to the room in which lay await the embodiment of malignant evil. Both peered in turn to ascertain that Sarah Jane was located where society had deemed most appropriate given that the death penalty was the finality that many would have preferred but an option that the law had long since withdrawn.

"Right she's there. Let's depart this unwelcome glimpse of Hell." Jack however remained still, staring through the glass. Craig rested a re-assuring hand on Jack's shoulder. "Jack, she is in there. Safely locked up where she belongs. Come on."

"I'm not so sure." said Jack. "It just doesn't look quite right to me."

"For fuck sake we're not going in!" protested Craig, his fear openly betraying him as his compassion for his troubled colleagued evaporated.

"All I'm saying is let's look just a bit more closely. We can't actually see any facial features at all and she is lying very still."

Nurse Purdom agreed to look closely and carefully and after two full minutes had elapsed they reluctantly concurred that she was unnaturally still. "Oh God oh God Oh God, let's go in then."

They pressed codes, swiped a card through a reader and undid two manual latches before sliding the door slowly and quietly open. Still there was no trace of movement. Cautiously they inched forward and at first so quietly then increasing louder called her name. They exchanged a glance then Craig moved forward and began to pull the thick single duvet of toughened unwelcoming fabric from her bed; then suddenly from behind them without a hint of warning came a howling shriek which fired terror through their souls as they anticipated imminent mutilation at the slashing hand of Primrose. Peering through crossed arms they had thrown instinctively across their fear clenched faces they turned to see nothing; and the ripping echoing screams subsided to a vibration. In the corner sat a phone awaiting a voice message to be accessed.

"Good morning guys. Oh how I so wish I could have seen that moment. I'm sure neither of you were expecting that. Anyway, thank you for allowing me to share your vacation condo. The happy memories will live with me forever. I promise I will give it a five star appraisal when I submit my report to the holiday guides. Oh, and by the way, probably just as well

I'm not here. Look under the pillow. Heads up here, it's neither a tooth nor a coin."

Craig unsteadily made his way to the pillow, his legs threatening to surrender their purpose and his arms trembling despite his best efforts to disguise this shame. Sliding the pillow aside his trembling was replaced by frozen rigidity as waves of chilling fear vacillated up and down his spine.

"Just how?" he thought. "Just how?" as he revealed a can of pepper spray and a broad glinting 15 inch hunting knife. Not just this moment but any time in the past, they both visualized in savage graphic detail how she could have left a slab of assorted butcher's cuts sourced from finest quality psychiatric nurses before they would even have had time to gasp their last ever terrified breath. The twisted monster may well also have pinned labels on them too.

A few hours earlier a dark figure was exiting the periphery of the clinically arranged trees, the darkness surrendering to a faint diffuse light allowing the basic features of the landscape to reveal their form to facilitate their negotiation exactly as had been planned to the minute by Sarah Jane Primrose. She moved to step onto the road when from nowhere a car brushed past at speed with only her most unnatural alacrity saving her from certain injury at the very least.

"Have you never heard of fuck'n headlights you fuck'n moron?" she frustratedly had to scream in the silence of her own mind. She was livid though; raging. The contempt which she mostly managed to suppress for her fellow humans was now palpable. Was the car slowing down, even going to come back perhaps? Oh how she wanted that; how she willed it. Her repertoire of retribution would surely ensure it would be the last journey that car ever made, at least with that driver. Her cold logic however regained control. "Why snack when a feast awaits?" she thought to herself as she melted into the landscape intent once more on sharing her darkness with the audacious world that had sought to confine her.

Chapter Twenty Six

Detective Inspector Buchanan was sitting in his usual chair in his usual coffee shop. His life was falling into a routine of repeating stability. Each day he arrived with his newspaper and was served a cup of coffee. There he would stay for perhaps two hours before rising to leave where he would make his way to the river after settling his bill, tipping generously and picking up his sandwich and coffee to go, always ready and prepared without asking. It didn't matter what the weather may be like, the walk followed by his lunch either sitting out or in a shelter from the rain was the modus operandi.

The first time he requested coffee from this welcoming but trendy café (he learned that they didn't like it being referred to as such) he was subjected to an avalanche of options in words which he did not even recognise as his native language. With much composure that day he allowed the enthusiastic young benefactress to sing her recital of bewildering choice, paused, smiled and said, "milk and two sugars please". Thereafter, good morning and a smile sufficed in ensuring delivery of his beverage. After several months a second girl joined the staff but she clearly had been briefed in her induction. Like the other she was polite, smiled and greeted him warmly with a few words but didn't intrude upon his world. She had a soft melodic southern Irish accent and he was never quite sure whether she actually had two eyes as a long severe angled black fringe always covered one; and the other had an iris that went through an array of most unnaturally vivid primary colours from one day to the next. What never changed colour though was her black nail varnish to match her black lipstick and also the narrow black lines so carefully and artistically curving beyond the corners of her eyes; or perhaps just one eye. Quite often he would note that she was reading a magazine dedicated to tattoos. He could understand, well just about anyway why there were those who chose to partake in body art; but read about it? Just what was there to read?

Young people coming and going was very much a feature of the city of Dundee as it was the home of two Universities and an array of colleges. Did the one eyed girl attend college he used to speculate? Art? Drama? Hairdressing? In the fullness of time his passing curiosity was furnished with an answer. Particle Physics. This rested uneasily with him for a while revealing a stereotyping prejudice of which he was unaware, not a little ashamed; and sought to exorcise.

In his entire life he had never actually even visited this city once despite it being less than a hundred miles away, and for that it served one cold purpose. No street, shop, view or riverside sunset reminded him of precious moments with his beloved wife Mary, stolen from him by evil. The sad truth was that he deeply wanted to end his own life and had so every single moment since left alone, images gouged into his mind that tortured him every night before rescued by uneasy sleep, and lay await to pounce as he emerged from the respite of semi stupor early every morning. Did his wife scream and cry as the acrid poison threw her stumbling over furniture as she grabbed at curtains, ripping the fittings from the wall? Did she try and shout out his name as she choked and suffocated on the thick oozing foam that erupted from her mouth and nose? There was now little joy in his life. That journey was over, but there was still one final destination; and one final job to complete before he could "retire".

There were many places of course other than this city that he had never visited and where he would have been similarly shielded from the pain of beautiful warm reflections now turned harsh and cold, but there was a second reason for choosing this town or city over all others. Dundee had another recent immigrant, Amelia Rosenberg. Anyone would probably understand why he perhaps believed he had a duty to protect and look out for one of Dundee's recent undergraduates, but only since the now notorious escape of Sarah Jane Primrose did he and he alone appreciate the full disturbing irony.

Amelia and a core of friends occasionally visited the coffee shop which had become his second home but not in the ritualistic manner in which he did himself, so rigid that anyone may be forgiven to suggest that OCD was at play.

The memories for DI Buchanan are still vivid of that morning he walked into the Coffee shop with the newspaper under his arm, headlining with the terrifying news of Miss Primrose's abscondment. As fate would have it Amelia was there that day with two of her fellow Philosophy students. She acknowledged him with a warm smile and was about to return to continue with her conversation when DI Buchanan, asked, "Amelia, do you have a moment; in private if that's OK with you?"

"Of course." She arose and turned to her friends, "We can continue with our conversation on whether we believe that Jean Paul Sartre would have dunked his doughnuts in his coffee or not when I get back."

This was becoming something of a running gag when DI Buchanan first enquired about what a group of Philosophy students discussed in coffee shops. He was soon put right that it certainly wasn't Philosophy and inadvertently set them off on a tangent on what the collective noun might be. Although not a regular occurrence, in fact quite rare, it was not the first time DI Buchanan and Amelia had sat together so it passed without comment from her friends. She had actually passed on her address so that he could pop in any time. The Inspector of course said he would be delighted though both knew it would just never happen. He did though know exactly the location from his frequent low key walks down her street.

Amelia just sensed as she walked to his table from perhaps subtle context, facial expression; just something that a moment of some gravitas awaited. DI Buchanan was quite aware that even such young and talented academics did not slavishly follow the early morning news as his own generation did, and in fact early mornings themselves were something of a rarity, nor did they pick up nor even glance at news stands as a general rule. And why bother he had to concede to himself when each carried the world's media in their pocket, that was when their electronic font of all knowledge was not glued to their hand. The Inspector had of course been notified directly and immediately about Primrose's escape although having retired from the force many months earlier.

They sat down together at his usual table. He motioned to speak but words did not come easily though both knew they were not really necessary. Amelia was already concluding what the Inspector already knew. He opened the newspaper in front of her. PRIMROSE ESCAPES MOORLAND. The tabloids used somewhat more colourful language but all papers ran with the same lead. If neither knew what to say before, now they both really felt robbed of the power of communication. It was obvious what had to be said but mental rehearsal made every option seem so glib. Eventually the Inspector however felt that he must complete the ritual. "So you be especially careful now Amelia." When he looked down his hand was resting on hers yet he had no memory of doing so nor even contemplating such a manoeuvre.

She completed the play. "Yes I will, and you too, and remember that invitation for coffee remains open." She stood up and returned to sit with her friends who were not in the least interested to enquire.

For many months that followed DI Buchanan continued to frequent the coffee shop, constantly reflecting that his decision to move to Dundee as a precaution had now, unfortunately, proved to be necessary.

"DI Buchanan?" a voice enquired hesitantly.

"Yes. How can I help?"

A police officer with ID to hand said, "I was told I might find you here. We need to talk." After a short exchange they departed together.

"Your coffee and sandwiches Richard!" Colleen shouted after them as they were disappearing out the door.

"Just raffle them Colleen."

Chapter Twenty Seven

A crowd was already assembled around the hole in the ground in which the remains of Sarah Jane Primrose were to be dumped. No one present was minded to contemplate more reverential language nor protocol which even alluded to respect or dignity. This was not a body to be laid to rest, releasing a soul from the discomfort of incarnate burden but rather a repugnant reprehensible abomination to be cast deep into the dirt. The chosen plot had been selected well away from all others and was actually never intended to be a burial site at all. In time, in very little time nature would reclaim the land, and the soft permeable headstone with the most basic and lightly etched inscription, would weather and crumble.

Approaching the grave came the lone hearse: everyone baulked at the thought of being part of a solicitous attendant cortège. It passed a lone figure who looked up before returning to the careful and dutiful task of dusting off leaves and grass from recently laid flowers placed on a carefully tended grave most possibly a victim of Primrose, the estimate being around 30 but death tolls well beyond this figure often speculated upon.

The long black vehicle swung around in an arc allowing all to see the most basic of casks most certainly not adorned with flowers. Most rapidly the coffin was rolled out and prepared to be lowered into the ground. Not for Sarah Jane Primrose would names be called out to take light strain of honourable cords.

"Wish you were still alive so we could burn you at the stake," came a sudden anguished cry from the crowd, "so we could listen to your screams and your fat spitting and burning."

The sobbing figure of retired Primary teacher Mrs Flood was led away as someone else added, "Be assured Margaret, that is exactly what will be happening to her right now."

Once more silence fell over the darkening scene, everyone staring like they could see through the cask to the rotting remains within. The coffin was dropped with such haste as to cause it to thud into the wet ground beneath. The minister began to say a few words which rapidly decayed to mumbles and a few rapid hand gestures and signs of no real discernible meaning. Where normally a few gently cast handfuls of soil would be scattered into the grave, shovels of soil from a team of diggers rapidly and quickly covered the box below. By the time all assembled began to drift away the coffin of Sarah Jane Primrose was deeply buried beneath rocks and soil. This is what they had come to see. Almost as if staged managed for effect a mighty flash of lightening brightly illuminated the morbid grey scene and an explosion of thunder literally shook the hearse. Rain rapidly began to fall which expedited the exit of those remaining. The grave diggers however stuck to their task.

There was to be no ceremonial gathering today; no steak pie and a few drinks as was the tradition in Scotland, to share happy memories through glazed bloodshot eyes and forced laughter strangled by grief. Everyone went their own separate ways or in small family groups. DI Buchanan and DI Christina McKay, had arranged to meet up with Amelia at a local hotel for lunch. DI McKay had been brought in to replace Richard Buchanan following his immediate leave of absence then retiral following the murder of his wife. Joining them would be Detective Constable Jason Melrose who was very much involved in the sordid discovery on the moors. He had replaced Detective Watt who had been transferred to another division due to irreconcilable damage to his marriage following the notorious Sarah Jane interview. There would be the pretext of small talk but in reality there was much detail that both Amelia and DI Buchanan wanted to hear.

They had pre-booked a secluded window table which looked down the full length of a local loch from a close but elevated vantage point. Any other day it would most certainly have been a topic of some enthusiasm such was the splendour of the view as mountains stretched steeply and imposingly either side. Today however it was a welcome backdrop but nothing more.

"A pint Detective Inspector?" asked the young DC.

"Thank you very much. That would be just great. A pint of something local; and please, Richard if that's OK."

"And a Gin and tonic for you Christina?" immediately sensing that perhaps that was not OK.

"Thank you Jason," she replied with mischievous emphasis on his first name, "and a sparkling water too please."

"Amelia? Coke? Fresh orange and soda?"

"Thank you very much. A Pinot Grigio would be lovely thank you."

Soon after, they all had a meal in front of them which they had all chosen with reluctance and disinterest but now suddenly found it most welcome. Pleasantries had been exchanged but they all knew what needed to be discussed, and for many reasons.

"Jason, I believe you were the first to be called to the scene," started DI Buchanan.

"That I was yes. We received a call that someone walking on the moors had discovered a body and I was immediately dispatched to investigate."

"And what exactly did he find, and why was he there at all? It's bleak and featureless."

"He had driven there with his dog. He liked the solitude he said. Anyway it wasn't actually him who found the body really."

295

This got the more acute attention of Amelia and Richard, though not that they weren't paying attention in the first place. "Are you actually ready for this?" The silent and barely disguised stares of annoyance were sufficient reply. "The dog brought him an arm; a black badly decomposed arm." He paused theatrically taking full command of centre stage.

"I'll take it from her Jason," interrupted DI McKay perhaps fearing Richard and Amelia would miss their train in 5 hours time. "The dog doing whatever dogs do led him to a derelict bothy where a seriously decomposed body was found which had clearly also been grazed upon let's say."

"Zombies!" said Amelia. She didn't know where that came from but any tension that may have existed was totally blown away.

With some difficulty DI McKay continued. "It looked like perhaps she had seriously underestimated the harshness of winter conditions on the moor and frozen to death, and was subsequently picked upon by crows, foxes and who knows what else as she began to thaw in the spring."

"She might have been the teenage genius or whatever but she couldn't have been that bright. Bashed in tins of food everywhere that she had tried to open against rocks or anything else that came to hand because she forgot to pack a tin opener."

Richard and Amelia exchanged the most surreptitious of glances. "And her clothing? Maybe warm enough to go shopping in Edinburgh but that's about it." The glances were repeated.

"I may come over as quite foolish here. Police procedure is not my forte," Amelia enquired with reluctant necessity, "but how was it confirmed that it actually was Sarah Jane Primrose?"

"The DNA tests confirmed it to be her beyond all reasonable doubt." That was sufficient to dispel doubt both DI Buchanan and Amelia had to concede to themselves, "and also she was still wearing her hospital wrist band with her name on it, Sarah Primrose." Suddenly the doubt came flooding back.

"The menacing voice mail?" DI Buchanan asked but in truth, no longer really interested. "I was told it was sent from Edinburgh. How does that all fit in?" suspecting exactly how really.

"Clearly one of Miss Primrose's sleepers let's call them sent it for her to put us off the track."

"It appears that it worked," said Amelia quietly but really intended just for herself as she looked outwards into blank space.

DC Melrose apparently taking some offence where none was intended defensively added, "The real issue is just how was she able to escape in the first place. That's where the blame should lie; the finger pointing."

DI McKay leaping to defuse a bomb that was never intended to be lit quickly interjected, "There is little purpose trying to apportion blame. We all know how cunning and manipulative she could be. Today we witnessed a dreadful nightmare being brought to a long overdue conclusion. Let us all just end the day by dwelling on that comforting thought."

Amelia would normally be torturing herself with guilt at the thought she had offended someone. That was just so alien to her very essence. Her thoughts were elsewhere however; and they were not in any way comforting.

Goodbyes were said as a taxi arrived to take DI Buchanan and Amelia to the station. Both were heading straight back to Dundee that night. Amelia, because her parents made it quite clear they were not coming home from Majorca early just to witness, "the bitch being planted," and Richard because there was just no way he could ever return to the village other than to the cemetery.

On the journey home they mostly drowsed and exchanged few words. There was no need. Something was just wrong; they both felt it but neither could articulate it with reason nor justification.

Chapter Twenty Eight

DI Buchanan was on his usual vigil in these hours of darkness. His route would change but his purpose never did; and the focus was always the basement flat in which Amelia lived alone. She frequently had friends staying with her, often for the night and on those occasions he would feel sufficiently at ease to desert his post if perhaps not entirely comfortable to do so. As he ambled slowly alone in the dim amber light he thought back to his chance meeting with Amelia as he sat down at the river. This was no longer a routine however. All routines were now a thing of the past. Their purpose or rather abandonment was for one particular observer. His hope was that a misleading message may be inferred by one specific covert spy. They did not exchange many words but they did exchange cryptic messages as if trying to protect the other by such circumspect discourse as the very occasional aeroplane filled the long but not uncomfortable silences.

"How strange that Sarah Jane Primrose would not be sufficiently prepared for the severe cold of the moors."

"Indeed, most unlike her," the DI replied, "and still wearing a hospital wrist band."

"Yes, and a name towards which she was expressly hostile," added Amelia.

"I'm led to believe that the 'little something' Sarah Jane left for you was just a twisted deception."

"Yes well neither I nor the police found anything that had been left in my bedroom." Amelia and Amelia alone knew this to be untrue.

As another plane was coming into land at the city airport which was not exactly an international hub they stood up as one and slowly departed in opposite directions. "Best get going Amelia before we are caught in the crush from the Airport." Amelia smiled at his harmless sarcasm and waved him good bye.

Events brought his attention sharply back to the present. There was something just not quite right. Did someone move behind the curtain? Was the lighting just very subtly different from normal? There was a subliminal trigger that compelled him to investigate. An embarrassing moment perhaps lay just seconds away. He could live with that. He knew there was an alternative with which he could never live. Considering back up the DI reached to pull out his phone before remembering that it was charging by his bedside.

Amelia was totally relaxed under the clear blue sky that looked down upon her as the boat on which she lay was so gently rocked by crystal clear water that quietly lapped onto the nearby shore. A mattress filled the shallow sided vessel making her feel especially snug and cosy in the gentle warmth. Beside her lay Dean with whom she went to school. How long ago those days already seemed. White fluffy clouds began to form and drift by. Soon they were exchanging names for the vague shapes they formed. A sheep, a duck; a horse perhaps. The vague shapes began to take on crisper clearer detail and they commented on just how amazing this was. Shapes turned to smiling fluffy white faces. The clouds started gathering in number and white was replaced by grey and smiles with menacing sneers; cold unwelcoming grey squeezing out all trace off blue as they merged together. Amelia was no longer feeling quite so comfortable with what was happening. Her discomfort increased rapidly when she realized she was now totally alone. She looked to the shore but in all directions was endless still grey water to every horizon. Her breathing began to become more difficult as a force began to press down upon her chest. Rain drops were starting to drop around her producing dark expanding circles in the grey void. Rain drops also began rolling down her face accompanied by a warm sweetly scented breeze; a sweet vanilla scented breeze. Amelia's eyes sprang open in terror to see a feather being gently brushed back and forth across her face, a feather held in the hand of Sarah Jane Primrose.

"Surprise!"

Amelia squirmed beneath the sheets.

"Don't try to get up Princess Amelia. I've tucked your sheets in nice and tight to keep you safe and snug."

Reaching across the bed for a box she continued, "Look sweet Amelia I have bought you some chocolates. I'll open them shall I?" as she pulled gently on a pink ribbon and sprung open the delicate small box. "Oh look how pretty they are? Everyone different but all have a smooth white surface and a soft sweet filling. When I chose them I so thought of you. Let's share one shall we? That will be so romantic. It will bond us, make us sort of engaged don't you think?"

"OK stop right there. The game is up Miss Primrose and I've already called for back up."

"No you haven't," replied Sarah Jane calmly. She was of course taken hugely by surprise by this intrusion but gave no outward indication of this, didn't even look up, and rapidly processed the situation.

"And what's with, "the game is up!" Seriously? What's my line? Fair cop guv? You've got me bang to rights and ain't that the truth?"

Sarah Jane only now casually looked up and said, "Well are you coming in or not? Are you a vampire or something? Do you need an invitation to cross the threshold? Amelia and I are having a party aren't we precious?"

DI Buchanan moved forward from where he had been standing to block the exit and started walking towards the bed.

"Stop right there matey," and in one smooth movement with the skills of a conjurer a bottle appeared in her hand from which she squirted some liquid onto the open box of chocolates. Immediately foul smelling smoke began to rise from the box and the white chocolate turned black and started twisting, bubbling and growing from the box to the sound of hissing. The inspector froze on the spot.

"Wait a cotton pick'n minute!" Sarah Jane said in theatrical overplay. "This isn't L'amour de Shag. In fact, unless I'm mistaken," she paused for dramatic effect as if any were really needed, "this is concentrated sulphuric acid! This is counterfeit rubbish! Let this be a lesson to us all boys and girls. If an offer seems too good to be true, it probably is."

She began menacingly moving the bottle back and forward close to Amelia. "Just imagine what that might have done to poor Amelia's face; or eyes. You know what? If this had done damage to such sweet countenance as this, I would have been livid. I would have been straight back to the shop and said, money back now!"

She returned her full attention to the DI. "DI Buchanan, you look shaken. Perhaps you should sit down. In fact I insist and on that chair right there. And could you turn the lighting up just a bit sweetie, but not too much. Don't want to ruin the ambience. Now lock the door behind you, oh and another thing, would you collect a couple of tie wraps from the bottom of my bag on your way?"

Richard Buchanan knew he had absolutely no option. Whether he tried a quick lunge or ran to get help Amelia would suffer blinding horrific burns irrespective of his choice.

Slowly after closing the door and turning the key in the lock he made his way towards the bag and began to search through it. Immediately terror and repulsion consumed him as he fought to camouflage his horror. Clearly what lay ahead for Amelia was a sustained grotesque sexual assault, then death; and perhaps not even in that order.

"Not those things on the top you silly sausage. Those are gifts for Amelia. What you are looking for is right at the bottom of the bag," she mocked as the bottle remained threateningly close to Amelia's face.

"Now put one in a great big loop round the arm so you can slide your hand through it soon but first tie your other hand to the chair."

DI Buchanan complied, mostly. He tied one wrist to the chair then slid the other through the loop as instructed but positioned the grip half way between his wrist and elbow then really tightened it with his teeth with all the strength he could summon which was completely to Sarah Jane's satisfaction.

"You know something officer? I wouldn't go getting a super hero costume just yet. You break into a house to rescue folks from a fire and end up getting rescued yourself and now this. What do you think of your knight in shining armour my lady?" turning her attention once more to Amelia. "Can you think of a name for our vigilante hero here who keeps the streets safe for us wittle girls?" she mocked in a childish voice. "We'll come back to that Inspector. Maybe you can think of a name while we play. You do have a very good seat but well, what we're about to do is not exactly a spectator sport," and at this she turned and smiled at Amelia after licking her finger and gently dragging it down Amelia's face, eventually to rest it upon her lips.

Amelia had been lying mostly motionless as she knew she must. Sarah Jane's invisible web of perception seemed almost able to detect every thought, and just as DI Buchanan had tried but failed to restrain his horror at the contents of Sarah Jane's bag, Amelia too had consequently also failed to do likewise in response. He gave little away but it was enough to stimulate the most subtle tremor of facial expression from Amelia.

"I can tell that you are absolutely desperate to see the treasure trove of presents I have for you. Well good news my sweet sweet Amelia. No more sleeps till Christmas!"

Sarah Jane was now forcibly pushing her finger between Amelia's lips and repugnant as it was, at least she was not yet being exposed to the terrible unknown which lay await. That was not to last. "I'm teasing you Amelia. That just won't do," and she turned slowly then moved towards the plain black bag that lay open against the wall. At least it gave her a second to ease just slightly free from her linen restraint. Momentarily she had thought of biting down on Sarah Jane's finger but she knew that DI Buchanan was in no position to seize the moment and nor was she; and she knew also that at best they would at most get one and one moment only.

"Now what shall we open first? Leave the biggest till last? That's what I.."

"So who was in your coffin then?"

"JUST WHO THE FUCK CARES?" The room reverberated with the rage and venom from Sarah Jane's outburst. "I was talking to Amelia!" she snapped aggressively. "It was just my fuck'n sister! Just don't you EVER interrupt..." she stopped in mid sentence and dropped whatever she had in her hand back into the bag. After a few seconds of barely restrained anger on her face as she stared into empty space she calmed herself and turned to the DI.

"I would have come to that but since you have asked." Once more she fell silent to gather her thoughts. She may have been so rudely interrupted but the unfolding of this little chapter like all others would be in her terms.

"We'll call her my sister, that bag of scarcely differentiated stem cells. I knew it might serve a purpose one day but was never really quite sure how. You know what it's like. You have an old piece of junk or whatever and you can't bring yourself to chuck it out just in case one day it might come in handy for something."

With considerable trepidation Amelia felt it purposeful to speak. To what immediate purpose once again she really had no idea. To buy time? What was the choice?

"I thought your sister was doing fine?" To Amelia's immediate relief she provoked no more than sneering laughter from Sarah Jane.

"You are absolutely right my Amelia. She was indeed doing just fine. OK she was profoundly deaf, blind in one eye and the other so damaged it would struggle to read letters two foot high, but that was scarcely a problem since her brain was so fucked it scarcely served more than to keep her heart pumping, control a few chemicals and functions to turn liquidized food into shit."

Both DI Buchanan and Amelia were aware of the trauma which had left Charlotte Abigail Primrose so totally dependent on 24 hour supervision, but she was mentally responsive to the love and selfless care she experienced; concepts literally alien to Sarah Jane. She was also physically never considered to be under immediate threat of a catastrophic medical event.

"Let's cut to the chase. She died. A mercy killing really."

Richard Buchanan was not minded to enquire further. Did Sarah Jane carry out the deed herself or did she employ yet another useful and obliging contact? Unless she volunteered to disclose further detail he genuinely did not want to know; and it would just serve to nurture Sarah Jane's twisted theatre of self gratification. Neither he nor Amelia were to be spared further elaboration however but thankfully it was brief.

"I wonder what suffocation is like? And face down on a pillow! Someone should get into big trouble for that you know. She is meant to be turned periodically; like a joint of meat."

Sarah Jane paused so DI Buchanan judged it to be reasonably safe to speak.

"This doesn't help with some unanswered questions. The body that was found in the hiker's hut on the moors was DNA checked." This time it was the DI who paused hoping it would obviate the necessity to articulate further enquiry knowing the depravity of what horrors awaited. Sarah Jane remained stony: she wanted the question specifically asked.

With all the attention on DI Buchanan, Amelia once more had the opportunity ever so slightly to loosen her bondage.

"I was actually aware of you sister Charlotte Abigail Primrose's sad death," making great emphasis of her name in a futile gesture of humanizing her in Sarah Jane's mind. "I also knew some of those who attended her funeral." More silence followed. Sarah Jane was determined to crush out every morsel of discomfort from her inquisitor.

Richard Buchanan took a deep breath. "How did the remains of your sister end up in the moors wearing your clothing and hospital wrist band? Did you yourself actually exhume the body? Did you dig her up and remove her from her resting place?" His tone, clenched fists and flushed face were betraying his complete revulsion and rage. Unknown to him it was soon to get so much worse.

"Do these look like the hands of a gravedigger?" she appeared to snap but was really sneering as she thrust out her beautifully smooth manicured hands with distinctive black nail varnish; black nail varnish he had seen before.

"Oh my goodness me. Did I just hear a penny rattling off the bottom of your empty concrete skull? Short dark, hair, one eye covered, some make up, a dodgy Irish accent and you are fooled? I hope you never got asked to an identity parade! Be as well lining up 5 penguins."

"Colleen."

"Well done Sherlock."

"Well perhaps just as well you were never quizzed about Physics then," he responded in lame retribution, and immediately regretting it the moment he did before Sarah Jane's lips had even parted.

"Electromagnetism? Thermodynamics? Higgs Boson? What would you like to know? And just don't get me started on String Theory, we could be here all night!" Of course she would have fielded such enquiry with consummate ease Richard Buchanan realized all to late. Not that it mattered. He knew she wanted further questions to elucidate the chilling detail of her sister's fate.

Once more turning her attention to Amelia she continued, "And here is your super hero who travelled all the way to Dundee to keep you safe from me and how many times was it? Three, four that I served you both coffee?" then turning to the DI, "And once I even mistakenly called you Richard and you didn't twig. How many lost opportunities to give you a very special coffee Amelia." Gesturing with her head towards Richard Buchanan she scoffed theatrically, "I wouldn't have wasted any on Inspector Idiot, and he clearly is an idiot."

"OK Explain?" Richard asked with indeterminate purpose and absolutely no appetite really for elaboration.

"If I must. What did I tell you about routines once upon a time? Dangerous things I warned you but oh no. You know better. Once you learned of my death you never again came to the coffee shop on a regular basis or went to the river. You bought the deception hook line and sinker."

"I stopped my routines to draw you out," Snapped DI Buchanan angrily. "There was no way on God's Earth that you would have kept on a hospital name bracelet far less one that said Sarah Primrose."

Joining in with a nod of agreement which clearly riled Sarah Jane, "And neither of us believed that you would be ill prepared for the harsh weather."

"Oh so you consulted did you?" her displeasure still ominously on display.

"We didn't have to," said the Inspector, "It was so obvious."

"And was it also obvious that I was at my own funeral?" It was the turn of Richard Buchanan and Amelia to be surprised then immediately rebuked themselves for being so. "Who do you think was the lone figure tending a nearby grave?"

Sarah Jane was about to become her own self again as control and further opportunity for repugnance presented itself.

"What do you make of that nasty bitch Mrs Flood mouthing of at me? A bit of respect at a funeral if you don't mind!" Somehow her audience sensed there was more atrocity to follow.

"How ironic that she thought she was at my funeral then later I was at hers Comical really. I wonder if they ever caught that, 'Six foot white male with a moustache and distinctive tattoo," she mimicked from the news, "that pushed her in front of the express train to Edinburgh?" She wasn't finished. "They really pass through the station at a hell of a speed. Don't think there would have been much to bury! So many people comforted me at the funeral lunch of my beloved favourite primary school teacher. The sausage rolls by the way? They were to die for. I had never actually heard of Margaret Flood in my life before I was laid to rest in front of my sobbing admirers."

Sarah Jane's captives turned to each other both wanting to convey so much. Even had they elected to communicate directly and risk the deranged wrath of Sarah Jane they would not have known how to verbalise their feelings. Both felt guilt; both wanted to express that the other should feel none.

With a second endeavour to buy time and then hopefully ever so slightly ease her linen constraint, Amelia introduced the subject of Sarah Jane's escape grudgingly conceding to herself that she was presenting her with a further opportunity for self adulation.

"I have been in the hospital in which you were receiving treatment," Amelia worded her gambit with stinging intent.

"My treatment, as you call it. Go on."

"The security we went through to get in was very stringent. I'm guessing it would be even more so for inmates to get out."

"Treatment! Inmates! Make your mind up Princess Amelia! So how did I do it? Is that your question? Don't be shy."

With disturbingly insane reliability Sarah Jane fell silent. Amelia knew what was required. "So how did you escape?"

"My goodness. I thought you were never going to ask. OK and first of all it was nothing to do with sex. There is more than one string to my bow you know. It would seem that every man who ever walked the Earth has an Achilles dick, but variety is the spice of death." She paused, "God I'm good! No this time I caught or rather contrived a trap to snarl a nurse helping himself to Charity funds. Cretin Aid or something. I don't know. Anyway suddenly I had another little helper." Taking a deep breath and shaking her head she said, "Embezzlement. How shocking! I was disgusted and from such a noble cause too."

"Nurse Proctor was guilty of nothing," Interrupted DI Buchanan. This gained Sarah Jane's full attention and she forgave the quite heinous crime of interruption.

"You have earned my audience. Continue."

"When you so horribly murdered my wife you also killed Nurse Proctor's precious sister. Together we and not you contrived his crime for your benefit and then facilitated your escape. Surely you must have thought it was just a bit too easy, no?"

For the first time Sarah Jane was forced to reflect on that, but then had to enquire, "Why?"

"I'll tell you why? Who do you think was driving the car that so nearly killed you as you stepped onto the road that night?"

There was a long silence as DI Buchanan bowed his head; a silence that only delayed the inevitable.

"Oh my God Amelia, this just gets better and better. The gift that just keeps on giving." There was glee in her face like had never been seen before. "And here we all are together. Such sweet serendipity." Turning her uncontrollable joy to Amelia she said. "I just know the delicious irony of all this is not being lost upon you?"

"It was the right thing to do." Amelia's coldly presented assertion was such a mood killer and not what Sarah Jane wanted to hear. It moved DI Buchanan to raise his face slightly also if perhaps not his expression of deep guilt and shame. "You would have got out one way or another. At least this way there was a chance of wiping you off the face of the Earth. I would have done the same if I could."

Sarah Jane's face turned cold again as she almost took on the demeanour of a child in a huff. "Well whatever. Here we all are and we have Inspector Idiot to thank for that."

DI Buchanan felt sufficiently but undeservedly forgiven to resume his particular line of enquiry. "OK then, back to your sister. How was it done, and I've absolutely had it with your 20 questions game."

"Oh calm yourself Inspector. Can I do anything for you? Scratch your nose perhaps?" From the far side of the room she dragged over a small stool and sat down in front of him tantalisingly close; deliberately close.

"OK a little story. Firstly it was the undertaker. He dug up the body, filled in the grave, took it to the moors, dressed it." She paused for effect again. "I'm boring you both. What you are both aching to know is why? Just why did he carry out this quite reprehensible exhumation? You are both ahead of me here really though. You know it was blackmail. Boring," she said dragging the word out with teenage sarcasm.

"Blackmailed him with what though? That is what has you on the edge of your seat isn't it Inspector? Well that and the tie wraps. Enough of this teasing Sarah Jane," she chastised herself mockingly. "I won't go into sordid detail let me just say that he looked after his charges very well. Hear what I'm saying? I would like to think he at least got them flowers or chocolates before his romantic evenings with the freshly deceased; and I'll tell you he wasn't at all fussy. Young and thin. Old and fat! Actually to hell with sensibilities. Boy could he fuck like a bunny once he got going?"

DI Buchanan's face turned stony grey as Amelia realized that evil had finally reached the lowest level of hell: as Amelia realised that Sarah Jane Primrose was possibly about to make a rare but catastrophic error of judgement.

Staring coldly and directly at Richard Buchanan through eyes with nefarious intent, she slowly and so carefully articulated, lest she spill one heinous drop of her odious toxin, "Wasn't that the undertaker who looked after your wife?"

The time for subtle clandestine exchanges with Amelia was gone. With one arm primed for escape he lunged forward breaking a single tie, but with the speed and slight of hand displayed many times before, a blade appeared in Sarah Jane's grip and just as quickly disappeared into Richard Buchanan's ribs where it remained. In the same flowing movement she turned back to her more precious captive but with one hand now free Amelia used the full momentum of Sarah Jane, grabbed her hair tightly and pulled her onto the bed as a further blade exploded through the back of her blouse skewering her to the sheets.

"Thanks for the present you vile repugnant bitch!" Sarah Jane Primrose looked momentarily stunned then quite remarkably regained her composure.

"Touché Amelia." Looking up to meet Amelia's eyes she said, "You will tell them I said that won't you? You will tell the world those were my final words?"

Gripping and twisting Sarah Jane's hair ever tighter as blood poured down the long glinting knife Sarah Jane had gifted her all those months ago Amelia met her stare imprinting one last image on her retina before her evil dark eyes would see no more and said, "I will tell them, Sarah Primrose, that you howled and squealed, and cried for your mummy."

For the first time in her foul rancid existence anxiety gripped Sara Jane's face, the devastating epiphany dawning upon her in those final moments, that the signature of her demoniac reign of terror would be recalled for posterity and so unjustly by such a whimpering fearful epilogue. That was the anxiety gripped face which Amelia watched breathe its final hideous breath, before kicking and pushing the tangled bundle of dead meat and blankets off the end of her bed to tumble and thump onto the floor.

Quickly Amelia swung her legs around and stepped onto the floor by which time Richard Buchanan had already removed the deeply embedded knife from his body and used it to cut the remaining tie before agonisingly pushing himself upright on the chair. Amelia grabbed her phone from a bedside drawer and began to tap the screen.

"No!" Richard Buchanan said loudly then pausing said more quietly, "No Amelia, please don't do that." Amelia lowered her phone. "I'm going on a date. How do I look?"

Amelia rested her hand upon his as he had once done to her. "You look fine." He gently tensed his own hand in response beneath her caring touch.

He raised his eyes slightly upwards. "Put the kettle on Mary I'll be up in minute." Turning back to Amelia he said, "A favour please. Take the keys from my pocket, go back to my flat and turn my phone off for ever. My poor wife must be hoarse the number of times I've listened to her voice in recent months." He paused then continued, "and the first chance I get I'll ask Jean Paul Sartre about the doughnut thing."

A slight smile appeared on his lips, he closed his eyes and released one last soft breath. Tears chased each other down Amelia's cheeks but tears of warmth; tears of release. She knew this was not a moment of sadness.

Grabbing a long hooded cardigan she slipped it on, removed his keys to her own pocket, then unlocked and eased open the door of her flat, leaving in her wake the extremes of humanity. As she made her way up the concrete steps from her basement apartment, steps which were so pleasantly cool on her bare feet, the sun had just made its welcome appearance to a backdrop of clear blue sky. Hazy mist rose from the glistening streets and a milk float hummed past on its morning duties. As she stepped onto the pavement two joggers glided past her running in synchronisation while lost in their own music. Across the road in the wooded grassland some birds were bringing to an end their dawn chorus as a dog excitedly tumbled and fell in enthusiastic pursuit of a teasingly elusive tennis ball thrown from afar.

Amelia tapped numbers on her phone, said what had to be said while walking a reassuring distance from her apartment, one in which she would never set foot again and sat down on a cold concrete step awaiting what ever emergency services may soon arrive. Her senses had never been more in tune, her perception never more lucid; her soul never lighter.

Made in the USA
Columbia, SC
29 October 2017